A Room in the Forest

Randy
Enjoy the journey to Haida Gwaii
Heather Ramsay

Copyright © 2025 Heather Ramsay
01 02 03 04 05 29 28 27 26 25

All rights reserved. No part of this publication may be reproduced, stored in a retrieval system or transmitted, in any form or by any means, without prior permission of the publisher or, in the case of photocopying or other reprographic copying, a licence from Access Copyright, the Canadian Copyright Licensing Agency, www.accesscopyright.ca, 1-800-893-5777, info@accesscopyright.ca.

Caitlin Press Inc.
3375 Ponderosa Way
Qualicum Beach, BC V9K 2J8
www.caitlinpress.com

Text design by Vici Johnstone
Cover art by Maryanne Wettlaufer

Edited by Pam Robertson

Excerpt(s) from A FIELD GUIDE TO GETTING LOST by Rebecca Solnit, copyright © 2005 by Rebecca Solnit. Used by permission of Viking Books, an imprint of Penguin Publishing Group, a division of Penguin Random House LLC. All rights reserved.

Printed in Canada

Caitlin Press Inc. acknowledges financial support from the Government of Canada and the Canada Council for the Arts, and the Province of British Columbia through the British Columbia Arts Council and the Book Publisher's Tax Credit.

A room in the forest / by Heather Ramsay.
Ramsay, Heather, 1969- author
Canadiana 20240473000 | ISBN 9781773861678 (softcover)
LCGFT: Novels.
LCC PS8635.A46444 R66 2025 | DDC C813/.6—dc23

A Room in the Forest

A NOVEL

Heather Ramsay

CAITLIN PRESS 2025

*To all those who have been lost,
and then found the islands of the people.*

Leave the door open for the unknown, the door into the dark. That's where the most important things come from, where you yourself came from, and where you will go.

Rebecca Solnit, *A Field Guide to Getting Lost*

I

Frontier, Alberta
End of April, 1999

1

Lily sat in a new-to-her Dodge Colt, hands on the steering wheel, ready to burst out of the chutes. She'd made up her mind to go and nothing could stop her. Certainly not her father, in his old terry-towel housecoat, scratching at his shaggy blond hair.

"But you just got here." His right hand pressed the latch on the protruding belly of her red hatchback and the hood popped. Lily sighed. One night in her backwater hometown on the edge of the foothills and she'd had enough. She'd reacquainted herself with the Van Halen posters in her bedroom. Her fuzzy blanket slashed with a purple and orange sunset. That damp, cold, basement smell. It had all been achingly familiar, but she'd barely slept.

Brian was causing further delays. He checked the oil, which Lily had to admit she hadn't even thought of doing. Luckily he found a half-litre in his too-packed-to-park-in-garage. As the sun crept to the lip of the eastern horizon, he was now fussing about something else.

"Belt's a bit loose." Brian poked his head around the open hood. "Won't take a minute to change. I've got everything you need right here."

Okay. Maybe she hadn't thought everything through. Like the safety of a $300 car she'd bought from a police auction two days before. Or the short turnaround time on her trip home. Brian had been expecting her to work at the family furniture store. That's why he'd paid for her college accounting course in the first place, so Lily could spend her life reconciling the cash register. Adding up daily receipts. But she didn't want to spend another summer in Frontier's most boring store, let alone undertake a career in bean counting.

Besides, she'd switched to forestry. She just hadn't told Brian until last night. She'd thought about heading straight west from Calgary, instead of coming home first. She could have spared herself all the familiar back roads. The brown fields, ranchers out repairing fences and white-stemmed poplars still bare as brooms. She could have spared herself Brian's shocked reaction. The pineapple, ham and cheese falling off the pizza slice he'd been about to bring to his mouth.

When she'd first arrived, Brian had been bubbling over with plans for the store diversifications she'd suggested as a way to bring in more customers. Too bad he thought adding antiques was a better idea than a cappuccino machine. He never quite understood what she meant.

"I should make sure all the lug nuts are tight. You never know," Brian said. Trying again. He did always want to help.

Lily pulled at the black toque that flattened her dark curls and shifted in her black puffy vest—the one with hand-sewn orange patches over the holes. *You look like the Michelin Man in that thing.* Her mother's voice. Arlene had always hated Lily's choice of clothes. *Why hide your figure? You'll be sorry when it's gone and no one even noticed.* Arlene always wanted someone to notice. But her mother had long since left and Lily would make her own choices.

"Dad. I have to go."

"Pretty small, this tin can." Brian polished the headlights with his housecoat strap. "Are you sure you can trust this thing on the highway?"

Could she trust anything? She was moving into the unknown. Her career plans switched based on a poster—one where two women in hard hats measured a stand of trees. Light sprinkled through the forest in the same magical way as the pictures she'd seen in a magazine. The one she'd found in the clinic last summer—after the worst thing she'd ever done.

"It's fine, Dad." But what did she know?

Brian slammed the hood down and came around by the curb. Lily could feel him kicking the tires—running his hands along them, assessing the wear on the tread. The night before, she'd spread a map out on the kitchen table to show him where she was headed—an eighteen-hour drive, then a six-hour ferry ride to the Queen Charlotte Islands. Brian had traced his finger past Banff, up to Jasper and west along a ribbon that led to the dagger-shaped archipelago out in the Pacific Ocean. Then he was quiet for a long time.

"Your mother went there once," he finally said.

But Lily already knew that.

Last summer, when he'd come to pick her up in Calgary, Brian couldn't remember where he'd parked the car. She'd told him she needed to research accounting courses at the library, but really, she'd needed to make sure that all traces of Jeremy were gone. The orange Tang smell of the clinic. The nurse calling her name. She had no idea how she made it through that hour. The magazine must have saved her. The giant trunks. Pillows of moss. An oasis of green. Brian had leaned over her shoulder as she flipped through it at the stoplight and was startled when she said the name of the place.

He'd said Arlene had been there, but when she'd asked what he meant, the beeping pedestrian signal started and then they walked right past the clinic. Lily almost died hoping the nurse or the doctor didn't come out and ask if she was okay. Then there'd been the charade with Brian trying to find the car. The A&W colours of the Calgary Tower. The tall naked statues at the Calgary Board of Education building. She never brought up Arlene and the forest again. What did she care where her mother had been?

Lily was not going to a group of islands off the west coast of British Columbia because of her mother. She was going for her own reasons, even if she couldn't fully articulate them to anyone else.

"Lily! Wait." Her little brother Ryan—their mother's favourite, their father's clone—burst out of the house. He'd grown so much over the winter. Fourteen. Same age as she was when their mother left.

Ryan tried to stuff an old shoebox through the window of her car. "Take it. It's Mom's."

"I don't want anything of hers." Lily tried to push it back, but Ryan wouldn't give up.

"Dad says its from those islands. Where you're going."

"Oh my god. Fine." She tossed the box onto the passenger seat.

"Okay, Lily-bug." Last night, Brian had started calling her that old nickname. As if she was eight. As if she might buzz around his every word again. He knocked on the window ledge and then reached in and scratched at her toque as if he was trying to ruffle Lily's dark curls. "Just like your mother." He probably meant her hair—Arlene's was wavy, and Lily's downright unruly. Still, she didn't like the comparison.

"I'll call!" Lily turned the ignition, cranked the wheel and waved, but she didn't look back.

2

"Away, away," Lily chanted as she slid through the back roads out of town. Anywhere but Frontier. Two days of driving and a ferry ride. Then she'd finally be among the old growth. Sitka spruce, red cedar, western hemlock. The dripping mosses. The colourful lichens. She let the wind play with her arm out the open window and inhaled the stubbled landscape. Forestry facts flew through her mind. Maple seeds spin like helicopters and travel long distances before they land. In order to reproduce, evergreen spores must be connected by wind.

A song about a dyslexic heart ended. Darwin, one of her classmates, had made a mixed tape for her. He'd followed the rest of the class to one of the big outfits in northern Alberta, where precision mills maxed out the number of two-by-fours. Not some backwoods forestry company on the northwest coast with one junior forest tech job. Darwin couldn't believe she was going to the Queen Charlotte Islands. He told her it would be like going to Siberia, but with more rain.

But she didn't need Darwin and his advice about jobs any more than she needed Jeremy and his antics at the horse races with the concession stand girl in the Coca-Cola t-shirt.

Six bells at the Sea Raven, Monday morning. That's all she needed to know.

The secondary road spat her out on the highway heading to Banff. *Open your heart and your desires will be fulfilled. The universe will provide.* Her mother's stupid voice again. As if Arlene should be giving advice to anyone.

Lily looked over at the shoebox on the passenger seat. Arlene, who always took the last scoop of ice cream. Who'd forced Lily to tamp down her hair with pink pastel barrettes. Who'd left with that rancher even after being the hairdresser winding baby's breath through his new wife's hair. Jane's Addiction ended, and next song came on: Pearl Jam. Electric guitar grunge. Darwin's soundtrack was a welcome distraction.

Lily cruised through Banff National Park's gates and sped past the exit that led to the tourist shops and motels. The car speaker crackled and the liquid heat of Chris Cornell started up. Something about breaking a rusty cage. Past a grove of Engelmann spruce and subalpine firs. Alberta trees were like matchsticks compared to the pictures in the magazine. Lily couldn't wait to see the real things. Ancient trees with elephant-sized roots diving into debris-littered soil.

She stuck her head out the window. Why would her classmates want to work somewhere that reminded them of everything they had ever known? She had a job with a different promise. Even the name sounded otherworldly. Totem Timber.

Scrotum, Jeremy would have said.

Argh... she did not want to think about Jeremy.

After Banff, Lily followed the white-blue Bow River, which was tumbling back in the direction of home. She saw mountaintops touch the sky. The snow sinking into streams that fed lakes. The wet rocks and mud of spring.

Your mother's like a thunderstorm, Brian always said. Lily did not want to be thought of as any kind of weather.

After Lake Louise, she veered up the ramp to the Jasper Parkway. She'd never been this far before. "This Monkey's Gone to Heaven." The Pixies. Darwin had better taste in music than Jeremy. There was that. She'd barely heard of any of his bands before. She turned up the volume and then saw a sign for a lake and a glacier. The start of the river that wound all the way back to Calgary.

Lily thought about her own origin story. Born in Calgary, November 1980, but so what? She knew nothing else. Arlene had no beginning. She was there and then she wasn't—had never even talked much about her parents. Assholes. Drunks. Father mean as a snake, somewhere out in Saskatchewan. Lily had never met them—wasn't sure if they were alive or dead.

Lily needed to stretch her legs. She flicked her left signal on and got into the turning lane, then parked and stared at a thick glob of ice hanging down at the back of the lake. The air, still and cold. The clouds grey. A trail leading into the distance. A beginning. She hopped out of her car and and the wind picked up. An old fast-food bag blasted across the lot and she pulled her toque low over her ears. Lily had been the one to leave this time. She shivered and thought about getting her puffy vest, but she wouldn't be turned back so easily. She stayed on the path to the lake.

A guy with a large German flag on his backpack came up behind her as a slab of ice heaved into the murky blue. "Holy shit, did you see that?" he said.

"Ya. Cool," she said, and then tripped on a tree root and grabbed at a picnic table to steady herself.

"Nice spot for a picnic," he said over his shoulder as he passed. She wanted to tell him she wasn't out in the elements for such a trivial thing. She had escaped another summer of customers trying to turn on lamps that weren't plugged in. She'd escaped Arlene's betrayals and Brian's disappointments.

"How far are you going?" Lily called out to the hiker, but he didn't even look back.

Lily stopped for gas in Jasper and the guy at the counter offered her a job, but she looked at all the colourful Gore-Tex people crossing the streets and knew it wasn't where she belonged. She bought some chips and beef jerky and by the time she got over the Continental Divide, she was moving with the water again. She lost the flow for a time, then found it, white and heaving against the highway. Sections of calm and then a drop. A raft bounced through the churn. Helmeted adventurers in neoprene with paddles all in. By then, she was tired and things seemed less clear. Why did she need to travel so far to start a new life? She could've stayed in the mountains; she could be riding these waves.

But no, she wanted the trees.

Trees make houses, she'd told Brian. And furniture. And flames. As if these were reasons to go work among them. He still hadn't understood and kept shaking his head. *Lily-bug, Lily-bug,* he said. Arlene had caught a ladybug once and passed it to Lily through her cupped hand. When it pinched at her skin, she whined and tried to shake it off. Arlene wasn't sympathetic. *Everything bites,* her mother said.

The road continued, like a gash through the green, and her stomach growled. Not a soul on the streets in McBride. A sign yelled RESTAURANT, but the room behind the pink curtain was dark. Lily started to feel empty and afraid.

You can't eat trees, Brian had said the night before, as if that made sense. Lily rubbed at her grumbling belly, then remembered the chips she'd bought back at the gas station. Damn rights, she was prepared. She didn't need a town full of tourists. Or a group of fellow students. Or Brian's ham and pineapple pizza served on soggy cardboard. She would survive on her own.

The cassette stopped and she flipped it again. Nirvana, "Come As You Are." She ate chips and daydreamed about the forest ecologist who'd taught her ecosystem mapping field course. A nerdy, broad-shouldered grad student from some coastal place that sounded like a rock and roll band. He'd been so jazzed by conifer species that she'd memorized the different needle bundles of jack pines and balsam firs. Meanwhile he couldn't even remember her name. Lucy. Louise. Lillian. Still, she tried to impress him by identifying every tree she drove past. White spruce. Lodgepole pine. Western red cedar.

Her foot tapped the brakes. Really? It couldn't be?

Furry arms of cedar drooping onto the road? Shaggy bark this close to the Rockies? She wiped her greasy hands on her jeans and groped in the back for the map. The ecologist had pointed at a scene projected on a wall: *Western red cedar found at low to mid elevations along the BC coast.* Lily had barely left McBride. No way was she anywhere near the ocean. She clutched the wheel with one hand and looked at the map for a second, then the blast of a transport truck horn popped her attention back to the road. Lily cranked her wheel to return to the right side of the centre line, then banked off into a pullout to catch her breath.

The word "crash" jumped out of the tape deck. Not today, Lily thought. She rolled down the window and left the cassette playing. Such great bass lines. She nodded her head to the music. The trees were cedars, alright. Scale-like leaves, no needles. No mistaking. What was this music? Hole, Darwin's favourite female grunge band? No. Another name like that. She mimicked the beat on the steering wheel. Had the grad student gone back to the coast for the summer? If all else failed, she could go look for him. Shack up and learn to play guitar. When the song turned to reverb, the name of the band came to her—the Breeders. Not her favourite idea. Lily had other things to do. She turned off the car and the music stopped.

A strip of pink flagging tape fluttered on a branch as the Colt's engine ticked. According to the map, she had at least two more hours to Prince George, then eight to the coast. She got out of the car and stretched. The air smelled like the bottom of a chest. Lily moved toward a sign with writing burnt into the slab of wood: *Ancient Forest Trail*. She reached out to touch the silvery bark and the breeze blew the cedar boughs apart. Lily entered the maze with her thoughts stirring like beads in her palm. She remembered the doorway to a hall of mirrors—peer one direction and you find your way through, peer another and you're lost. Lily turned back toward the road for a moment, unsure if she should continue. But the branches had already snapped back into place.

She'd been eight when her father encouraged her to go into the funhouse without him. Arlene had told her not to be a scaredy-cat and then she'd gone to get a corn dog. Lily wanted to prove that she wasn't afraid so she'd navigated the zigzag staircase, the shifting floors, and then made it across the swinging bridge. Still, she'd screamed when a neon skeleton touched her hair. A man in faded jeans, like her father's, brushed past and she thought he'd come to help, but when he turned a corner, she couldn't figure out how to follow his never-ending reflection. She hadn't cried, although she wanted to. Instead, she picked herself up, and found her way. Brian, with her little brother in his arms, tried to clap his hands as she stumbled out of the funhouse and onto the fairground. Her mother, as usual, was nowhere to be found.

Lily continued along the path and thought of the tricky way the grad student had told her to memorize Latin plant names. Remember the first two letters of each word. For example, LyAm. That was his name. Liam, but also the mnemonic for skunk cabbage. *Lysichiton americanus*. A broad, fan-like green leaf, with one central yellow curl.

Skunk cabbage indicates moisture, he'd said, and smells like rotten meat, but Lily inhaled as she stood beside one and wasn't so sure. The plant smelled a bit rank, but also like something newly alive.

The breeze blew at a hunk of old man's beard lichen and it dropped at her feet. Lichen are fungus, plus one or more types of algae, Liam would have said. She continued past the curled brown tongues of the awakening ferns. Her arm brushed against the rigid spears on a stalk of devil's club—OpHo, or *Oplopanax horridus*—its spiked leaves about to unfold. *Don't be fooled and pick their soft-looking leaves for toilet paper*, Liam warned. You won't like it when their spines break off in your skin.

A sunbeam broke through the canopy and she moved up the path from the damp devil's club ground to a patch of feather moss.

15

Feather bed. Just a short break, Lily promised as she slid to the forest floor. These cedar trees. Ancient like in the magazine. She leaned into the softness and dozed.

Soon she was tangled into a time when she'd awakened to Ryan snoring beside her by a pond not too far from their house. Mom, he'd said as she'd nudged him. It's just me, Lily said, and gathered him close. Arlene had left her children alone in the woods as if they were part of a Grimms' fairy tale. Not Disney. No fairy godmothers. Nothing cute about it at all.

Lily sank deeper into the moss and tried to push thoughts of her mother away. Her mother and her betrayals. She wanted to stay in this room in the forest and not be bothered by anyone at all.

Lily counted five deep breaths, as the little bird sounds twirled and she dozed again, until a car door slammed and she was jolted back into reality again.

"This must be the trail," a woman's voice said.

"What makes you think there's a trail?" said a male.

"I heard the old man at the next table talking about it. The enviros are trying to save this patch from logging."

A van door slid open and another female voice sounded through the trees.

"What old man?"

"At the café in Dome Creek," said the first woman.

"We were at a café?"

"Oh Sissy, you were dead to the world." Another male.

Lily only heard four voices, but to her they sounded like an invading force.

"Shut up, Blaize. You guys left me in the van? Assholes. You didn't have pie, did you? Tell me I didn't miss pie," said Sissy.

"I had bumbleberry," said the other woman.

"Apple," said the first guy.

"Lard crust. You wouldn't have liked it anyway," said Blaize.

"Bullshit. No one cooks with lard anymore."

"It's supposed to be marked with a ribbon," said the first girl. "Plus someone else is here. Oh, there *is* a sign. Ancient Forest Trail. We found it."

Lily couldn't see them, but they sounded as close as if they were on the other side of her bedroom wall. Arlene and Brian fighting. Her mother storming out.

The van door slammed.

"*Assstrid*... What if I don't want to meet whoever is in there?"

"What are you on about now?" said Astrid.

"What if it's a monster?" said Sissy.

"In a Dodge Colt with Alberta plates?"

"Magic does what magic wants."

"You better stay out here then."

Lily pushed herself to standing. Why did they have to disturb her beautiful room? She did not want to talk to them—or anyone.

"I'm not staying out here alone, waiting for an axe murderer to walk out of those trees," Sissy said.

"So lock yourself in the car." Footsteps started through gravel.

"Shut up. I'm coming."

The sliding door closed and there were more footsteps, and then Lily could tell they'd all entered the forest.

"Check out the lichen. It's dripping," Astrid whispered.

"Why would someone throw orange peels here?" said Sissy.

"That's fungus. Look at this whitish one. They call it cat's tongue," said Blaize.

"Is it edible?"

"Supposedly, but you'd have to pick a lot to get a meal."

"Fucking loggers," Sissy growled. "You've got to be kidding."

"Kidding about what?"

"Look at this place, Blaize. These are the biggest trees I've ever seen."

Lily flattened herself against one of the giant cedars. She felt silly hiding, but who had invited them? She'd felt so relaxed, for so brief a time. If she could just slip out, she could continue on her way undisturbed. But then two of them started on the loop one way and the other two went the opposite direction. They were closing in.

"These are big, but I don't think they are bigger than the ones on Haida Gwaii," said Blaize.

"You and Haida Gwaii," said Sissy.

"You'd love it."

"I love it here. I can't believe they want to chop these down. It's like a cathedral."

"You better start praying."

"I will. I mean what kind of murderer would kill these? I get that we need wood and everything. But this place is *sacred*," Sissy said.

"Hey, it's a loop. I see you guys."

"Do you see the other guy. The monster or whatever?"

"I think it's a girl," said Blaize.

"What makes you think that?" said Sissy.

"I just do." Lily looked in the direction of the voice and saw him in a straight line through the trees. He smiled and put his finger to his lips, nodding toward the others. She didn't understand, but he started talking loudly again and she took her chance. Her feet moved in a trajectory that angled toward her car and away from all of them. When she popped out of the forest, she was farther from the vehicles than she thought, so she started to run. Gravel sprayed under her feet. The others must have heard her, because they started shouting and running too.

By the time she pulled back onto the highway, they had all burst out of the darkness. Never mind. Their car faced the other direction. Heading to Alberta. She would never see them again.

Two hours later, Lily passed a sign that announced the city of Prince George. The highway led down a steep hill, across a huge brown river and into the wide valley. Rain sprayed off the hood as she cruised over the railway tracks. Her windshield fogged. Lily cracked her window and blasted the defrost. The air smelled of smoke and crusty socks.

Downtown lasted about five blocks and then she was out the other side. Lines of semis geared down and expelled diesel breath at an intersection with another major highway. Turn right for Vanderhoof, Burns Lake and Prince Rupert. But Lily had been on the road for almost ten hours and there was no way she wanted to keep driving. A sign pointed to Mr. P.G. Man, an eight-metre cartoon figure with a log-like body and a doorknob-shaped head. She stared at him for a moment, but neither he nor the map gave clues as to where she might find a campsite, so she turned her car back downtown and pulled up to a motel. Paying $39 a room seemed like a lot, but probably wasn't. She got a room key from the proprietor and just as she was closing the door, the minivan pulled in. Holy crap. Lily clicked it shut and held her hands over her ears, but Sissy and the gang went at it again, as if they were right in her room.

"What a drive."

"I need to take a crap."

"Oh my god, Blaize. Can you not tell us every time you have to poo."

"Just get a key. I'm touching cloth."

"Hey, isn't that the same Colt with the Alberta plates?"

"Far out, the axe murderer is staying at the Downtown Motel!"

Weirdo hippies. Lily threw her stuff on the bed and used the cord to pull the drapes. What kind of karma did she have to bring these people to her again? *The universe provides.* Thanks, Arlene. Lily kicked the door stopper just to hear it boing and wondered how things were at home. That noise used to make Ryan laugh. She'd knocked the one in the kitchen when she came home the night before, but it hadn't pulled Ryan out his video game. Lily had to march right up to him and drop her pack before he'd even say hello. So much for the little boy whose favourite hiding place was a cupboard like the one in *The Lion, the Witch and the Wardrobe* that Brian had set up in one of his bedroom displays at the store. How many times had she pretended that she didn't know where he was? How many times had she let him find her by hiding in plain sight?

She looked at the telephone beside the bed, then picked it up and called. Ryan answered, of course.

"Hey."

"How was the drive?" he said.

"Fine. I'm not there yet. I'm just in Prince George."

Ryan didn't say anything and she could tell that he had no idea where that was—and that he didn't really care. He didn't show much interest in anything outside of what he'd always known. No self-doubt. No worries about who he was or what he was supposed to do.

"Did you stop at the candy store?"

"Where?"

"In Banff."

"Of course not."

"That's too bad. You used to love going there."

"No time. I had a long drive. Prince George is like four hours west of Jasper. And I've still got eight more hours tomorrow."

"Wow. Couldn't get far enough, eh? Just like Mom."

"Whatever. Mom's way the hell in Costa Rica with her rancher boyfriend, so that's a little farther. And it's not like I'm not coming back. Anyway. How's Dad?"

"I don't know. I should go check on him though."

"I'm sure he's okay."

"Listen Lily, you don't understand. He hasn't been doing well."

"Cripes. It's just a summer job."

"Well, it's not like you gave him a lot of notice. Anyway. Mom called the other day."

"So?" said Lily.

"It got Dad talking about her. He told me about when he asked her to marry him."

"What? When?"

"Before you were born. But she up and left instead. A week later he got a call from some place named Prince Rupert and he had to get out the atlas to figure out where that was."

"That's when she went to the islands?" said Lily.

"Yeah. He thought he'd never see her again."

"Really?" Lily said.

"But then she came back. That winter. In January or February, he couldn't remember. He asked when your birthday was again."

"November!"

"Ya, ya. I know. I told him."

"So what? What does that have to do with Mom?"

"I don't know. Apparently she showed up and acted like nothing happened. Knocked on the door and moved back in. They never did get married."

"Well, that's a happy ending." Maybe there was something about Arlene going to the Queen Charlottes after all. Something that had made her mother feel good. Mostly Lily remembered her being mad.

"I don't know. It seems more complicated than that," Ryan said. "Anyway, she's coming back."

"Coming back where?"

"To Frontier. She wants Dad to sell the store, so she can get half the money."

Lily pulled the receiver away from her ear. Jeezus. "Speaking of money, this call is costing a lot. I better go."

She hung up, went into the bathroom and turned on the shower, undressed and stepped in. The spray bit her back and she twisted around to get as much of her body under the heat as she could. She tried to put her face under the water, but the needle-like jabs made her turn away. She lathered and scrubbed. *Pussy, pits and tits.* Her mother's voice again. Crude instructions through the door of the bathroom, as if Lily couldn't even get her own personal hygiene right.

She did not need Arlene. That was one of the truest facts of her life. She wished Arlene had nothing to do with the Queen Charlotte Islands. That her father didn't always remind Lily that she and her mother looked alike. That Ryan hadn't mentioned their mother at all.

A thud in the pipe swept all the voices away and the spray of water went cold. Lily tensed and splashed at her body to remove the slippery soap. Then she turned the shower off and shivered as she rubbed at herself with the motel's crappy white towel.

She'd never felt so unsatisfied.

3

A cheeseburger was the only way through any of this. Lily popped her head out the motel room door. No sign of the nosy neighbours, so she crossed the road to a pub, but as she pushed her way inside Lily knew she'd made a mistake. Sissy's voice shrieked out of the first booth and Lily could see the four of them out of the corner of her eye. They all stopped talking as she passed and the whispers began. Over in the shadows, two bikers shot a round of pool. She thought of putting her quarters on the table as she had done so many times back in Frontier, but that was how she met Jeremy. Not something she wanted to repeat. So she walked up to the bar instead.

The bartender sneered as she ordered a Traditional Ale.

"You from Alberta?" he said.

Couldn't she just walk into a pub and remain anonymous?

"The beer," he said. "We just started getting them. Most people drink Molson's in here."

Jeremy's brand. Disgusting sweet corn taste. Stupid idea to come to a bar. Lily looked at the jean jackets and leather vests. The men in red plaid. What was the point of moving forward, if you wound up in the same place you left behind?

Her stomach grumbled. "Can I order a burger too?"

"What kind?" He spoke as if she'd asked for a snake.

"Cheeseburger. With fries."

"Good. Not like those vegetarians over there." She didn't have to look to know where he pointed. "They think everyone owes them black beans. And can I get salad with that?" He made a funny voice and hand-flapping gestures while punching her order in. "Rabbit food."

When the bartender raised his eyebrows at something behind her, she resisted the urge to look back. He was full-on scowling over her shoulder by the time Lily felt a touch on the back of her arm.

"You're the monster."

She turned to face a mop of dreadlocks tied back with a string.

He wore a black t-shirt under a tan vest and had an old army canteen slung across his chest. She knew his name was Blaize, but she didn't say anything.

"I recognize your coat. I could see it through the trees. You saw me, too. I know you did."

"So?"

"So... what were you sneaking around for?"

She shrugged and turned back to the bar. "I didn't want to talk to anyone."

"Well, that was then and this is now and I won't let you get away so easily." Blaize leaned into the counter and asked the bartender for a pitcher of Canadian. Lily caught a whiff of his animal smell, mixed with mud. She didn't think she liked it, but as he brushed against her shoulder, she inhaled again.

"Okay hippie. Nice try. Are you wearing shoes?" The bartender put his hands on the bar and peered over the top of it.

Lily looked down at Blaize's paddle-length feet.

"No shoes, no shirt..." the bartender said.

"No service." Blaize finished the statement for him, then pulled a pair of flip flops out of his pocket and slipped them on.

"Dropout." The bartender pushed through the swinging doors into the kitchen.

"Asshole." Blaize turned back to Lily. "Come sit with us."

Lily looked over at the booth and saw the other three waving. "Why should I?" she said.

"Because you know you want to." Blaize lunged forward, bending one knee, then spread his arms.

"What the heck are you doing?" Lily said.

"Warrior pose," Blaize said. "Yoga chest opener. You should try it."

Lily watched him lift his arms over his head like a prayer and wanted to say *not likely*, but the bartender came back with a jug of beer and her cheeseburger. Before she could do anything Blaize snatched them both up.

"That's not your beef, ya hippycrite," said the bartender.

"Put it on our tab," Blaize said, and turned to Lily. "Come on."

He walked back to his friends and dropped the plate on the table. One of the girls—dreadlocks tied into a medusa-like bun on top of her head—gagged at the scent.

"That's worse than the pulp mill." Still, she shoved over and Lily knew by the sound of her voice that this was Sissy.

"They say pulp is the smell of money." Blaize stole one of Lily's fries. "So which crew are you with?"

"Watch out, vegan. They're probably cooked in lard." Sissy poured a glass from the jug of draft and tried to pass it to Lily.

Lily shook her head and lifted her darker beer. She took a long swig and said, "Totem Timber."

"Must be a new one. Are they in the Muskwa–Kechika or up near Terrace?

"The Charlottes," she said.

"Oh my goddess. You mean Haida Gwaii," said Sissy. "The Queen Charlotte Islands is the colonizers' name."

"Um. Okay." Lily had no idea what Sissy was talking about. She turned to Blaize for help, but he just raised his eyebrows.

"It's the sacred home of the Haida and they rule the coast. You better watch what you say if you're going to their territory. Right, Blaize?"

"Okay, okay, Sissy." Blaize turned to Lily. "I thought planting didn't start there until fall?"

"Planting?"

"Tree planting. That's what you're doing isn't it? I saw the caulk boots in the back of your car."

"I'm a forest tech," she said.

"Shit. You're going there to cut trees down?" Sissy snorted. "Good luck."

"I'm not a logger. I'll be doing surveys."

"Duh. For cutblocks," said Sissy. "Totem Timber. That's rich. Talk about appropriation. Things are heating up there again, right Blaize?" He didn't get a chance to respond before Sissy started again. "Blaize says there's going to be protests. It's all he can talk about. I'd watch out if I were you."

"Is that why you ran out of that other forest? Where we saw you earlier today?" asked the other girl at the table.

"What?" Lily looked at the blonde with bangs, who had to be Astrid.

"Guilt," Astrid whispered. "The forest knows."

"Don't be silly," said Blaize.

"What? She ran," said Astrid.

"I heard some logging company guy killed himself there because of a big protest," said the short-haired, bearded guy. Lily stared as he ran his tongue over his lips. Was that a metal ball at the tip?

"Christ, Jake, that was over a decade ago, and he died of a heart attack," said Blaize.

"Or heartbreak," said Astrid.

"Whichever. People don't like loggers there," Sissy said.

"Especially white ones."

"Logging is evil."

"First it was smallpox."

"Now it's clearcuts."

The group kept volleying comments back and forth and Lily couldn't keep up.

"They'll eat you alive."

"If you're lucky they'll just run you off the islands."

"Forget forestry. Come with us. We could use another chick on the crew," said Blaize.

"But if you guys are planting," Lily channelled an argument from her forests and society class, "it's because someone's been logging. So you're still making a living off the forest industry."

"Yep, she's got you there," said Jake.

"We're trying to fix it," said Sissy. "Rehabilitate the failings of Babylon."

"Oh. Right." Lily rolled her eyes, but she didn't know what Sissy was talking about again. Babylon? Wasn't that some ancient empire in the Middle East? Anyway, they could have their tree planting. Lily wasn't going to crawl over burnt stumps with a bag full of seedlings. No thanks. She wanted to work in the forest.

"You better have a look at this." Sissy pulled a huge book out of her bag and flipped through pages of grey poles, carved with faces, in front of rows of windowless wood houses. Lily saw canoes pulled up on a crescent-shaped beach. A beak poking out of a moon. A crouched animal with its tongue sticking out.

"What is this?" To Lily, the photos looked like something out of a forgotten dream.

"Those are totem poles in front of villages on Haida Gwaii before white people came."

"Wow. Is that what it looks like now?" she said.

Sissy scoffed. "Are you kidding? The missionaries cut the poles down and burned them. Called the people heathens and then sent their kids away to residential school."

"Whoa, slow down, Sissy," said Blaize.

"What? This was only a hundred years ago. Smallpox wiped out whole villages on the islands. Now she's going there and hasn't got a clue," Sissy snapped at Blaize, then turned to Lily. "You'll see what's changed. Then you can decide."

"About what?" Lily said.

"The land and who should have a say over what happens to it."

"Most logging takes place on Crown land, so the public has a say." Lily repeated words she'd been taught, but her face went hot from not knowing. She had never seen pictures like the ones Sissy had. Totem poles lining a beachfront. Totem Timber. She knew nothing at all.

"It's unceded," said Sissy.

Lily thought the conversation had turned back to tree planting. "Seeds? I thought you guys used baby trees."

"Oh my lord. Unceded. In other words, stolen."

Lily still didn't get it.

"You are cute, but clueless. Whose land do you come from?" Sissy asked.

"What? I'm from Alberta."

"Indigenous land, sister! Which nation's land do you live on?"

"I live in Frontier," Lily said. "It's a town, not a reserve."

"Where's this town of yours?" said Sissy.

"Just south of Calgary."

"Probably Blackfoot."

"What's that got to do with anything?" Lily shook her head, but on some level, she knew exactly what Sissy was talking about. Treaties were signed and Indians lived on reserves. That was all she'd ever been told. She'd seen teepees set up at the Calgary Stampede, and fancy dancers during the Grandstand Show, but Lily had only been to a reserve once, in grade six. They'd been bussed to a multicultural assembly. She remembered doors with no stairways leading to the houses. Cars with no tires. All the kids brought potluck dishes that were supposed to reflect their ethnicity. Jars of sauerkraut and platters of shortbread. Lily's mother had scoffed and sent Ritz Crackers and Cheez Whiz. *Tell them we're from right here.*

"Earth to Lily. *Jay-sus.* I don't have all week to explain this," said

Sissy. "It's pretty much all stolen. Even if Indigenous people supposedly signed treaties back in the 1800s, the government didn't play fair. In BC, the colonizers didn't bother to sign any agreements at all. They just took the land. We're on Indigenous land right now. Lheidli T'enneh."

"Okay. Okay. It's my first job, alright? I didn't think about whose land it was," Lily said.

"You think that'll get you off the hook?" Sissy picked up the pitcher and poured the dregs into Lily's glass and Astrid went to get another jug. "They're Haida, okay? On Haida Gwaii. It means 'Islands of the People' and it'd be good for you to remember that."

"Got it. Thanks." Lily thought of the article in the magazine she'd found at the clinic. Young men with black lines painted on their faces. Holding a line. She'd read that the whole southern half of the islands had been protected. A national park or something, and loggers were never allowed there again. That seemed like a big win, right? Wasn't that enough? Besides, people still had to make a living. But Lily kept those thoughts to herself.

"I've got to pee." Sissy bumped Lily's hip to push her out of the way.

The room spun as Lily stood. How many beers had she drunk? She tried to stretch, but her puffy vest got in the way. She took a step, then the music shifted from high-pitched metal to a familiar guitar and bass twang. Her mother's favourite song. Something about cold, late nights and a pretty man.

Sissy slithered out of the booth, dreadlocks writhing. The music accelerated and Sissy twirled her arms in the air, and then before Lily knew what was happening, Sissy had grabbed her hand, and spun herself into Lily's chest.

"You're going to be eaten alive." Sissy leaned back as if Lily were dipping her in a kind of ballroom dance. Ann and Nancy's voices, a bar full of bikers and Lily trying to stay upright.

"By the bugs?" Lily was trying to act cool.

"By the energy. It's a wild place. Not everyone can handle it." Sissy gyrated out and then back. Brian could dance like that, but Lily's mother would never follow.

"You haven't even been there." Lily tried to mimic Sissy's tangled moves, like she would try to follow her father's after Arlene gave up. Hands held up, then over shoulders, and winding around again.

"Blaize told me. He spent a season mushroom picking."

"Mushrooms? Like drugs?" said Lily.

"Those too, but no, chanterelles." She wrapped Lily in toward her this time and whispered in her ear. "You've got a lot to learn."

The guitar twanged and Lily's face turned red. She felt all eyes in the room turn to them. She heard whispers like the ones she'd heard all her life. About her. About her mother. About what kind of girl she'd turn out to be. Lily had had too much beer.

"Little logger girl. Out of all the places, what are you going there for?" said Sissy, whirling again.

"Why shouldn't I?"

"So many reasons," said Sissy. "But there's something else. I've got a feeling about it."

"What do you mean?"

"You tell me. It's like something's oozing out of your pores. Some big fat question. But what does it have to do with Haida Gwaii?"

Lily yanked her hand out of Sissy's and thought of her mother, running off after Brian asked her to marry him. Arlene phoning from Prince Rupert and Brian having to look it up in the atlas. The shoebox Ryan had shoved into her car. Lily was not following her mother. She had a mind of her own and Sissy should mind her own business. Lily was about to say so, but the bartender poked her on the shoulder.

"If you want to dance, find a man—each of you. And get your dirty hippie asses onto the actual dance floor."

Sissy waggled her tongue at him.

"Degenerates," the bartender said.

Sissy laughed, kissed Lily on the lips, then took off toward the bathroom. Lily stood alone among the tables in the middle of a Prince George pub, burning from Sissy's touch.

"I wish I was going to Haida Gwaii." Blaize came up from behind and put his chin on her shoulder. "That place is like a back-to-the-land mecca. Stick a frying pan out and the fish jump in. Berries dripping off the bushes. Deer so small you could chase them down and kill them with your bare hands."

"I thought you didn't eat meat," said Lily, pulling away from him.

"I'm more of an opportunivore, but don't tell Sissy," said Blaize as he tried to encircle her waist. Lily dodged him again and let the momentum propel her to the bar.

The bartender sneered when she tried to order another round. "The tab's been closed out. People don't like tree planters in this town."

"I'm not a tree planter. I'm a forest tech." Lily slurred a bit and considered heading back to her motel room, when a body bumped against her again. It wasn't Blaize this time.

"What's a nice girl like you doing with those rat bags?" A skinny guy with a leather vest put his hand on her back.

"Hey," she said. "Don't touch me."

He lifted his hand like he'd been shocked.

"I'm just trying to be nice. Don't have a conniption."

"Is he bothering you?" Blaize came up beside her.

"I can handle this," Lily said.

Blaize ignored her. "The lady told you not to touch her."

"Ya, what are you going to do about it, clown?" Skinny guy pushed up his sleeves and Blaize sucker punched him in the gut.

"You little prick." The guy tried to grab Blaize, but the hippie did a ninja move and kicked him in the ass. Another guy with a handlebar moustache pushed in and a dude with a long beard flipped a table. Sissy walked out of the bathroom just as a beer bottle flew past.

"Jesus, Blaize. What have you done now?" He was hunched in the middle of the room in fight stance while more patrons swarmed. Then the bartender rang the huge cowbell that hung above the bar.

"Tree planters get out!"

Heart was still playing and Sissy gyrated one more time, then she grabbed Lily and pulled her out the door. Blaize, Astrid and Jake spilled out behind them. Sissy picked up Lily's hand and pressed it to her cheek, then ran it down her neckline. Lily pulled away, just as her fingers brushed the top of Sissy's breasts. "Fights are sexy," Sissy said. "If you need some consoling, I'm heading to my room." And without another word, she splashed across the road to the motel.

Lily stood there speechless.

"She wants you," Blaize said. "And Sissy usually gets what she wants."

"She wants everyone," said Astrid.

"Until she doesn't," said Jake.

"I want to go to Haida Gwaii," said Astrid. "You're lucky."

"Good place to hole up for Y2K," said Blaize.

"You're always going on about Y2K," Astrid said.

"Well, if the grid's going dark at midnight, New Year's Eve 2000, you might as well be somewhere with a lot of wood," said Blaize.

"Whatever. World's ending no matter where you are," said Astrid.

"It's all going down," agreed Jake.

"No one's going to survive," said Astrid.

"I've got to go," said Lily, interrupting the doomsdaying. "I've got a long drive in the morning." They all crossed the road to the motel together, and Jake and Astrid disappeared. Only Blaize walked Lily to her door.

"Thanks, I guess," she said.

"For what?"

"For fending that guy off."

"Anytime."

Lily could feel the rain starting up again. For a second, the drops just pattered, and then they began pummelling the ground.

"We'll drown if we stay out here," she said.

"No, you won't." Blaize reached into his pocket and pulled out a ball of blue glass. He brushed it across her cheek and then rolled it down her shoulder and into her hands. She closed her fingers around it and felt the smooth sides, the seam in the middle.

"What is it?"

"It's a fishing float. Keeps you above water," he said. "I found it on Haida Gwaii. You should have it."

"I don't know what to say."

"Just say yes to everything."

"Ha. With advice like that what could go wrong?" Lily paused and then said Sissy's name.

"She's like a thunderstorm. Big weather, but it blows off," Blaize said, then he bent to try to kiss her, but she pushed him away.

"Jesus. You're with Sissy."

"You could be with both of us," he said.

"Way too complicated," Lily said.

"Okay. How about, I'm with you right now."

"I have to go."

"It's all good. But you should still change your mind and come with us. Planting is way more fun than logging."

"No, thank you." Lily wriggled the room key into the lock and waved him away.

4

Lily pressed her back against the closed door. She'd left the window open to air out the stale cigarette stench and the sulphur had seeped in. The pulp mill. The smell of money. Lily touched her stomach and felt the ache—of desire and emptiness. She thought about Jeremy and all the things that were and could have been. He'd cheated on her and then he'd left before she could even tell him that she was pregnant. Ugh. She heard the moan from the next room and the banging. Sissy's voice like a tendril. Blaize's trumpet-like grunts. She crawled into her bed and pulled the covers over her head.

Keep moving forward was her new mantra, so Lily was out the door before five a.m. She found a black and white page from Sissy's book tucked under the windshield wiper. The sweep of beach and the line of poles. The tree-planting company's name and phone number had been inked into the weeds by the water. Lily curled her fingers around Blaize's talisman in her vest pocket. A float. The blue of the ocean. She didn't know what to think. About tree planters, loggers, her mother. About Haida Gwaii. The warm air from the defog dislodged the light film of ice that had formed on the windshield. She revved the engine and hoped the noise wouldn't bring the tree planters to life.

Giant trucks passed loaded with logs. Flocks of geese angled north. Silver clouds ballooned like a pillow fight. She drove by a sign for beaded artwork and leather moccasins. A roadside toilet. A town with an A&W. Orange and brown. Her father liked to get Teen Burgers when they went to the city. He'd offered to take her there after picking her up last summer. She'd come out of the clinic and stared at the orange and brown of the Calgary Tower. She'd thought about disappearing into the forest of skyscrapers, but instead she waited at the library until Brian found her and brought her home.

Whose land do you come from? What a thing for Sissy to ask.

Lily put on another of Darwin's tapes. On one side, a band

called the Rheostatics played and a painter talked in between tracks about the sky going from blue to white to black. Then the real rain came, soaking the road in front of her. The storm hit so powerfully that she thought the darts might dent her hood. *Your mother is like a thunderstorm.* Sissy is too, according to Blaize. Lily was better off without either of them.

Rain pinged off the pavement, as if it originated from there, and Lily couldn't see the lines on the road or a car length in front of her. She just about slammed into the back of a Winnebago and her mother's shoebox slid off the seat. Lily's arm shot out the way a parent would try to protect their child. But it was too late. The contents tumbled onto the floor. Seashells. A feather. A photo. She angled over toward the invisible shoulder as far as she dared, put on her hazards and prayed that no other vehicle would sneak up behind and knock her into the ditch.

Lily picked up the pieces of her mother's unknown life from the Dodge Colt's floor. The opalescent insides of a shell. A billowy scarf. A photo of a cabin. A beautiful orange and grey feather that Lily stuck into one of the vent holes on the dash. A few minutes later, the storm blew over, just as her father always said it would. She pulled back onto the highway and a car honked, so she pressed on the gas.

Trees. Hills. Trees. Small towns with cartoon names: Burns Lake, Smithers, Hazelton. Soon she found a river again. That was something. The blue-green carried her past mountains. At Kitwanga, she pulled off at a gas station to fuel up. A big wooden sign indicated a crossroad leading north to Alaska. Bear Glacier. Someplace called Stewart. Mud-covered trucks parked outside the red-roofed store. She went inside and found "Forestry Feeds My Family" bumper stickers on a spinning rack. A deer head with spiky antlers mounted high above the tires. An island of salt and vinegar chips. In the diner, bearded men in foam-mesh baseball caps lifted thick creamy coffees to their mouths. Lily pulled a book off the postcard rack: *How to Stay Alive in the Woods.* "A complete guide to food, shelter and self-preservation," it claimed. If she couldn't have someone like Liam or Blaize, maybe she could have this book. She picked it up, along with a postcard showing a row of totem poles, and went up to pay.

Lily gestured at the postcard as the cashier rang things up. "Are the poles nearby?"

"Just over there," the cashier said, pointing toward the river.

"Like, still standing?" Lily asked.

"Unless something's changed since breakfast." The young woman gave Lily a withering look.

"Are they Haida?" said Lily.

"Are you kidding? They're ours."

"Okay, thanks," Lily said. Sissy would be shaking her head. *Clueless.* "So head toward Alaska?"

The cashier rolled her eyes. "Not quite that far."

Lily pushed at the door and heard the girl scoffing to a man eating his burger and crinkle-cut fries. "City people," she said.

Back at her car, Lily still burned from the sting. How should she know where the totem poles were? She thought the girl might have been happy she'd shown an interest. She turned the postcard over and read that the poles could be seen from the Indian village on the other side of the bridge. She started up her Colt. Fine. Time to start learning.

A little brown sign named the river. Skeena. On the other side, a track-like road led along the bank. Lily passed an old wooden church, then saw the carved faces, arms and legs. Human and animal. Bodies with stories she did not understand. In *The Lord of the Rings*, trees could lift up their skirts and join the fight for something greater than their long and quiet lives. But these were something else. Poles as beautiful as the forest they'd come from. Maybe Sissy was right. What was the point of lumber? People need houses, but they tuck the beauty behind drywall.

Lily looked around for someone to ask or a sign that explained things. A small car filled with people drove past. Lily waved, but no one looked back. A man with a cigarette walked by. She said hello, but he didn't turn. The air brimmed with smoke and cold and she had southerner written all over her, just as the girl at the gas bar said. She put her car into gear, crossed back over the river and continued west.

At Terrace, the blue granite of the mountains shone in the sunlight, then came a turnoff to some place named Kitimat. Later, a diner in the middle of the forest offered seven kinds of pie. She roared past all distractions and drove into a landscape of glistening walls. The map told her the water was still the Skeena, but the river had become as large as a lake. Waves lapped at small islands in the middle of the flow and ice sparkled on purple peaks up near the sky. A train roared beside her lane, too close for comfort, and at a narrow bend, a torrent of water fell straight from a cliff and pummelled her car. Her hand searched for the wiper as the liquid slid down the windshield, blurring her view of it all.

If nothing else, she'd always have this drive.

As she entered Prince Rupert, she passed banks and hotels, a Greek restaurant with a special on samosas. But she couldn't stop. After two days of driving, the ferry was leaving in less than an hour.

She found the terminal and parked in a line behind a shiny black truck with dual wheels. A dually, Jeremy would have said. Would she ever tell him what she did?

Lily got out to stretch by the hood of her car. She tried to remember Blaize's warrior pose. A row of phone booths made her think of calling home again. Her mother had called Brian when she'd gotten to Prince Rupert. But Lily didn't know what else there was to say.

Dually-guy hopped out of the driver's seat and started checking all his straps. His wife stuck her head out the passenger side and called him back. The back box was bungeed with everything one might need to survive the end times. Giant packs of toilet paper, diapers, cases of Kraft Dinner and cheap beer. A toddler's bike. He glared as he bumped past her to his back gate. Lily shifted, but held her pose. Roll your shoulders back and down, she thought.

"All drivers report to their vehicles for loading." The announcement crackled through a loudspeaker and Lily took a deep breath and got back in her car. Vehicles started up and a minute later the little family in the dually charged forward, leaving her in a cloud of exhaust. She followed them into the depths of the boat and parked as directed by the uniformed staff.

Lily shut off her car and sat for a moment, taking more deep breaths. She looked at her map and traced her finger through the blue water. The Queen Charlotte Islands. Haida Gwaii. This was it. She was about to get lost.

2

Haida Gwaii

5

Lily had never been on a boat and started the voyage by walking laps around the vibrating deck. The sage green water so full of salt and froth. The dark islands sliding by. When she got cold, she found a seat in the front lounge near two boys constructing card tunnels on the floor. One pushed a Hot Wheels through the entrance and the other waited for it at the other end. If the car didn't make it, the deconstruction began.

Then a storm hit. The blur of salt wash hit the windows as the ferry plunged into each wave. The boys whooped like bull riders while an elderly lady in a hand-knit cardigan calmly tugged at flat twists of woody rope. More waves broke over the deck and the lady kept working. Lily's knuckles stretched around the base of her chair. She wished she'd called her father before she'd left. What if she never made it to the other side?

Two rows over, Dually-guy and his pregnant wife fought to get their toddler to lie down. When Mom got up and left, Daddy had to physically restrain the little girl. "Mommy doesn't want you right now." The little girl bawled.

Fathers. All their bullshit about providing a stable home. Lily had mostly grown up in the furniture store. A room full of fridges that didn't keep anything cold. Dozens of ice machines that promised crushed or cubed. She could hear her father offering the luxuries of automated frozen water, but at home, they never had any of the things her father sold.

As the storm deepened, the boys' card constructions collapsed. They moaned and rolled around on the floor. Lily wanted to curl under the seats too, but first she wanted her sleeping bag. She stumbled to the car deck as a wave smashed against the side of the boat. The rivets strained and somehow she made it to her car. She lifted the hatchback and tried to pull her inflatable mattress out. The boat pitched one way and her body lurched. She yanked at a stuff sack and it rolled under the wheels. A crewman in dark coveralls spotted her and ordered her to get back above deck.

Another violent motion and she grabbed what she could of her gear, slammed the back down, then ran for the stairwell. Upstairs, she found a bathroom and her insides crumbled. The ferry shuddered and groaned. Arlene, so full of storms, had never talked about boats.

When Lily finally stopped heaving, she attempted to stand, but the nausea came again. Finally, she clutched her sleeping bag like a pillow and stayed close to the throne. She must have slept because the next thing she knew, the engines slowed and a crackled announcement promised they would arrive in half an hour. The bathroom door opened and Lily, still locked in a stall, tried to stand.

"Gross. Fucking reeks." Lily could see the pregnant lady through the crack in the door. She patted at her hair in the mirror. Smoothed her hoodie over her sweats. "Fucking men. I can't believe I'm going through this again." She ranted her way into a stall, then farted loudly, flushed and slammed her way out to the sink. Water blasted from the taps. Her hand whacked at the paper towel dispenser and the paper dropped to the floor. Lily waited until she'd left and came out and splashed water on her face, rubbed her finger up and down on her teeth and pulled her toque back on. Dads were definitely a pain, but moms were not in Lily's good books either.

Back on the car deck the vehicles roared to life and the same crew guy who had shouted at her to get off the deck yelled at her to get into her car. Lily felt the boat thud against something and the wide bow doors opened. She thought of the gap between the trees at the entrance to the Ancient Forest Trail—the curtain of branches whisking aside, offering a new life. She'd been happy there, for a moment, until Blaize and the others had stumbled into her peace. Until Ryan had told her a story about their mother coming back.

Six bells at the Sea Raven, Monday morning. That was the only thing that mattered. Rick, the boss, said to turn left off the ferry. Right? But she was forced to go straight through the lights across the highway, then loop around to an intersection that said Masset was one hundred kilometres to the left. She swore he'd said the town was a five-minute drive.

Lily hesitated at the pointy edge of the median and vehicles split past, like a river rushing past a stone. Finally she turned right along a road that hung on to the edge of the dark green ocean. She opened her window to breathe the quiet, damp air. A minute later she saw a sign that announced the town.

When the houses started clumping closer together, a community emerged. The first commercial building was the Sea Raven Motel, with a restaurant attached. She breathed a sigh of relief and kept driving.

She stopped at a shop with red and white notices in a window—Purex bathroom tissue, twelve rolls for $9.99. Kraft Dinner by the caseload for $19.99. Everything Dually-guy had already bought. She pulled in and grabbed smokies and buns. A $10 bag of apples. A bunch of celery and a jar of peanut butter. Survival food. When she asked at the checkout about camping, an old man by the front door offered advice. "You vant camping? Try the graveyard." He pointed west, where red gashed the dusky sky. She must have looked stricken because he added. "Mein Gott. Don't worry. It's a proper campsite."

She hadn't been worried. Silly. Follow the road and take the left at the end. She passed a rickety dock lined with peeling-plank boats and a fenced field where a nut-coloured terrier and a blue heeler vied for the same Frisbee toss.

Lily continued past a tire store, a 1950s-era hospital and a freshly stained plywood high school. She started to relax. She loved all the wood. Cedar shingles on a half-dome roof. A trailer with an add-on. A houseboat on a platform that had been rammed onto shore. She found the intersection the grocery man had described and turned left into the darkness of trees. A giant puddle blocked the entrance of one pullout, a pile of garbage another. Tin cans, banana peels. Was that a diaper? Lily felt her mind spin as she started to question everything again. Her career path, her voyage to the islands, her need to get away from everything she'd ever known. One hundred metres later, the road ended at a cemetery gate.

Silly. It was just the graveyard, like the old guy said. Next to a campground. Lily stepped out of the car and saw a grey mushroom curled out of the earth like a rising finger. Across the wide mossy lawn, all crosses and cairns, the falling sun glimmered against the water. She moved through the rows, reading off names from fifty to a hundred years before—Moore, Beattie, Cochrane. A laughing sound led her to the rocky bank. She would have been glad to find company in this eerie place, but she looked through the chain link and saw no one else.

Back at her car, a sign pointed to the tent sites. She would not be afraid of a graveyard. She pulled her gear out and tripped over roots. Chattery, nattering sounds turned out to be squirrels. At the end of the path, she found a spot that looked straight out onto the beautiful calm bay.

She started building a campfire. Sticks layered like a log cabin, as her mother had shown her. Arlene snapping the branches into semi-uniform lengths, building the walls, shoving paper in. When it worked, it was magic. Brian would find long green willow boughs to roast the wieners on, and Lily would be allowed to sharpen them to a point herself. But if the fire didn't start—that's when Arlene's storm season began. Soon they'd be back at the car, then gliding out of the hills toward home. Brian trying to reassure everyone that he liked boiled hot dogs better anyway. Lily and Ryan trying to stay quiet.

With the structure ready, Lily still needed paper, so she wandered back to her car. She couldn't burn Sissy's photo of the Haida village. What about the photo of the cabin, a chip bag or her BC road map? She could burn the shoebox. But why did she need a map anymore? She followed the dashed line from Prince Rupert to the base of the shield-like islands. The map only showed one road. Not exactly a maze. She crumpled the paper, walked back to the firepit and tossed it into the cabin.

Lily whittled a cooking stick. Two smokies later, the sun was gone and she could hear sizzling noises coming from the fire—or the muddy beach? Maybe both. Lily pulled her sleeping bag up like a blanket and sat in the doorway of her tent watching the embers and the night sky fade.

She woke to a child calling. Was it all alone? She got up and immediately found herself in the graveyard. This time she tripped and fell into a headstone. It turned into a silver totem pole. And then she heard a wailing sound. She went to the fence and realized the noise was coming from the water. A form emerged from the darkness. She did not want to meet this thing in the night and she turned to run. Then she heard gnashing, chewing sounds and knew the creature had her by the toes. She thrashed and kicked. The entity chased her—and she woke to the sight of a large brown dog in the doorway of her tent. Legs splayed, it alternated between woofing and snapping at the grocery bag at her feet.

"Frida. *Freeeda*. Get over here. Now! Oh my god. Is someone in there? Come, Frida, come." Seconds later, a woman roped her arms around the dog's haunches and yanked it backward out the door. In the dull light of dawn, Lily scrambled up, glad to find herself fully dressed. The shopping bag contained remnants of the open pack of smokies. Stupid. Hello. Who leaves food in their tent? Who falls asleep with the door open?

"Are you okay?" A bookish woman with blue glasses stood over her gargantuan brindle dog, now leashed and laying chastened on the ground. "Bad girl," she said. The dog coughed against her collar like a chain smoker, and strained toward the grocery bag.

"Sorry. There isn't normally anyone camped down here at this time of year. Did she do anything to you?"

"She ate my breakfast," said Lily.

"I can give you money, or..." the woman started to say.

But Lily looked at her watch and panicked: 5:40 a.m. She had twenty minutes to get to the Sea Raven. Lily started pulling pegs and poles, stuffing everything into her pack.

"Don't worry about it, I've got to go," she said. "I can't be late."

6

Lily pushed into the diner at 5:57 a.m. She heard a guy at the counter growl something about Totem Timber. "Yep. That's me," she said, panting.

"Damn." He scanned her up and down.

She looked him over too. Brown foam-mesh trucker cap, unruly hair just shy of matching, a moustache that could almost be described as handlebar. He reached down to check his zipper and Lily could feel her eyes widening, but she forced a smile.

He tapped his wrist. "You're late."

She started to protest, but he shoved a styrofoam cup of coffee at her. "Six bells. That's when we head out. Not when you get here. You had breakfast?"

"No."

"Well, you missed out." He pushed past her and out the door. She rushed to follow.

"I'm fine." But Lily's hand went to her stomach to quiet the rumbling.

"Just don't come crying to me when you're hungry. Let's get this show on the road."

"Wait, Rick..."

He turned back. "You don't know much do you?"

Lily had hardly said three words, but this guy thought he had her all figured out.

"I'm not Rick," he said finally, then bounced down the steps toward a white truck with "Totem Timber" written on the side.

"But, I thought you were the boss..."

"Not everything is what you think, girlie... Name's Larry. We'll be on the same crew."

Lily stood on the step, disoriented. She wished she could come up with a smart retort. To Ryan, to Sissy, to this guy. She wanted to tell him not to call her girlie too, but she let it all slide.

"Cat got your tongue? Deer in the headlights?" Larry opened the truck door. "Thinking of bolting?"

"No, no. It's just that... Look out for that raven!"

A black bird swooped out of a tall tree and grazed the back of Larry's head.

"Mongrel!" He waved his arms in the air and it set down in the back of the truck, then croaked and started pulling at gear with its beak. Larry charged forward and it hopped onto the box rim, then flapped toward him again.

"That's no raven. That's a crow. He's after me every time. Fed him once and now he thinks he's my frickin' dog."

"The same bird?" Lily was skeptical.

"Yeah. Old One-Leg? He's easy to recognize," said Larry. "Most people can't see what's right in front of their noses though."

"I didn't notice," she said.

"Don't know the difference between a raven and a crow either. Nope, you don't know much at all." The crow called out again and flapped onto the roof.

"So what's the difference?"

"Ravens are larger, with big necks. Ruffled feathers. Plus they hang out alone."

Lily looked at Old One-Leg, by itself, with messy feathers all over its body, and wondered if Larry really knew what he was talking about.

"Crows are smaller and travel in groups. Except this guy. He can't keep up. Bit of an outcast." Old One-Leg cawed and scratched around in the restaurant eaves. Poor thing seemed hungry and Larry didn't seem to care.

Larry reached into the truck and pressed the horn. "You coming?"

"What about my car?" Lily had parked in a patch of gravel overhanging a slimy green beach across the street. "I can't just leave it here."

"You call that a car? Looks more like a soup can." He marched over and ran his hand over the hood, then stalked around to the passenger side and peered in the window. "Sandhill crane."

"Sorry?" she said.

"The feather in your dashboard. Grey with rusty tips. The males paint themselves to be more attractive to their mates. Where'd you get that?"

"I don't know. It was my mom's."

"Mate-for-lifers."

"What?"

"The birds. Good dancers too. Now let's get a move on. Forestry doesn't just happen."

"Okay, so my car?"

"You could leave that thing just about anywhere. Nobody'd want it." The crow called again and Lily saw it tossing papers out of Larry's open truck. She nodded toward the commotion and Larry yelled "Bugger!" then ran across the road, threatening it with a rock.

"If you're that worried, you can drive back up to the ferry landing and park there," he called back.

"Where?"

"Just follow me," he said.

Fine. Lily hopped in and reached into the back to gather her stray bits. The package of jerky she'd bought back in Jasper. Her bag of apples. She looked at the picture of the cabin and wondered again where it was, then tossed it in her mother's shoebox with the purple scarf. But she pocketed the tiny compass.

Larry sprayed gravel as he charged ahead and Lily gunned her little Colt to keep up. Silver water on her right and cars coming past her on her left. At the ferry landing, Lily was surprised to see the big white boat still there—smoke coming out the stack, cars loading into its wide-open mouth. One last chance to bolt. But no, she could handle this guy. She could handle anything.

Lily flicked her signal just after the terminal and pulled over on the ocean side, behind Larry's waiting truck.

He leaned out the window and called back to her. "Happy?"

"Here?" She thought he would lead her to a parking lot, but her car still teetered on the edge of the road.

"This is as good a place as any. Now get in. Time's a wasting. And we've got someone else to pick up."

Lily didn't have much choice. She grabbed her pack, tossed it into the back of the truck, and as soon as she hopped in, Larry took off. Around the corner, he veered below the main road and the black and white image from Sissy's book rose to greet her. The same crescent bay, fronted by sand and water, but the wood houses with giant beams and poles clustered in front were gone. Only one hundred years ago, Sissy said, and in their place, houses like you'd see in Frontier. Lily craned her neck as they passed one house with beams like in the picture. It even had a silver pole out front. Was it from the black and white photo times?

"So this is Haida Gwaii?" She spoke to fill the dead air and immediately wished she'd kept quiet.

"You mean the Charlottes? Or are you one of those?" Larry said. "People keep changing names for everything. This is Skidegate. The reserve. Or around here they call it the village." A second later, he stopped in front of a small white house. An old lady puttered in a garden that took up the entire front lawn. Larry beeped, one short, and then loud and long, until a young baseball-cap-backward guy bounced down the steps. He threw his stuff in the back and pulled the door open, forcing Lily onto the hump.

"Bye Gran," he called and the old lady looked up and waved.

"Chaz meet Lily," said Larry.

The young guy grunted what could have been a hello. Was he Haida? If this was the reserve, he had to be. But what did Lily know?

She knew she didn't like Larry's driving. Chaz was barely settled in with his seatbelt on when Larry pressed full-throttle on the gas. Lily lurched forward, off-kilter, and grabbed the dash to avoid bumping shoulders with either of them.

*

She was jolted awake when the truck bounced off the pavement. Lily remembered the ocean and then curves, trees and grass. It had all gotten to be a bit much and she'd closed her eyes. Now they were deep in the forest, no ocean in sight, racing along the rawest road Lily had ever seen. Sharp grey rocks and giant trunks in the ditches, still bleeding pitch. The radio squawked static and Larry careened through tight turns and burst over crested slopes. Lily bobbed in all directions. When her body tilted against Larry she felt cool. When she bumped against Chaz, she felt fire.

"Hey!" Chaz reached across Lily and slugged Larry. "Why don't you slow down?"

"Stop yer whining," Larry said.

The radio crackled again: "Leaving the hammer."

"Where are we headed?" she said.

"Into the bush. Where do you think?" Larry said.

She slid her hand into her pocket and squeezed Blaize's glass ball. He said it would keep her above the surface. She had to swallow to keep everything inside.

"Coming down the chute." Lily heard most of the rattling over the tiny radio speaker but missed what Larry said back into it before he pressed harder on the gas. The back end swung like an angry cat and Lily felt certain they were on on the verge of losing control. Then Larry cranked the wheel and skidded into a pullout on the driver's side.

"Are we taking a break?" Lily reached over Chaz for the handle.

"You sit tight," Larry said. A second later, a giant box with a crown of timber arcing over the top came into view. The truck wheels were as tall as their vehicle. Shaggy bark dragged in the mud and the snap of a remnant branch cracked against the passenger-side door.

"Road pigs." Larry snorted as the truck rumbled past. The second it was out of the way, he cranked the vehicle back onto the gravel and gunned it again.

"How did you know to pull off?" Lily said, still in shock. Larry just smiled.

Ten minutes later, the radio crackled again. Another gravelly voice: "Down the chute. Forty-eight." Larry said something back and swerved off to the side again. This time a truck rumbled past in seconds.

"Holy cripes," she said. "That was close."

Larry swung out onto the road. "Empty forty-eight," he said as they passed a small yellow number tacked to a tree: 48. She saw Chaz and Larry make eyes at each other.

"Fine," Lily said. "I get it now."

"It's magic," Larry said.

"He just knows," Chaz added, and they both laughed.

They drove on and on, rocking and sliding, skidding around corners, veering to the right on a Y. Lily was desperate to escape again. Surrounded by trees, but unable to focus on anything, she prayed for the radio to squawk and dreaded it at the same time. Then without warning Larry swung to the side and cut the engine. For good this time? She looked up the road for an incoming monster, but there was nothing.

"End of the line," Larry said.

Lily held the dash for a moment longer. "Is this where we camp?"

"Camp?" Larry laughed. "This is where we work!"

Chaz spilled out and Lily tumbled after him, gulping air. She tried to catch his eye. Make an ally. Recover her breath. But Chaz went straight to the back of the truck.

Chaz kicked off his sneakers and pulled on his big spiked caulk boots. "Where are yours?"

Where *were* her caulk boots? She looked in her backpack. Under her backpack. Throughout the truck's box. Could they have jumped out during one of Larry's insanity swerves? She racked her brain but couldn't remember putting them in the truck. Then an image came to her and she froze. The frigging ferry ride. Her frantic grab at her sleeping bag as the waves crashed. Her boots piled on top. She could see herself moving them to the car deck. She could not see herself putting them back.

"Fuck," she said.

"None of that language, young lady. This is a class-act logging show," said Larry. "You ready?"

"My caulk boots," she said.

"Get them on, girlie."

"I can't. I left them on the ferry."

"Oh for Christ's sake," Larry said.

"Language, old man." Chaz pulled two high-viz cruiser vests out of a tote box and put one on. The other he tossed to Lily.

"I told them hiring a girl was a bad idea," Larry said to nobody in particular.

Frigging ferry. Frigging truck. Frigging men, Lily thought.

Chaz ripped open a chip bag. Ketchup. She couldn't stand that fake, sweet smell. It made her think of carnival rides. Generators chugging. Her dad standing outside and Lily about to enter a maze. She took a deep breath, then looked past her coworkers and saw what she'd come here for—the quiet of the trees. Lily bent over and tied her hiking boots extra tight. "Okay, now what?" she said, standing straight and tall.

"You ready?" Larry said.

"Yup."

"No crying about lost boots?"

"Nope."

"Well, then," Larry continued. "Now we head into the forest to lay out blocks and measure the value of trees." He pointed to a thick, dark line of trees on an air photo. "Methodology: keep walking due north on this compass line until we get there. Think you can handle that?"

Chaz put on a pair of headphones and clicked a CD into his Walkman. Larry went back and buzzed around in the truck as Lily put on the red fieldwork vest Chaz had handed her.

"No problem," she said, and tried to believe her own words.

"Not so fast." Larry, arms crossed, blocked her path.

"Now what?" Lily forced herself not to burst into tears.

"Bear spray and a hard hat. No one's allowed into the woods without 'em."

She looked at her woefully ineffective shoes and wondered how a loose hunk of plastic would save her. Could she keep her toque on underneath? The cayenne pepper in the aerosol would probably offer more protection.

"Do we need to worry about bear attacks?" she said. Darwin had tried to scare her off with the size of the black bears on the islands. Largest in the world. Massive heads and biggest molars of any bear on earth.

"Never heard of one in all my years," he said. "Not like on the mainland. But rules are rules. So, where's your compass?"

A compass. Duh. The grad student would have laughed. They'd supplied them at school, but Lily had completely forgotten to get her own. She fumbled in her pocket for the miniature one from her mother's box.

Larry looked at her and laughed. "What the hell is that going to tell you?"

"Outdoor air temperature sixty degrees Fahrenheit," she said with a shrug.

"Cripes. Take a real compass," said Larry. He dug one out of the gear box in the back of the truck. "Do you even know how they work?"

Yes, she knew, she wanted to say in a snappy tone. Did he think she could go to forestry school and not learn how to use one?

"And you might as well carry the first aid kit too," Larry added, handing a small red case to her. "Lord knows you'll probably be the one who needs it."

"Thanks," she said, deciding that staying quiet was better than causing a fuss. She attached the compact first aid kit to her belt, then turned the compass dial to make north meet up with the red arrow. And with that she was ready to head into the forest.

But first, they had to get through a layer of crusted slash—stumps wider than any trees Lily had ever seen. Larry and Chaz marched as if they were on a groomed path while Lily's ankles shifted in the loose fabric of her hikers. She stumbled over branches and kept having to retie her laces. The guys leapt up and over obstacles with two firm steps while she had to work out strategies using elbows and knees. She missed how high her stiff leather caulk boots rose onto her shins. Shit kickers. She and Darwin found them at a second-hand store after the first weekend of field school. Not very ladylike, her mother would have said. Nope. But those rows of fang-like spikes meant she could cling to any surface. Stumps, logs, hummocks. Everything except rock. How could she have left them on the ferry?

She crossed the old clearcut and a stick narrowly missed her eye. Imagine tree planters trying to hack through a place like this every day. Tripping, scrambling and attempting to dig down to find soil so they could plant the seedlings they had to schlep around. She almost grabbed at a prickly plant, but then she didn't. Devil's club? Not usually in a clearcut, Liam would have said. But she couldn't stop long enough to identify it. She needed to keep up.

Once they got into the forest, everything changed. The quiet of the canopy. The soft, feathery footfalls. She forgave all that had happened before. All the driving, distractions and doubts. Lily had finally walked into the centrefold of the magazine.

Chaz marched on ahead and Lily would have been happy to be alone to soak it all in. But Larry hung back. Every few minutes he would spin to point at a plant. "What's this one?"

Lily couldn't even think, let alone spit out an answer before he spoke again.

"Fairy slipper orchid. I thought you'd been to school. How about this one?"

She thought she recognized the small green leaves, but couldn't remember the name.

"Single delight, not yet in bloom." Larry acted as if plant identification was a dare. He brushed his fingers through fern fronds and muttered something about maiden hair and swords. Then a bird called and he stopped dead.

"Winter wren. Like typewriters in a New York City newsroom," he said.

A few more steps and more calls through the trees. "Varied thrush. An eerie whistle followed by a deliberate pause."

Lily tried to spot the small creatures but couldn't focus on the flickering. Townsend's warbler. Ruby-crowned kinglet. Pacific-slope flycatcher. Three syllables. *Pseet. Ptsick. Seet.* Larry's constant chatter made her think of Arlene. *Don't call me mother anymore,* she'd said when Lily was thirteen. *You're almost grown yourself. I don't mind being a little kid's mom.* Lily's little brother had barely turned seven. *But I'm too young to be yours.*

"Little secrets," Larry said. "Most people don't see birds. They just walk on by without realizing the world is full of things they've never noticed."

An hour in, Larry had ditched her too, and she felt relief. She followed the compass line and stared at the forest floor, finally allowed to think for herself. Yes, Larry, she'd taken plant ecology, but she'd mainly focused on Alberta species. The Rocky Mountain slopes, the parkland and boreal. He hadn't given her a chance to explain. She thought of the wood lilies back home. LiPhi. *Lilium philadelphicum.* How red the star-shaped blooms could be when they were backlit by mounds of grass.

In this forest, she recognized a twisted stalk as part of the lily family. She touched the elongated stem, its accordion leaves, but she had no idea what to call it. Nor the tongue-like thing she'd seen unfurling out of the moss. Did she need to know everything's name?

A curtain of sun curled around the shaggy tree trunks and Lily stopped. Where exactly were those guys anyway? *How to Stay Alive in the Woods.* That girl in the gas station at Kitwanga scoffing at her. Lily would survive just to prove a point. What had she read? *If you stray from a bush trail, look for a new sign that you recognize and don't lose that starting point.* She scanned the ground and found a boot print in the mud, then squinted into the flattened light. Was that Larry's yellow jacket flashing through the trees? Could she hear the rap music buzzing through Chaz's foam-covered headphones? Nope. Only the sound of her own breath.

Lily looked at her compass again. The needle still pointed northwest—a bearing of 315 degrees. That was something. She knew all the paths at home: between her family's furniture store and the high school, down the back alleys, the tall grass between the sandstone bank and the barbershop. At home she couldn't choose a wrong direction; here she could blink and she'd be lost.

"Hello," she said to no one in particular. She reached into her pocket and worried Blaize's glass ball in her palm. She thought of that little tree-planting crew—Sissy, Blaize, Astrid and Jake—so sure of their purpose, marching through slash. Calling back to each other. Nights around a campfire. Huddled like small birds keeping warm.

Lily sighed. When would she find a place where she fit in? A noise came from behind a tree, as if someone cleared their throat. "Larry? Chaz?"

No answer. "There are no monsters here," she whispered.

Lily finally got to a creek and hoped it was the one Larry had pointed out in the air photos. She looked down the banks and found a huge spruce sprawled across a steep drop. Beer-like suds foamed on the dark ale of the water below. She considered staying on her compass line and skidding through the water, but then noticed a gash where the men must have pulled themselves up to the top of the log. If they could do it, she could too. But when she tried, her hip wouldn't stretch far enough, so she reached along the trunk to find a handhold. A broken, not-too-rotten stub of a branch would do. She heaved her belly onto the girth. A metre up in the air and she still had to rise to standing. She got one foot onto the log and braced to bring the other up. Then, as she pulled herself out of a squat, the land on either side fell away. Lily swayed above the rushing water and the wide swath of bark suddenly seemed as thin as a tightrope.

"Did I mention I'm afraid of heights?" she whispered to nobody again. She couldn't go back and she was terrified to go forward. Who did she think she was trying to move through this forest?

Lily commanded her soft brown hiking boots to move, one step in front of the other. Weren't they keeping track of the new girl? No complaining, Larry had said. God. All of a sudden she had to pee so badly. Brian told her not to panic at the threshold of the funhouse, let your instincts guide you. Bold advice from someone who'd sent a child into a room full of shifting floors.

Once on the other side, she exhaled. Safe, an umpire would have said. Then Lily turned to find a way down and caught her toe. That's when Chaz emerged from the woods.

"Holy shit." Chaz rushed to catch her slow-motion fall. Her foot was tangled in a vine and he teetered. Then the moss slid out from under him and they both fell down the bank and into the creek.

Lily was on her ass, and Chaz was on his knees between her legs, foamy tea-coloured water flowing around them.

"Oh my god," she said. "That didn't go well."

"What were you doing up there?" He was churlish, when he'd been so sweet the moment before.

"What did it look like? Crossing the stream," Lily snapped back.

"Might have been easier to just walk through it in the first place, like we did." He pointed at the blackened trail, moss disturbed, huge boot print on the other side. She saw their path clearly from this new perspective and wasn't sure how she could have imagined that they'd teetered across that log. But what of it, she'd succeeded. Almost.

"I was trying to keep my feet dry?" she said, finally, laughing.

He laughed too. "How'd that go for you?"

"Fine until you came along." Lily pushed past him up the steep bank, grabbed her hard hat off the moss and stuffed it back onto her head.

"Where the heck is Larry?"

Chaz shrugged. "I thought he was with you?"

"He was barking out plant names for a while, then charged on ahead. I haven't seen him for an hour."

"Weird. I guess you're lucky you didn't get lost."

"Wasn't luck. It was skill," she said. "I followed the compass and stayed in your tracks."

"Right." Chaz looked up at the height of the log over the stream. "Took guts to cross that."

"Thanks," she said, and then realized how badly urination needed to happen. Chaz was too close for comfort, but she didn't care. She tottered behind a tree and tugged down her pants. After the flow slowed and her heart returned to its normal pace, Lily stood. She couldn't believe she'd just peed in front of a guy. She turned to face him, but he wasn't paying attention. Chaz was fiddling with his Walkman and looking unhurried, as if he belonged to the forest. Or the forest belonged to him.

They found Larry leaning back on a mossy knoll, feet up as if he was sitting on a reclining chair.

Chaz laid into him. "Where the heck were you? She just about killed herself falling off some log."

Larry shrugged. "Must have been a test."

"Jeez," Chaz said. "If I hadn't shown up, she'd still be wandering around out there."

"I was fine." Lily tried to stand up for herself. "Right on course. I would have found my way."

"Well, if Chaz is going to go back looking for you all the time, I guess we'll never know," said Larry. "By the way, I radioed camp and they contacted the ferry. They found your boots and they're going to ship them in with the next supply run."

"What? Oh my god. Thank you!" Larry might be annoying, but he was Lily's instant hero.

She still had no idea where camp was, or what other challenges might unfold, but she felt sure that once she had her caulk boots, she wouldn't need Larry or Chaz looking out for her. She'd be fully prepared to make her way through this new world.

7

As they drove down the bumpy roads at the end of the day, Lily held her elbows to her sides and braced her feet on the floor of the vehicle. The day in the forest had been beautiful, but exhausting. She couldn't wait to set up her tent on a cushion of moss and make a cup of tea with her camping stove.

But when the road sloped out of the green, they moved into a huge clearing filled with giant machinery, ATCO trailers and sheds.

"Here we are," said Larry.

"Where?"

"The logging camp. Your new home," Larry said.

Lily's mouth still hung open as Larry pulled up beside a clean-cut man in a tucked-in plaid shirt. "Rick! This here's Lily. The new girl," Larry said.

She peeled her back off the vinyl seat to say hello and felt Chaz stiffen, flattening up against the bench to hide. Not that Rick paid attention to either of them. He barely grunted back.

"Prick," Larry said once Rick was out of earshot. He rammed the truck into drive and rumbled toward an arcing metal garage. A number of Totem Timber trucks in varying states of decay were parked outside. Some with logos and some without. Larry pulled up beside one of the most dilapidated and the three of them hopped out. Chaz immediately took off and Larry shook his head.

"So that's the boss?" said Lily.

"Guess so," said Larry. "Not that he ever gets his hands dirty. Or knows what's really happening on the ground… Taught him everything I know. Just like his son."

"Don't even start," a voice out of the darkness interrupted Lily's next question. Who was Rick's son?

"Lily, this here's Mac. Head mechanic and major asshole," said Larry.

Lily took the greasy hand offered by a short, brown-skinned man in coveralls. Was he Haida too?

"Larry's always had an inflated sense of his own importance," said Mac.

"Ya, well, I've seen them all come and go. Rick used to be the lowest man on Totem's pole. Brand new forest tech like you, Lily. Now, he thinks he's indispensable."

Lily had more questions with every thing being said. Larry and Mac insulted each other a few more times and she stopped herself from asking the obvious. If Larry had so much experience, why was he still a forest tech?

Anyway, who cared? She looked around at the jumble of shacks and mud and walked to the back of the truck to get her pack.

"Where do I set up my tent?"

"Tent? You're as green as grass," Larry laughed. "Looks like no one else is going to show you around, so come on."

They passed stumps jutting out of bare dirt on the denuded land. Bunkhouses teetering beside boulders big as houses. More metal sheds and ATCO trailers. The broken remnant of a five-metre-wide spruce tipped on its side.

"Pushed over by a D8 Cat," said Larry. "Then the buggers never finished the job." She couldn't imagine how the rest of the massive tree had been removed, but Larry continued on anyway. "A line loader hooked the pieces one at a time and loaded them onto the back of logging truck. Worth fifty grand a hunk. That was twenty years ago. Clearing this place has been a frickin' war."

"Looks like the loggers won," said Lily.

"Damn rights."

But Lily couldn't help being disappointed. A wood-cutting operation and nothing made of wood? They walked through the mud to the last trailer in the compound and Larry hopped up the steps and knocked on the door.

"Get lost," said a female voice.

"Renée, it's Larry." He aimed his words at the screen covering the window. "I've got someone for you."

"Who? That boy you work with? He can come in."

"No, its your roommate."

"I don't have a roommate."

"You do now. Rick said she'd stay with you."

Not a peep from inside.

Lily whispered to Larry, "I've got my tent. I can stay elsewhere."

But a second later, an older woman with a cherry-coloured scarf wrapped around her head pulled open the door.

"Tabarnac. I forgot about dat." Silver disks jangled from another scarf tied around her hips. She looked Lily up and down. "Well, don't just stand there. Get in."

"My bag is in the truck," Lily said.

"You go get that, Larry. And then you can get lost," she said.

Larry backed down the steps muttering about a crazy Quebecois witch and Renée threw churchy-sounding swear words—asti, câlice, tabarnac—back at him, before slamming the door.

"Okay, fine. You stay here, but keep away from my side of the room." Renée attached two giant hoops to her ears and Lily stayed in the doorway, surveying the space. Sarongs billowed down from the ceiling. Colourful clothes lay flung on what might now be considered her bed. Dirty cups on the bedside table, a bra on the lamp. A shelf holding an electric kettle. Several boxes of Celestial Seasonings tea. Renée had claimed every inch.

"Women. Always messing with other people's things. I don't like living with dem," she said, marching around, plucking underwear and t-shirts off of Lily's side of the room. "What you doing here, anyway?"

"I'm working… uh, I'm a forest tech." Lily stumbled, trying to find the right words.

"No, really. Why here? Why dis place?"

Again with this question? As if someone couldn't just arrive on these islands. "I answered a job ad."

"Tabarnac. Where did you come from anyway?" Renée kicked at a pair of red Doc Martens until they tumbled under her bed.

"Alberta," Lily said.

Renée groaned. "Why these women from the flatlands keep coming here?"

"They do? When?" Lily thought of her mother. Would Renée have known her? They looked about the same age, but Lily couldn't imagine the circumstances that would have brought lipstick-wearing Arlene into contact with this belly-dancer type.

"Yesterday. Last week. Twenty years ago. I don't know. But dey come dreaming of trees. Den find out its not so easy."

"What's not easy?"

"It's dark, Alberta girl. And dangerous. And nothing is as it seems. Don't you forget it."

"Okay. Okay." Lily just wanted to sit down. Unpack her things. Have a moment.

"De forest. De storms. De men who don't know how to tie down tings."

Lily tried to pay attention but her mind wandered back to the tangled place where she'd spent the day. Less than a year ago, she'd had no idea that such large trees existed. Now she couldn't believe any of the trees in Alberta were considered a forest. What a joke.

"And don't get mixed up with de dynamite ones," Renée continued.

"Dynamite what?"

"Men. Stick with me, young lady, or you're going to get lost."

"Okay, what about them?"

"One of the blasters blew up another guy's truck because he never cleaned his shaving out the sink." Renée emptied water from a bottle into the electric kettle and flicked the switch to boil. "And you stay away from my man." She shuffled her tea boxes, the smell of cinnamon wafting as she plunked a bag into a cup. "Dey call him Cookie because he's the cook, not because he's sweet. If I even catch you—"

"Don't worry about me." Sheesh. Renée poured the water and Lily wanted so badly to ask for a cup, but the woman didn't seem to notice.

"Now Chaz. He's the boss's son, but he's alright. You can have him."

"Rick is Chaz's dad?"

"You don know dis? It's okay, the young one is not like the big one. Didn't even grow up with him," she said. "Little boy was raised by his grandparents in Skidegate."

"What about his mom?"

"June? What about her?" Renée threw her soggy tea bag into the garbage.

"Where is she?"

"She took off."

Lily closed her eyes and tapped the back of her head against the door frame. Mothers taking off she could relate to.

"How long have you lived...?" But before she could finish her sentence, Larry was up the steps.

"What? She won't let you in the room?" He pushed past Lily

and dropped her backpack on the floor. He nodded his head toward Renée. "Don't listen to anything she says. She's effing crazy."

"Eff you, logger man." Renée shot Larry the finger as he pushed past Lily again and hopped down the stairs. "Dat guy is the biggest pain," she said. "Watch out for him too."

"Larry? He's harmless, no?" Lily said.

"He's not what he appears to be. Remember that." Then without notice she grabbed a sweater and marched out the door, sloshing liquid from her cup.

Lily sighed and looked around the room. Her stomach rumbled, but no one had mentioned meals. Wasn't Renée's boyfriend the cook? She picked up her bag and hauled it onto her bed. Opened the top. Her beef jerky and bag of apples fell out. She walked over to the kettle and flicked the switch. Lily chose a soothing chamomile out of her roommate's stash and started unpacking her things. No need for a rescue. No need to ask any more questions. Lily was happy to be left alone.

She woke up ready to face camp again. Her roommate hadn't been back all night, but Lily followed her nose and found the cookhouse. Renée—in a plastic hair net and breakfast-bloodied smock—slopped the scrambled eggs onto her plate with the same wrist-snap she used for everybody else. Lily picked up some toast and fumbled toward the maze of tables strewn about the room. A guy with a cook's outfit sat alone at one of the first tables and she gravitated in his direction.

"Sit with yer own," he said, after Lily made eye contact with him.

She veered away. Down the centre aisle she saw Rick with a freckled-faced, straight-out-of-high-school type guy. They both wore new Levis and matching button-down plaid shirts. The boss's clean-shaven smile looked like an offer, but Lily had been warned. At the next table, a clutch of heavy-duty mechanics waved her over. Grease pigs, Larry had said. Someone whistled.

A guy, loud and lean, in a white t-shirt and leather chaps, called to her from another table. "Stay away from those letches and come over here."

Lily hadn't fathomed how many people would make up this operation. She'd pictured a few forest techs and an outhouse. But this place was a small town—with its own complicated subcultures.

Instinct, and everything Renée had said the night before, kept her clear of most of them. Finally, she picked an empty table in the back and sat down. When she looked up from her breakfast, she saw Chaz waving at her. Larry sat beside him, shovelling in his eggs.

"Over here," Chaz beckoned. "You're with us."

8

"Look what I have to deal with." Larry took his hands off the steering wheel and waved them around as they drove past the fresh growth sprouting on the sides of a new logging road. "Lily. Green as grass…"

Chaz nudged her and moved his eyes over to the wheel, as the truck angled toward the ditch. She grabbed the bottom, turning it just enough to get them back on track, then snapped her hand away as Larry took control again.

"And Chaz." Larry continued his yapping, pressing harder on the gas. "More experienced, barely. But still, a papa's boy."

She could see Larry sneak a look at him, wanting a reaction. Lily side-eyed Chaz too and saw he wasn't going to bite.

Larry went on. "With a crew like this, we'll be lucky if we get anything done this summer."

Then Larry skipped like a record over the summer's plans. Lily imagined the DJ scratch version in Chaz's headphones. *T-T-T-Totem to take out 220,000 cubic metres*—the company's allocated cut.

"We've already slowed down due to bad log markets in the past few years," said Larry. "Can't even sell some of the goddamned wood we've got on to the ground."

Apparently the Americans were to blame. *T-T-T-Tariffs*. Raw logs and tariffs.

"American mills are so friggin' hungry for our wood, but we get crapped on for selling raw logs. Meanwhile Canadian mills keep shutting down because they can't compete. And the bureaucrats tasked with getting us out of this? Bunch of liars—or losers. They're always passing blame onto everyone else."

Lily tried to conjure what she'd learned in her forests and society class again. Raw log exports were profitable for British Columbia because foreign countries pay higher prices for logs and pay their millworkers less. But others argue that Canadians should be milling their own wood, even if the lumber ends up costing more. Keep more jobs here. Hard to disagree with that, she thought, although

Sissy probably would. Keep them standing, she'd say. Instead of feeding the dirty capitalist machine.

"Tariffs killed more than a few forest companies in the last few years," said Larry. "Next thing that'll screw us is the pine beetle. Those bugs are just getting going. Then we'll have dead trees standing and a glut on the market. You wait. In a decade, the whole industry will crash—again."

Lily looked at Chaz, who rolled his eyes and shook his head.

"We've had too many lean years." Larry took his hands off the wheel again and shrugged. "Can't even keep the workers on the islands." Chaz nudged Lily again and she steadied the vehicle. "Then we've got Chaz's people to worry about."

"Rick?" asked Lily.

Larry shook his head. "Haidas. Protests or court action. Either way, they're going to claim this whole damn archipelago. And they might just win."

"Run the whites off the island," said Chaz.

"That's what your people seem to want. Meanwhile the whites continue acting like they own the place."

"But the Haida do?" Lily said.

"Never gave it up or signed it over," Larry said. "Not like where you come from. In Alberta, the government parlayed and made promises and still the Indians got screwed."

"Unceded," said Lily.

"Seedlings come after they log," said Chaz.

"I mean the land hasn't been surrendered," Lily said.

"Ha!" Larry said.

"I was joking, Lily," Chaz said.

Lily turned red.

"Anyway. We can't keep any of these hornet nests happy. One way or another everyone's got bills to pay and logging's one of the only steady jobs on this rock," Larry said.

"People could be teachers, or work for the ferries?" Lily said.

"Jesus, city girl. That's not how it works. No logging, no workers. No workers, no families. No kids. No schools. No teachers. No little coffee shops. People don't seem to get the economics of keeping food on the shelves in a place like this," Larry said.

"I'm not from the city." Lily wondered if this lecture would end, but Larry kept going.

"Never mind. We've got goals to meet. Got to get at least three forty-hectare blocks laid out this summer or we won't max out our allowable cut. Then Totem Timber will be screwed anyway."

"We have to keep our noses to the grindstone," Chaz said in a singsong imitation of Larry.

Larry snapped his head toward Chaz and the steering wheel jerked with his gaze. "You got a problem?"

"Just keep your eyes on the road, old man."

Lily tried to nudge the wheel back to the left as the back end of the truck started weaving. "Okay, Larry. Slow down."

He steered into the slide and the truck got its purchase and snapped into line again. "I've got it under control, girlie."

When Larry finally pulled over, Chaz hopped out and went to the back of the truck to get his gear. "You still don't have your caulk boots, city girl?"

Lily looked over at Larry, hoping for an update on her boots, and got nothing. She bent to tighten her laces, then stood and faced Chaz. Best defence is a good offence. "So Rick's your dad?"

"That's what they say."

"But you're Haida?"

Chaz didn't answer. Silence: also a good tactic. Lily's mother used it all the time. Ignore questions when you don't like the topic. Lily waited in case he was just thinking about his answer, but the whine of two-stroke engines in the distance filled the dead air.

"If you two are done with family history, let's get at it," Larry said. "Stypes and the boys are logging a block on the other side of the valley and intend to hit this side before the end of the summer. Your dad might run the company, but I'd be more worried about those boys being out a paycheque if we don't get these surveys done."

"I'm not too worried." Chaz pulled a small orange plastic box out of the back. "Maybe you should carry this," he said to Lily.

"A hip chain? Cool." She took the box and tugged at the string. In one of her classes, she'd been shown how to thread one like a sewing machine. Lily tied the end to a sapling and a gossamer line spooled out behind as she walked. She liked the idea of staying connected to the start, even if just by a meagre thread.

"It's not like a trail of crumbs." Larry started off into the trees. "It's for measuring distance once you get to the boundary of a cutblock."

Larry took huge strides compared to her shuffle. Chaz bounced as if he was walking on a beach, but Lily couldn't walk as fast, with or without caulk boots. Besides, she couldn't help staring at everything. Not only the monumental trees, but the white-lipped shelf fungi. The rotting logs nursing new trees into life. Fern fronds curled like tiny fists. A flicker of light. A sound. What was that bird again? She could hear it typing away. Lily's line unspooled as she chased the men's shadows through the maze. Peer one way and you can see your way through, peer another and you're lost.

When Lily came to the edge of a slope, she looked down at the trees, fat and tall. Pumpkins, Larry said. Massive thirty-metre-high cedars. No twisted trunks or folded buttresses at the base. Fewer branches meant not as many knots burrowing into the heartwood. More money. She could hear Larry's voice in her head, but she couldn't keep sight of him. Lily checked her compass and the amount of string she'd unspooled—750 metres. They were supposed to stop a kilometre in by a small creek. She should stop wasting thread. She picked up the pace, her steps crunching over the tiny tree-like moss. Then she heard the crack of a branch and called out. She looked back and the gossamer line free-floated behind her. Something had snapped.

"Guys?"

Nothing. She started trotting. A minute later, she jumped when Larry cleared his throat.

"Run, Lily, run."

Lily hadn't seen him in the shadows, kinked hair puffing out from under his hard hat. A bit of moss on his moustache.

"Lost again?" he said, walking over to her.

"No. Are you sneaking up on me?"

"I was right there. You weren't paying attention. Not a good idea in the forest, by the way."

"Why not?"

"You're on the edge of the world, girlie. Not much farther you can go. If you keep running, you might plunge into the abyss." Larry, a doomsday prophet in an acrylic sweater with a thrift store dress shirt underneath. "Here, tie this around that big cedar." He passed her a roll of pink flagging tape.

"Why?" He was moving through the mounds, measuring the

space between thick columns. She couldn't figure him out. This guy had twenty years of hard-slog bush work under his belt, yet he was still doing the same surveying job she'd signed on to for the summer.

"Your Elders didn't teach you to stop asking so many questions?"

"We were supposed to meet at a creek crossing. I thought the cutblock was farther in. Why are you marking trees here?" she said.

"Cripes, Lily. Green as grass. This is where we're going to put the road."

At lunch, she finally got to flop onto the pillowy ground and let the forest surround her like a room. Trunks wide as walls; the canopy, a textured ceiling. Quiet floating over her like an old quilt. She rested her head against the root of a giant cedar and a sunbeam touched her face. She curled her body into the soft step moss. This was it. What she came for.

Five minutes later? Ten? The thudding sound of footsteps brought Lily scrambling to her feet. Clods of peat dislodged under her hiking boots as she heaved herself to standing. The stomping could be her co-workers, but what if it was one of those legendary local black bears? They were a mammoth version of the species, Darwin had said. Unchanged since an age-old sea level rise cut the land link between the islands and the mainland. Larry said they never bothered people, but she couldn't believe everything he said.

So much for her cozy room. The requisite bear spray lay on a fallen log in the opposite direction from her non-negotiable hard hat. If the thudding were Larry, he'd hassle her for not wearing her protective gear. But a bear? A sharp pepper blast might be her only hope. She remembered a mantra from one of her courses: *Safety first. Safety first.* So she leapt across the forest floor to grab the hard hat and jammed it on her head.

"Hello," she called. "Larry?"

He'd probably tell her it was a grouse. Where the hell was he anyway? She hopped over the log to grab the bear spray too and saw a shadow lurch between two towering Sitka spruce. The figure, steady and confident, moved as if the forest floor was as smooth as a living room's.

"Chaz?" Lily couldn't help stumbling in the bouncy-house moss. By the time she reached the far side of the small clearing, whoever—whatever—it was, was gone.

"Working hard are ya?" Lily jumped, but it was Larry.

"Did you see that?"

"Did I see what?"

"The... person... or... whatever..." She pointed to the spot where the shadowy figure had slipped out of the grove. What had it been? Not a bear. Too skinny and upright on its hind legs. She watched Larry stare into the collage of ferns, and then he looked back at her and shrugged.

"I don't see anything. Whatcha been smoking? Got any more?"

"I thought I saw..."

"What? A ghost? There's no one out here but us. Now where's Chaz? Time to get shit done."

Maybe it had been Chaz? But no, they found him curled into the crotch of a giant hemlock. His hard hat rolled to one side and his fingers woven under his chin. Larry poked his butt with his spiky work boots. "Wakey, wakey."

Chaz jumped from ground to standing in an instant, his expression fierce.

"It's just us," Lily said.

He maintained the fight position for a second, then his wariness dissolved. "Jeez. Can't a guy get a little rest?"

"Between Lily and her sasquatch and you and your napping, we'll never get anything done." Larry tugged at the back of his pants. "These cutblocks don't measure themselves."

Chaz looked at Lily with his eyebrow raised. *Sasquatch?* he mouthed. She looked away. She never said anything about a sasquatch. Larry could make fun of her, but she didn't want Chaz to. And so the three of them set off again, walking deeper and deeper into the landscape.

Lily and Chaz pulled a d-tape around another giant spruce while Larry was off in the distance poking at his maps. Lily was past the six-metre mark. "This is the biggest tree I've ever seen," she said.

Even Chaz looked impressed as she finally tapped the two ends together. "Six point three metres." Chaz let the snaking end of the fabric drop and scribbled the number down in his notepad.

Lily looked skyward and tried to untangle the top from the canopy. How the hell were they supposed to record tree heights to the merchantable timber line? You had to back away, measure the angle between you and the treetop. But what if you couldn't tell where the jumble of branches ended and the sky began?

Chaz got the clinometer out, but he didn't have the angle right.

"That guy I saw at lunch," she said to stop herself from critiquing his technique. She wanted Chaz on her side. "He walked through here like it was his backyard."

"What guy?"

"The one Larry was talking about. Just before we found you out in that hemlock stand."

"He was probably one of ours. Stypes and his crew."

"I doubt it. Those guys are way over by that clearcut from yesterday." She'd gone over it in her head a dozen times, trying to picture what she'd seen. A whisper of movement. The shape of a man? He couldn't have been in forestry. He wasn't wearing a hard hat.

"Well, are you sure it was a guy? Like, he didn't have seaweed for hair?"

"What do you mean?" Was that a joke?

Chaz tossed a few spruce cones at a fork in a branch that he'd turned into a basketball hoop. "Forget about it. Besides, we need to get back to the truck."

He let her set their bearing toward the road and followed for a few minutes, before he held up his compass to check her line. "You didn't adjust for the declination, so you're off course. If we go your way, we'll overshoot the road."

Lily looked at the compass he'd given her and verified against the angle at the bottom of the map. She'd been off by a few degrees ever since she'd entered the woods. Rookie move. Worse than not keeping up.

9

Back at camp, Lily started peeling off her mud-caked gear in the doorway. "Do you know anything about a guy with seaweed hair roaming around the woods?" she asked her roommate.

Renée grabbed Lily by the arm and pulled her inside. "Monsters in de forest? What is wrong with you? Taking off your clothes in front of everyone. I'd be more worried about ones in camp."

"Oh. Sorry. Mud management. I'm just trying to keep this mess down."

"De room is already a mess, crazy lady. So, seaweed hair? You mean Gogeet?"

"What?"

"The half-drowned one."

"What does that mean?" said Lily.

"Dey come from a capsized boat, half-drowned, crawling in from the sea. Why? You saw one?"

Lily took off her socks. Her feet were ghost-white with yellow hemlock needles stuck between her toes. "Larry said it was probably a sasquatch."

"He should know better. Dere are no sasquatch here."

"Actually, he said I was imagining things. That I should forget about it."

"Well, he likes to forget."

"Forget what?"

"A lot. Anyway. You should forget about him."

"Who, Larry?"

"No, the Gogeet."

"Why?" said Lily.

"Supernaturals. Dey can be dangerous."

"I think he was just a man."

"A wild man," said Renée.

"A real man, and he looked like he knew where he was going."

After dinner, Lily showered, and then went to find the so-called rec hall where Cookie offered drinks. Chaz had mentioned it and then nodded his head in the general direction, which she guessed was some kind of invitation.

Once inside, she almost didn't recognize him, hair all slick without a baseball cap. A fresh citrus scent emanating from his clean t-shirt—or was that some try-hard cologne, like the Drakkar Noir that Jeremy used to wear? He waved her over and ordered without even asking what she'd like. "Two rum and Cokes."

"All I got is vodka. Homemade—from potatoes," said Cookie.

Lily crinkled her nose and ordered mint tea as she sloughed off her puffy vest. Chaz stared at her for a second, then turned to Cookie with wide eyes until he dug under the counter and pulled out a bottle of crème de cassis.

"How about a shot of that?" Chaz suggested.

"I prefer beer." Lily pulled off her toque and her dark curls bounced.

"Can't argue with that," said Cookie. "Too bad there's none in camp." He set out two shots and went into the kitchen to find a teapot.

Chaz held up the purple liquid and made as if to cheers with her. "Nice to actually see your hair—without that beanie you usually wear."

"At least it's not seaweed." She could feel Arlene shaking her head. *The boy is trying to offer a compliment.* "The guy. In the woods? Some Haida myth about being half-drowned?" she said, trying to play it cool. He looked as if she'd poked him in the gut.

"I don't know what you're talking about," he said. But it was obvious that he did.

Still, she was happy to drop it. At this point, she wanted a friend more than an answer to a minor mystery. "I don't know what I'm talking about either." Lily pushed aside the tea that Cookie had brought her and picked up the shot glass. "Can I at least get this on ice?"

Chaz laughed and got Cookie to fix up her drink, then he rattled off a few jokes. Why don't cannibals eat hippies? They're too hard to clean. Why did they invent Earth Day? So we'd remember what planet we're on—that kind of thing. He talked about the Canucks screwing up and missing the playoffs and how he was saving for an F-150.

"Why such a big truck?"

"So I can get out of here? What about you. How did you end up here?"

"I like trees."

"What's so great about trees?"

Lily shrugged. "Better than Walmart."

"We could use one of those," said Chaz. "First place I'm gonna hit when I get to the city."

"You can't be serious. Why?"

"Good cheap shit. You can't get anything on this island."

Lily laughed. Haida guy seeks crap from China. She wondered what Sissy would have to say about that.

"So what's this about heading to the city? What are you going there for?"

Before Chaz could speak, the front door crashed open and Lily watched five guys come in, lacing through the tables.

"Like an incoming tide," Chaz said under his breath.

"Fallers?" whispered Lily.

"Yep. That one's Stypes." Chaz nodded at the longest and leanest. She recognized his buzz cut and sharp nose. He was the one who'd tried to call her over to his table.

"Hey boys," Cookie called out. "You're back late."

"Yep. We've been logging our guts out." Stypes snapped the Husqvarna suspenders holding up his chaps and turned to Chaz. "So Haida boy gets the girl. Makes sense, I guess. Haidas get everything else on these islands." He slapped Chaz on the back.

"Fuck you." Chaz pushed back his chair and got to his feet.

"Relax, pretty boy." Stypes dropped some cash on the counter and ordered a round of vodka shots for the house. "I just bought you a drink, didn't I?" He handed one to Chaz. "Bottoms up."

The guys all raised their glasses, then downed the shots and swiped their mouths. Lily left hers on the counter.

"I heard your girlfriend saw a sasquatch." Stypes reached over to grab the extra shot and slugged it back without even looking at her.

"I heard the boys shot a bigfoot out this way years ago," another guy said. "Wasn't your uncle on that crew, Chaz?"

Lily watched Chaz take a deep breath, but he stayed silent. She could tell he was holding something back. When he'd gotten control of whatever it was, he spoke.

"Is that a new saw you've been using, Stypes? What's the chain speed?"

Nice deflection, thought Lily.

"Fastest out there." Stypes responded without a second's hesitation. "It's air-injected too. Heated handles."

"No way."

"Yeah, baby. Only the best for these paws." He held out cracked hands the size of baseball gloves, rubbed them together and picked that moment to turn and wink at Lily. "Paid four hundo. Heard Joey's old lady poured straight gas in his when he was home last. He went to buck up the firewood and the engine was cooked."

"What a piss off," said Chaz.

"Chicks. You can't trust 'em." Stypes winked at Lily again.

Another round of shots arrived and the boy talk revved louder. Chaz leaned into the bantering as if he was being twirled on a dance floor. Lily couldn't stand it any longer and shouldered her vest.

Chaz touched her arm as she got up to leave. "Hey, where are you going?"

"I'll see you tomorrow."

The guys cat-called after her: "We scare you off?"

Outside Lily's shoulders relaxed. Yuck. What a bunch of testosterone. Too much like Jeremy. All of them. She picked her way through muddy tire tracks and was almost at her door when she heard footsteps moving her way again.

"Hey." A man's voice. Lily pivoted, hoping it was Chaz, but Rick stepped out from shadows.

"Oh, it's you."

"Sorry to disappoint."

"I just thought you might be…"

"Somebody else. Story of my life," he said. "Lily, isn't it? How are you making out?"

"Not too bad."

"That's not what I heard. I heard you've had trouble keeping up."

"What? Who said that?"

"Larry. He's wondering if you have what it takes."

"He said that?"

"Pretty much. And you don't have the right equipment?"

She sucked in her breath. Thrown under the bus. "I left my boots on the ferry. Larry said they'd be sent in with the next food order."

"Right. When I hired you, you said you'd be prepared. Working in the bush would be no problem. Instead, I keep hearing that you're falling off logs. Getting lost. Trying to catch up." Rick shifted back and forth, his boots making suction noises in the mud.

Lily stuttered, tried to find the right comeback, but he cut her off. "We don't get a lot of women working here and it can be tough. For everyone."

"I'll be faster once I get my boots."

"Sure, but that's not my only concern. I heard the boys have been razzing you already."

"About?"

"Something about a sasquatch you saw today?"

Great, even the boss thinks she's a wing nut.

"It was nothing. I'm surprised you heard."

"It's not easy keeping secrets around here. And sasquatch sightings get people riled."

She wanted to tell him that she'd never said it was a sasquatch, Larry did. She wanted to ask what the loggers shot, or if he'd heard of the half-drowned one—what did Renée call him? The Gogeet. But really, she just wanted the conversation to end.

"You seem like a nice young lady." Rick patted her shoulder and Lily stiffened. "I'm just saying, this isn't the right place for everyone. It's never too late to turn around and go home."

"I'm fine."

The rec hall door slammed and Lily glanced over. Rick followed her movement and saw Chaz and the boys. "Best to stay out of Cookie's liquor stash too."

"Okay. Wow."

"Sorry to be blunt. Guys in camp don't always treat women well. Look, if you were my daughter, I'm not sure I would have let you come..."

"Okay, thanks for the advice. I better go." Lily said, but in her head she was screaming, *Prick, prick, prick!*

"Well, I hope your caulk boots show up."

f

Lily opened the door to her room as Renée rustled under a wool blanket. Her long black hair roped across the pillow and a silk mask covered her eyes. "How was the boy?"

Lily pulled off her shirt and reached for her pyjamas. How had

Renée known where she'd been?

"Okay." Not. Chaz was trouble, just like Rick said. So city, she thought. Too much hair gel and lemony cologne. What had she expected? That he'd be all quiet and noble? In his spare time carving poles? Cutting fish to dry over racks? No, he listened to Public Enemy and the Beastie Boys and she'd caught him staring at her tits. Too much like Jeremy.

Renée's words slithered like air out of a balloon. "Never mind. Maybe you'll see dat one again."

"I'll see him tomorrow," she said. "We're heading up Dunbar Main."

Renée murmured again in the dim room. "Dey say it was a mistake. Den something happen and he run away."

"Chaz?" Lily said. She climbed into her sleeping bag and picked up *Plants of Coastal BC*, determined to prove to Larry that she could remember the name of every plant she saw.

"No. De other one. He's not a wild man. He's Walker." Renée's words were heavy with sleep.

"Who? The guy I saw in the forest?" But she could tell that any further chance of talking with her roommate had been lost. Lily looked out the window at the ash-coloured sky. A mystery man walking through the forest, as if it were his home. No higher-ups nagging at him. No one making fun of his pace. The thought of him made her stomach ache. Was he half-drowned, or someone who didn't want to be found?

10

In the morning, Lily tried to ask Renée more about the man. Walker. Was that a name? Or an occupation? When was this? How could a man survive, just walking around in the wilderness? But Renée kept brushing her off.

"Arrête, mon chou. Questions, questions. Annoying Alberta girls."

So Lily grabbed her gear—still no sign of her caulk boots—and met up with Larry and Chaz at the truck. Chaz didn't mention their evening at the rec hall and neither did she. They tussled briefly over who had to sit in the middle (Lily, of course), then the three of them set off into the forest again.

Back at the end of the road, Larry held up his compass, tilted it this way and that, and then walked north. Chaz checked his compass line and fell in behind. Lily, her compass properly adjusted, rushed forward too, pushing to keep up. Rick's words followed her every step. *You aren't prepared. If you were my daughter, I'd have made you stay home.*

Within half an hour, she was panting, her knees bruised from a fall, but she hadn't lost them. Larry stopped in a bright spot in the dark forest and unfurled his maps. Lily wished Chaz were more chatty (hadn't they bonded in the rec hall?), but he stood by a spruce, peeling flake-like discs off the bark, then scraping his front teeth down the soft inner cambium. She'd read in *Plants of Coastal BC* that people used the inner layer of Sitka spruce bark as a laxative. She watched Chaz roll the material on his tongue, then spit it out.

"It ain't a cakewalk. We've got some issues to overcome." Larry pointed at the maps. "Like the Haida Forest Guards."

"Who?" Lily said.

"A bunch of white people the Haida hired to tell them what areas needed protection from white people," said Larry.

She waited for Chaz's reaction, but he was kicking a rotten log apart.

"Supposedly a goshawk nest around here." Larry circled his finger on the map. "That'd be a mid-sized bird of prey, in case that's your next question."

"So you must know the question after that too?"

"Sound like monkeys. Some call them chicken hawks," Larry said.

"Ha, ha. Actually, I wanted to know why—"

"They eat chickens. They've taken out a few people's prize hens."

"Not *why* they're called that... why do *we* care about them?" She looked at Chaz again. He rubbed his finger on his tongue where the bark had been.

"*We* don't care," Chaz said. "The tree huggers do."

Aha. Chaz was paying attention.

"Sure," said Larry. "But we do too. If there's one in this proposed cutblock, it means no logging for us."

"So they're protected?" said Lily.

Larry made air quotes. "According to the 'experts' these northern goshawks are a different subspecies than the ones on the mainland, which are not at risk. So lucky us. Ours are threatened." He re-folded his map so the marked area faced out and slipped it into an extra large Ziploc bag. "And logging threatens their habitat."

Lily nodded. At school, they'd watched slides of big men wearing "Save a Logger, Eat a Spotted Owl" t-shirts. Diners in mill towns "offered" them on the menu for breakfast, lunch and dinner. They talked about Save the Owl legislation that had shut down timber towns and put men out of work. Families forced to move. Then a picture of another owl, a migrant from the east that wreaked havoc on the Indigenous population anyway. The barred owls weren't picky eaters like the spotted ones. The newcomers ate mice too, but also grouse and ducks, growing bigger and hogging the best habitat. So was it the fault of logging or just environmental change, the instructor had asked.

"What about spotted owls?" she said.

"A cross between a muted rooster and a French horn," said Larry.

"We don't have those." Chaz shot Larry a look. "Only saw-whets."

"Saw-whets. Knife sharpening on a whetstone," said Larry.

"What's a saw-whet?" asked Lily.

"A miniature owl. Not endangered yet, just 'of concern' to the Haida," said Larry.

"How about marbled murrelets?" The instructor had flashed pictures of the dainty sea birds with their upturned beaks nestled on pillow-topped branches. He said no one knew where they lived until the 1970s when a tree climber discovered a nest high up in the canopy of the California redwoods.

"A smooth *keer, keer, keer*, sometimes in two syllables," said Larry.

"Shut UP!" said Chaz.

Unperturbed, Larry took out his compass. "We likely won't find a marbled murrelet this far inland, but they're endangered too."

"So what are we supposed to do about the goshawk nest?" Lily said.

"Knock it out with a stick?" said Chaz.

"Not unless you want to pay the $100,000 fine." Larry wagged his finger at Chaz. "Your father would like it if we didn't find it, but I don't think your uncle would."

"Leave my uncle out of this." Chaz pulled his hoodie over his hard hat like a cocoon.

"Don't get your knickers in a knot," said Larry.

"How about we get to work?" said Lily.

"Okay little lady, you win. Let's move."

Larry directed Chaz to stay on the lower level of the bench to measure a promising line of trees and Lily to hike up the rise to look for the nest with him. Chaz readjusted his headphones and his hard hat as they parted ways.

"Chaz's uncle?" Lily said.

"Chuck's on the Haida Nation goshawk recovery team," said Larry.

"Chaz doesn't like him?"

"He doesn't like me talking about him. And his uncle doesn't like Chaz out here in the woods."

"Why?"

"I don't know. Superstitious, I guess," said Larry.

"About what?" said Lily.

"Sasquatch?"

"Come on. There are no sasquatch here."

"Oh, you think you're pretty smart, do you? Who knows, then? Chuck quit logging so he thinks his nephew should too?" said Larry.

"He used to be a logger? Did you work with him?"

"If he's worked in forestry, then I've worked with him. Anyway, enough chatter, our job is to look for the white wash at the base of the trees."

"Paint?" Lily said.

"Bird shit. It's usually splattered below raptor nests. Should be young ones by now, so the goshawk won't let us get too close."

"What will it do?"

"Dive bomb. They're nasty," said Larry. "Like as not we won't see them though."

"But I thought the Haida Forest Guards already found the nest?"

"They said they did, but sometimes they're just as notorious for marking stuff in places they don't want us to log as loggers are for 'mistakenly' logging in places the Forest Guards have marked as needing protection."

"That's insane."

"Yep. Nobody trusts anyone. Not even families like Chaz's. Now try and keep up."

Larry moved with his chin high, scanning for signs. Lily watched as he skirted a sinkhole filled with mucky dark water, climbed over a fallen log and missed a patch of devil's club, all without lowering his gaze. She plodded behind him as the light changed and imagined the clouds above the canopy settling into a thick drape. Chaz was downslope, hooking one end of the tape to a flaked piece of bark. He got halfway around, then jumped as if he'd been struck. She watched him wipe his hand on his jeans and leave a white streak up one leg.

Larry was already ten steps ahead when a dark shape passed through the branches. Three flaps, a glide and a flash. Then came the screaming. The blue-grey shadow careened into a free fall. High above Chaz's head, Lily saw the untidy heap of sticks, red hemlock needles and pale green lichen resting on a branch. Cones of white fuzz peeked out the top.

Lily shouted at him but Chaz had his headphones on and seemed not to hear.

"Larry!" she called, changing her tactic, "do something!"

Larry yelled Chaz's name and made him look, but a second later Chaz took the strike. The bird whacked the top of his hard hat and knocked him down.

"What the...?" He hit off his headphones.

"Goshawk," yelled Lily. "It's coming back."

Chaz looked up as the dark rocket looped around for another try. He scrambled to his feet and ran, skidding head first under the safety of a scaly yew tree. Lily and Larry clambered down the slope toward him. The bird screamed, veered and then landed on a perch, staring at them with rabid eyes. The monkey-like noise rang through the forest.

Chaz was shaking and swiping the leaves off his lap. "Fucking forest," he said.

Larry pumped Chaz's arm as he helped him to his feet. "Congratulations, you found the nest. Still want that stick?"

They marked the spot on their maps and Chaz stayed quiet as they finished up the rest of the day. Lily wanted to razz him, but he seemed so pissed off that she left well enough alone. When they got to the truck and he slammed the door while Lily still stood outside, she couldn't take it anymore.

"Dude, take a chill pill. I've got to get in too."

"I hate this job." He opened the door but wouldn't slide over and got out instead, tapping his foot as he waited for her to take the middle. Then he got back in and slammed the door again. "I've got to get out of here."

"Right," said Larry. "Like, where are you going? To work at the gas station?"

"I'm going to the city," said Chaz.

"Please," said Larry. "What do you know about the city? And how are you going to get there?"

"I'm buying a truck. I'll have enough saved after this summer. Not that it's any of your business."

"What the hell for? You have a job. A place to live. Family. What are you going to do down there that's so much better?"

Chaz pulled his cap around and down so that it covered his eyes. "Find out what happened to my mom." He said it like a dare. Whether to himself or someone else, Lily couldn't be sure. Chaz crossed his arms tightly and slouched into the seat. Lily bumped against him as they drove, but neither she nor Larry said another thing.

11

If Lily's whole goal in life had been to spend time walking in the forest, she'd certainly gotten her wish. Each day brought more and more movement through the trees. Rain or shine, didn't matter. They were on a mission to enter the old growth, count trees, find their way back to the truck and repeat. Lily fell into the rhythm. Steady, but different every day. A little bit perilous. Watching, listening, she could feel the surface changing beneath her feet.

One morning, she woke up late after an overnight downpour. Rivers of muddy water rushed along the jutted tracks and she wondered if it was too soggy to work. Was that a thing? As she crossed the compound, the rain pummelled the tin roofs. She went to the cookhouse and grabbed a sandwich for breakfast. By the time she got to the office her hikers were soaked. She wondered for the millionth time about her caulk boots. Were supplies in? Grayson, the young guy in the button-down shirts who always sat with Rick, was on the phone as she went to grab the keys for the truck. He reached out, opening and closing his hand, as if trying to stop her, but she avoided him, got what she needed and left.

Outside, she watched Larry stagger toward the truck carrying a blue storage tote.

"I've got the keys." Lily waved them in the air. "And what about my—"

"Hand them over," he interrupted her. No hesitation. Nothing to give.

"I thought maybe I could drive?"

"Are you joking? I haven't seen this much rain since '84 when the whole side of Steep Mountain came down." He tossed the tote into the truck's box. "Covered a new road we'd just built. Just missed the truck the new guy was in. He thought he could drive that day too."

Chaz had arrived, squinting into the rain and pulling up his hood. Lily looked at him, pleading with her eyes: *Say something*. But Chaz just shrugged. Larry pulled open the truck door.

"Any news about my boots?" Lily said. "You said they'd be in with the groceries?"

"Did I?" said Larry. "My job is to transport you to the job site. Safely. And that's it."

"What a bunch of bull," Chaz whispered to Lily after Larry slammed the door. "He's the worst driver ever."

"Maybe you should see if he'll let you drive," she said.

"Yeah, right."

Chaz and Lily crawled in and Larry gunned it, spraying mud back at Mac's garage. Then he stopped just as quickly as he'd started.

"Hey," he said to Lily, "Run back and ask Mac for some elbow grease. We're going to need it today."

She nudged Chaz to crack the door and then started hoisting herself out of her seat, until she realized what he'd said. "Ha, ha." She sat back again and Larry and Chaz were were still chuckling as they hit Dunbar Main.

Larry took each bend at speed and started his yapping about all the territory they still had to cover. The truck wobbled over washboard and just before a pothole that covered the width of the road, Lily and Chaz looked wide-eyed at each other. Larry went straight through the middle without slowing down and the pooled water splashed up and over the windshield. Lily braced her arms against the dash.

"Brutal," Chaz said.

The truck radio crackled and Grayson's voice rustled onto the airwaves. Something Larry. Something that Lily thought sounded like boots.

"Christ. That kid is still in the office. He should be out in the field." Larry whacked the radio off, then continued on about Grayson and how much he sucked up to Rick. How he needed to get his hands dirty and do some real work.

"I want to hear what he's saying." Lily reached down to turn the sound up but Larry pushed her hand away and the truck swerved.

"Slow down," she said louder than she'd meant to.

His face reddened and he turned to stare at Lily straight on. Opposite reaction than she had hoped. He wasn't even looking at the road. Lily clutched the dash as the vehicle raced into another bend.

"Watch where you're going," Chaz yelled and Larry cranked the wheel. Lily held her breath.

"Larry!" The truck started to skid and Lily shouted as if that might help.

"Don't you worry, princess. We'll be fine. Just hold on," he said.

Lily had held onto Jeremy the night that now seemed a lifetime ago. Her hand on his knee as the tire hit the soft shoulder and the truck drifted into the ditch. Her arms wrapped around him later as they made out. A whole night spent hoping, and not hoping, that someone would come along and pull them out.

Larry jacked the wheel back a little too hard and Lily remembered the gut-punch she'd felt when her pregnancy test came back. First time lucky, someone might have said, if getting pregnant at eighteen was funny. Or if she'd ever told anyone. Arlene was already long gone. Telling Brian was a hard no. Lily remembered her throat filling with fear, then grief, as her life spiralled out of control. She'd gone to find Jeremy at the horse races to tell him, but he'd been making out under the bleachers with that concession girl.

Action. Distraction. Things had been moving too fast, and the next thing she knew, Lily could feel the teetering. The calm before the darkness. One last swerve before Larry rammed the front end of the Totem Timber truck into the ditch.

"Now you see why I didn't want you driving on these slick roads?" Larry held the steering wheel as if nothing had happened and casually reached over to switch the radio back on.

"You're a disaster, as usual," Mac said when Larry got a hold of him, but regardless he promised to come with the winch.

Larry pulled out his maps. "I'm going to sit here and make a few adjustments to our route. We'll be on our way in no time."

"Well, I'm not sitting around." Chaz opened the door and the truck groaned as he hopped out.

The rain had stopped, so Lily slid across the seat and jumped down too. She followed Chaz up toward the largest clearcut she'd ever seen. Tall, skinny leftover stems, bending with wet and wind. Bare limbs turned silver within nests of fallen bark. Chaz climbed onto a table-wide cedar stump and held his hand out to pull her up. She scrambled to the top without his assistance and looked across the debris field.

"Is this one of ours?"

"I don't think so. We're in Cradle Logging territory." Chaz brushed his hand over a small cluster of salal growing out of the tree's base.

"Whose?"

"The big licensee. They've got the volume-based cut in this area. Our chart areas wrap around the end of theirs."

"Which means?"

"We're only allowed to cut in adjacent areas. I guess that's what Larry is trying to figure out. Where their territory ends and ours begins."

"Larry's got it in for me."

"What do you mean?"

"He told Rick—I mean your dad—that I couldn't keep up."

"What? He's an asshole."

"Who? Larry or your dad?"

"Rick. Just call him Rick, okay? Never mind about him being my dad."

Fine. They're both assholes. Maybe Chaz is one too. Lily waved her hand at the clearcut to change the topic.

"So this is what we're here for?" She wondered how Blaize and Sissy and all the other tree planters were doing, frolicking in the slash. Happy, horny and healing the earth.

"Yeah. But we don't do cuts like this," Chaz said.

"What do you mean?"

"This is insane. They shouldn't be allowed to take this much at once."

"Really?" Lily wondered if Chaz was more like Sissy than she thought. She wanted to ask him about Haida land and who should be allowed to do what, where, but she didn't know how to begin. At the houses in the picture that Sissy gave her? The carved poles. The time before chainsaws. What did his people do before that to bring trees down? How did people survive? How did the guy she saw in the forest survive?

"Hey, Chaz. What would you do if you had to stay out overnight?"

"Where?"

"Here," she said.

"In the forest? Not going to happen," he said.

"But if it did?"

He shrugged as if she were joking, but of course he would know what to do. He was always picking at plants and eating them. He'd probably curl into a hollow tree, like a bear.

Her survival book said if you are stuck out for a night, find a boulder or a fallen log and build a shelter using that as one of the walls. Layer sticks and leaves to block out the weather. Gather wood for a fire. Then what? Stay calm. Find a water source. Eat bugs. Look for someone like Chaz. Or the hermit.

"You could take down a deer," he finally said.

"What?"

"If you were hungry enough in the forest."

"As if I could take down a deer."

"Serious. You'd be doing the islands a favour. They're only small and they're pests. Introduced by white people in the early 1900s because they were worried about finding enough to eat, and now they're decimating cedars and huckleberries."

"There were no deer before?"

"Nope. Used to be caribou, though, but those got hunted out."

"So I guess the white people weren't wrong?"

"About what?"

"The deer providing more to eat?"

"Yeah, as if Haidas weren't doing perfectly well before they came along."

"Eating what?"

"Salmon. Seafood. That's our mainstay."

"But you want me to catch a deer?"

"We're out in the middle of the forest, Lily. Do you see any fish?"

Lily didn't like his tone. She pulled her glass ball out of her pocket and started rolling it around in her palm. "So Gogeet is apparently just a guy."

"What are you talking about now?"

"That's what Renée said. She called him Walker. I couldn't figure out if that was his name or what he does. Then, I don't know. She hasn't been around and I haven't been able to find out any more."

"Well, that's quite a tale."

"Is it true? What do you know about him?"

"What? Me? Nothing," said Chaz.

"Come on, how could there be a mysterious guy wandering around in the woods and you haven't heard about him?"

"Some weirdo in the woods? That's got nothing to do with me," said Chaz. "Maybe you shouldn't be so nosy either." He snatched the glass ball from her. "Where'd you get this?"

"Who's being nosy now?" she said. "Someone gave it to me. Why? Are you jealous?"

"Ha. I've seen fishing floats a lot bigger than this. Still, it's pretty cool. Must have been someone real nice to give you such a gift."

"Nicer than you," she said and grabbed the ball back from him before jumping down off the stump. "I guess we better go see what Larry is up to."

"I guess," said Chaz, pretending like he was going to chase after her.

They scrambled up to the road and Lily couldn't help herself. "Why is Mac so agro toward Larry all the time?" she said.

"Who knows," said Chaz.

"Like, did he steal his girlfriend?"

"That's unlikely. Larry would not be Banger's mom's type."

"Banger? You know a guy named Banger?"

"Mac's son. He's my best friend... and it's a nickname. People have them around here."

"Okay, but why that one?"

"It's stupid."

"So? Tell me."

"It's something that happened a long time ago."

"What?"

"It's got nothing to do with you," said Chaz.

"Jeepers. That's obnoxious," Lily said.

"Who? You?" Chaz said.

"No," said Lily, "you."

"Takes one to know one," Chaz said, then slugged her in the arm and laughed.

The rain started up again, so Lily and Chaz jogged back to the truck. Larry jerked out of his snoozing as Lily opened the passenger door, then he started shuffling his papers, as if he'd been busy the whole time. They climbed in, just as a vehicle pulled up. But it wasn't Mac.

"What are you losers doing here?" A bearded guy in a dark green Ram truck with "Cradle Logging" stenciled on the side rolled down his window.

"Hey Fletcher," said Larry. "All good."

"You don't look good. You look fucked. But if you're out here looking for the a-holes who've been monkeywrenching around again, I might be persuaded to help you out."

"What are you talking about?" said Larry.

"We've been out marking cutblocks in the last few days and come back to find the ribbons gone. Other times stuff gets stolen from trucks while the guys are out in the bush. Gas gets siphoned. Lucky those boys were in radio range, because our mechanic had to drive out and fill them up again."

"Well, that's bullshit, alright, but I don't know why you'd think we'd be looking for them."

"Oh, I think you do, Larry," said Fletcher. "Seems to me you were implicated the last time this kind of shit happened."

"What? Eff you."

"No, eff you. Asleep at the wheel while someone dumps enough sugar to bake a goddamned cake into a loader tank. That's hard to swallow."

"Christ, Fletcher, are you talking about twenty years ago? That was some transient."

"Yeah, right. Rumour has it that hermit is still messing around out here. Gone wild or something."

"Don't tell me you believe in ghosts," said Larry.

"You know who I'm talking about. I heard he was a friend of yours. It's time that guy got hauled in.

"Nothing to do with me," said Larry.

"You're such a weasel." Fletcher jumped out of his truck and came toward them. Lily watched Larry stiffen and slowly reach for his bear spray. She waited for the shitstorm to begin, but at the last second the Cradle guy veered back for his winch and hooked it to the Totem Timber truck.

"Did you motherfuckers ever pay the use agreement for this part of the road?" he said as he got back into the driver's seat. "Don't just sit there, Larry. Put 'er in reverse."

Larry scrambled with the gear shift as the winch started turning.

"See," she said to Chaz.

"See what?"

"The mystery man. He exists. This guy even says so."

"This Fletcher guy? He's an asshole," said Chaz.

Lily didn't think he seemed any worse than any of the other

guys. He was pulling them out of the ditch. Plus she loved the gossip he was dishing. The hermit was a monkeywrencher?

The two vehicles growled, but within a minute, Fletcher had yarded the Totem truck back onto the road.

"We maintain these bastard back roads, then Rick thinks he can just use them like a damn highway." Fletcher spoke into his radio, then he turned back and said they couldn't go until he got confirmation.

"Yeah, of course we did," Larry said under his breath.

"Did what?" Fletcher was already out, unhooking his equipment. "Speak up Larry. Tell the world, not your moustache."

"I said, we paid."

"Bullshit. Where's the paperwork?"

"Got 'er right here." Larry made a show of going through the glove box, but then Mac pulled up with the tow truck. Mac and Fletcher's chests heaved, fingers pointed, there was talk of liability—retribution. Finally, they all decided that Larry would go with the Cradle guy and Lily and Chaz would head back in the tow truck with Mac.

"That guy is a piece of work," said Mac, as he prepped the dented truck for towing.

"Who?" said Lily. "The Cradle guy?"

"Not him," said Mac. "Larry."

"Larry? What about him? He's one of ours," said Lily.

"Ya, but you don't know the half of it, girlie. Not the half of it."

12

After all the truck shenanigans, Lily hadn't gotten her full quota of walking for the day, so she hit the beach after dinner. Or what passed for a beach beyond the rickety-looking dock. What the hell was she doing with a bunch of jerks in a muddy clearcut on the edge of a log dump lake? Or ocean—supposedly this was an ocean, even though she could see all the shores. Her ankles wobbled as she moved over the rocks and her smallest toe crushed against the edge of her boot. That she could fix, so she stopped, loosened the laces, looked back at camp. She had so many questions for everyone, but she didn't feel like talking.

 Maybe she should just walk along the edge and all the way out to the sea. Larry said a channel reached north to the open water. That's how the logs got to market. Soon, a big barge would grind its way down the inlet, load up, then drag them all out to a sawmill somewhere. Lily tried to picture the map of the island and think of where she was. Where her mother might have been. Where had she found that feather?

 Lily kicked a festering pile of seaweed, then recoiled as hundreds of lice-like bugs jumped into the air. A black bird gargled in the fading light. Raven or crow? It swooshed past her and landed on the slick black rocks. The bird's feathers ruffled at the neck as it poked at the barnacles. Raven, Larry would say.

 She looked out across the hilly islands covered in a light green glow. Most had been logged off and Larry said they'd greened up good. In the still light, she could see a mirror reflection of the trees in the water. Her toque-topped silhouette. She wondered what lay below the surface and tossed a rock in with a splash. The raven rose, squawking, and the ripples blurred her distorted shape. Lily stepped on a clamshell to hear the crunch and followed the raven down the beach. When she got near, it flew off again. The sun felt golden on her cheeks and the water pulsed with tiny waves. Was it going out or coming in? Or hovering in place, like a tiny hummingbird?

At a curve, she hopped over a creek, heard the raven again and when she found it, she noticed a cabin sitting back on a grassy clearing. She heard the slap of a door and looked back the way she'd come. She could just see the dock, jutting into the inlet. And here was a cabin like the one in the photo in her mother's box.

"Hello?" Lily called and moved closer to the building, but no one appeared. No one answered her knock, so she pushed at the handle and spoke again, just to be sure. The little space absorbed the sound.

Someone must live here. But who? The Walker? All these people acting as if they didn't know who he was and he lived right next door.

A pretty sparse life, though. The platform bed was a piece of foam with no bedding. She saw one cup and a plate by a makeshift sink. She flipped through the small shelf of books. A ragged copy of Colleen McCullough's *The Thorn Birds*, a coverless Louis L'Amour, a tall pebbled hardback with a thin green spine and a thicker book called *Queen Charlotte Islands: Of Places and Names* by Kathleen E. Dalzell. She pulled that one off the shelf and it fell open to a hand-drawn map. Masset Inlet to Juskatla West. The wriggled lines of an inlet that she recognized from Larry's maps as Totem Timber's stomping grounds.

Lily turned pages and saw that old villages had been everywhere. You could find ruins of lodges and even some town called Help-Received-Unexpectedly. Sissy would be all over a book like this. As she browsed, a paragraph about an old trail that led from the inlet to the west coast jumped out at her. "Little is known of who made it or why. Reported to be overgrown today." The book was written in 1973. If the trail had been overgrown then, it must have disappeared by now. Still, she was intrigued to see how short a walk it might be to the open sea, if anyone could find where to start.

The only other things in the room were a blue storage tote and a net bag full of light blue glass balls. Fishing floats keep you above water, Blaize had told her. They were bigger than the one she had. Would anyone notice if she took one? As she bent to try the knot, she noticed something that looked like aerial photos under the storage tote. When she knocked it, the lid tipped off and she saw the box was full of old flagging tape. Fletcher said someone had been removing markers from Cradle cutblocks.

She wanted to take a better look at the maps, too, but heard a raven call again. A noise outside. If the mystery man walked in, what would she say? Did you sabotage a loader? Is that why you're on the run?

As if. Besides, Lily saw headlights bumping through the trees. Whoever was coming to the cabin had a vehicle.

She'd better just go. Lily grabbed the door handle and her gaze landed on a scrawl of words pencilled onto the door frame. *April, May, June*. The months, or were they names here? Hadn't Renée said that June was Chaz's mom? She tried to decipher more letters beside lines that seemed to indicate different heights—*Larry* maybe, was that *Chuck?*—but then the raven screeched. She slipped through the door and took cover in the shadows where the raven had flown. The truck lights blinked off before it reached the clearing. When it got to the cabin, the door opened and someone wearing a baseball cap hopped out. The silhouette (a he or a she?) went around to the back of the truck and hauled two more blue totes into the cabin. Lily contemplated calling out, but the raven gurgled again.

"What?" She watched the bird tilt its head, its neck feathers rising like a mane. The cabin door slammed and the person threw a lighter tote back into the truck and reversed into the forest. Lily heard a whoosh above her head and the big black bird croaked, then swooped off the branch and flew back toward camp. She wanted to see what had been dropped off but the raven seemed to be telling her to follow, so she took the hint and left.

13

"Where's Larry?" Lily said the next morning when she met Chaz out by Mac's shop. "The Cradle guy still holding him hostage?"

"I'm sure he's fine. Something about making new maps so we don't have to use their road again," said Chaz.

"So the truck's okay?"

"Ya, Mac gave her a full run-through."

"What was that guy going on about? The sugar in the gas tank?"

"Something that happened years ago," said Chaz.

"Was it the hermit?"

"I don't know. I heard some hippie chick got blamed."

"Like Renée?"

"Maybe, but I doubt it. She'd never work in the forest again if that was the case." Chaz followed Lily to the truck and then tossed her the keys.

"You're letting me drive?" Lily ran around and jumped into the driver's seat before he could change his mind. She forgot about the hermit, the hippie and the flagging tape and concentrated on the road. Lily knew the route. They'd driven it every day before Larry dragged them into Cradle territory. Turn left on the road out of camp, then along the main line for ten kilometres, then the first right. Then follow the road around the bottom of the inlet, past a dark green lake and up through the fresh logging roads on the west side.

Rain had gushed again all night and the roads were still slick. Through the flicking of the wipers, Lily kept her eye out for strange movements. A deer could pop out of the trees at any moment. Or a hermit. When Lily leaned into the last turn, tires grinding over sharp crushed rocks, Chaz spoke.

"Good to know," he said.

"What?"

"You aren't perfect."

"Far from it," she said. "I may be slow, but I'm careful."

"No. You missed the turn. Back a hundred metres. This is the beginning of the road to another cutblock. But it's okay, we can start from up here too." Chaz pointed at a pullout and then started organizing their maps.

Lily continued a little farther and then rolled to a stop behind a white Jeep. "Looks like we got company," she said.

"Shit."

"Who is it? Gogeet?" Lily thought she was being funny, but Chaz stiffened. Hot, then cold. He'd been acting so nice again, as if they were actually friends, but some kind of shield kept going up.

"Let's get going. We've got a long day." Chaz went around to the back to grab his gear and called out, "Lily! Have you seen what's in this tote box?"

Her frigging caulk boots. "What the hell?" Lily pulled the box filled with bits of equipment toward her. "Did you put these here?"

"Nope. The tote was in the truck yesterday, though. I remember seeing it when we got back to the shop."

Lily had a vague memory of Larry carrying it out to the truck.

She snatched her boots and the barbs hit her shin. Fine. Fine. She kicked off her hikers and pulled on the shit kickers. Tightened the laces. Slapped on her hard hat. Hooked the bear spray to her belt. She tried to focus on where she was, instead of all the secrets everyone held. Totes filled with ribbons, and maps of what? What had she seen in the cabin? Who had been in the mystery truck? Not the hermit, surely. Maybe it was none of her business.

In the forest things were knowable, like which bird made the long, swooping whistle. Except she couldn't quite remember if it was the hermit thrush or the varied. Larry would know. He knew most things. Supposedly. Like he'd known where her boots were.

She wanted to ask Chaz but he was up ahead, as usual. Anyway, she didn't need him. She had her caulk boots now and she could move through anything. She heard the newsroom-typing bird. The eerie whistle again, and she walked on and on, the soft moss swallowing her steps.

A while later, Lily stopped at a huge shaggy cedar tree and leaned against it to settle the layers of her outerwear into place. The raincoat, the rain pants, the cruise vest with pen, notebook and compass filling the pockets, her hood over her hard hat. The first aid kit on her belt next to the bear spray. She pulled at the stiffness and marvelled at Chaz's ability to glide through the woods. Where was he? If she walked in another direction, would he even notice? She pictured the trail from the book she'd found in the cabin. The shortest distance to the sea. She could be halfway to the ocean before he even turned around.

"I thought you'd gone back to the truck," he said when she finally caught up to him.

"Well, I thought you might have just left."

"Nah, I wouldn't leave you out here."

She wanted to ask him about the names she'd seen in the cabin, but he just started off again. They were into it now. Far from any creeks and surrounded by trees—the big ones. The ones that had grown so high and so far apart that the space underneath them rippled with a glassy sheen of green. She crested the top of one tree mound and skirted around the flank to slide down the soft green trough to another. The forest was so open, the floor so clear, she could keep an eye on Chaz, even if he wasn't nearby.

The rain started up again and Lily drifted into a dream state. The forest transformed into shapes. She saw faces in tree trunks and dark patches that conjured bears. Cocooned by the hood of her rain jacket, steam from every breath blew back to her ears. She felt as if she was underwater. Swimming, floating. Entranced by the enormity of it all. Then, she saw the canoe.

In Sissy's picture, the canoes were pulled out of the water in front of the big cedar longhouses. It wasn't that long ago, Sissy had said. Lily flipped her hood off and approached the long, narrow, missile-shaped form. Its outline so solid, yet so clearly melting back into the forest. She couldn't bring herself to touch it.

"Chaz. Come check this out."

He walked back toward her, eyes trained on her face. "What?"

"You don't see it?"

He looked up, rain streaming off his chin, then around, scanning the trees. "Is it another one of those monkey birds?"

"Here on the ground."

His eyes dropped.

"A canoe," he said.

"It is, isn't it?"

"It's been carved right here." Chaz reached out with none of her apprehension and ran his hand along the moss. He walked down the length of it. She could see the bottom was carved roughly, not yet shaped into its hull, and the top was a solid mass of spongy green.

Chaz turned and crouched at the flared-out end, one eye closed to take in the line. "It's as big as the *Loo Taas*."

"The what?"

"A canoe carved in Skidegate in the 1980s. I remember them working on it by Gran's place. It went to Vancouver for Expo 86. My granddad and my uncle helped carve it and then Uncle helped paddle it back."

"What's it doing here?" she said.

"Looks like something someone started and never finished."

Lily reached out to touch it, but a movement startled her and she pulled her hand back. Somebody or something was coming toward them.

"Fuck." Chaz tensed and Lily looked for the Walker, but instead, four Haida men emerged from the trees.

"Chaz." A barrel-chested man in an old ski jacket, his long hair barely contained in a rubber band, stopped and put his hands on his hips.

"Uncle," Chaz said, then nodded at each of the older men in turn. One guy raised his chin to him, and the other one reached into his fanny pack for a cigarette. "Smoke?" But Chaz shook his head.

"We saw your Jeep. What are you guys doing out here?" said Chaz.

"Surveying," said Chuck.

"For…"

"Places that your boss shouldn't be in." Chuck's face changed as he noticed the canoe. "What have we got here?"

The men fanned out and Lily watched them trace the edges of the vessel like Chaz had. They crouched down, assessed the line. The cigarette guy pointed at the stump two metres back from the end and then he pointed to the far side and Lily saw remnants of the top of the tree crumbling into the moss.

"Good work, nephew. This is even better than what we were looking for."

"What were you looking for?" said Chaz.

"Heard you guys found a goshawk nest. They're protected by both Haida law and white man's. But this. This is amazing."

"Why? An old stump isn't protected by anything," said Chaz.

"This proves Haida jurisdiction over the land."

"Jurisdiction?" Lily said.

"Title, girl. We hold it. Your people usurped it. Now people like you and the boy's so-called father expect us to prove we were here first. Well, take a look at this Rick Reckless."

"It's just a bunch of rotting wood in a cutblock," Chaz said.

"Not anymore. This is a cultural artifact. I guess your buddy Larry will have to make a new set of maps."

"A different cutblock? Come on, you should talk. You destroyed a lot of forest in your day, Uncle."

"Time to make amends."

"What's that supposed to mean?" said Chaz.

"You'll find out." Chaz's uncle turned and nodded at his friends. "Let's go."

Chaz said something under his breath as they walked away. Lily thought he might have said "hypocrite."

"They're going the wrong way," she whispered.

"Don't worry. They'll figure it out," said Chaz.

To get back to the truck, Chaz and Lily moved like people possessed. Chaz chattered on about the canoe his uncle helped carve.

"One of his buddies found the tree near another cutblock. It was seventy-five metres high. Three metres around. It took a day to prepare a spot for it to fall. Then another day to drag it out to the road.

"Then the carvers spent months hollowing it out and my uncle helped build a huge fire on the beach."

"Why?"

"The sides spread when the hot rocks and water are put in, completing the shape."

"That must have been something to see."

"Yep. Then they took it down to Vancouver. Uncle, Mac, even my grandad, they paddled it at Expo. Then later, some people paddled it back."

"All the way back here?" Lily struggled with her breath. She was keeping pace for the first time.

"It took them two weeks up through the channels and when they were about to cross the strait, they had two choices, head to Skidegate or down to Lyell Island to join the blockade."

"What blockade?"

"To protect the southern half of the islands. There was a stand-off against the logging companies, the province, even the feds. People had to take sides."

They popped out of the old growth and back onto the slick crush road.

"Holy shit." Chaz stood staring at the empty space in front of their work truck.

"What?" said Lily.

"Uncle's car is gone."

"Not possible." She peered up and around the bend. "They couldn't have gotten back quicker than us."

"Yes he could. He's crafty, that one," said Chaz.

As they drove back to camp, Lily kept thinking of the young men, faces painted warrior-style, in the magazine she'd found. The Elders being led away by the RCMP. "So what did they do? Which way did they choose in the canoe?" she said.

Chaz had been quiet for a good long ways, but she poked him and had to repeat her question. He shrugged. "I was six. All I remember is that the land was saved, and when Uncle got back, he went logging again."

At the garage Lily turned off the truck. "I can't stop wondering how they would have gotten the canoe out of the woods back then." She tried to imagine water swelling. A wave reaching up from the ocean. No. Impossible. She knew from Larry's maps there was a high ridge between the west coast and their chart area. The inlet, then. Fingers reaching into green, pulling the canoe out with the tide. She looked over at Chaz, but he wasn't paying attention.

"Chaz, hello? Are you okay?"

He stared out the window. Lily shifted in her seat. She touched the door handle and looked sideways at him. If he wasn't going to say anything, she wasn't just going to sit there. Her elbow shifted to wrench the door open, then all of a sudden he spoke.

"I remember asking Uncle if he'd seen her."

"What? Who?"

"My mom. She went down to the city around the same time."

"For Expo?"

"No. She was looking for someone."

"Who?"

"I never found out."

Later, in the cookhouse, Lily shuffled behind Chaz in the line-up. Cookie released a pile of mashed potatoes onto his plate. She watched his tray dip, but Chaz didn't seem to notice.

"Wake up!" Cookie said, clanging his spoon onto the metal counter. "Or your pork chop will slide to the floor."

Chaz didn't even flinch and Lily had to push him along. They got to their table and Chaz's tray clattered down. Somehow, he pulled his legs over the bench and sat. Lily touched his arm.

"We can't log that block," she said.

"There's nothing we can do about it. Besides, if we don't someone else will."

"I don't care. That canoe is too cool." Lily stared toward the Totem Timber office door. When it opened, Chaz's dad walked out, and she leapt to her feet.

"Leave it alone," Chaz said. But she couldn't. She followed Rick to the meal counter. When she mentioned the canoe, he took her by the elbow and led her back to his office.

By the time she came back to the table, Lily's face had turned as crimson as Rick's shirt.

"How did that go?" Chaz asked.

She was silent.

"I've been thinking about it some more," he continued. "Maybe we could just change the boundary of the block. Or they could put a buffer around it... What did Rick say?"

"He said that loggers usually burn shit like that anyway."

14

When Lily pushed open the door to her bedroom, it crashed into the wall.

"Whoa," said Renée.

Whoa was right. Renée hadn't been around since she'd mentioned the Walker days ago. Now she shows up? But Lily didn't feel like talking with her, or anyone, so she just flopped on the bed and started tugging at her boots.

"What are you slamming around about?" said Renée.

"What a jerk," Lily said.

"The boy? He's young. Give him time."

"Not Chaz. His dad."

"Ah well dat is something else altogether."

"He's so dismissive."

"Entitled."

"Arrogant."

"Selfish."

"Oblivious."

The two women burst out laughing from opposite sides of the little room.

"Seriously?" Lily forgave Renée on the spot. "It's not just me? You hate him too?"

"Everyone does. Dat guy is only tinking of himself. That's it. End of story."

"But Chaz doesn't hate him," said Lily.

"Doesn't he?"

"I don't know."

"Tell me." Renée came to Lily's bed, shimmied her hips onto the thin mattress and shook a cigarette out. "Someting bad happen in the woods?"

"No. It's something we found."

"Ah. Dat old growth is pretty cool. What was it? Another goshawk? A bark strip?"

"An unfinished canoe."

"Ooh. In a cutblock?"

"Yes, unless we can change the boundaries."

Renée passed Lily the cigarette. "Off the chart, eh?"

Lily didn't like to smoke, it reminded her of Jeremy. But she twirled the cylinder anyway and then inhaled. Renée reached out, impatient fingers wriggling back and forth. "So a canoe? Like being carved? Back in the woods somewhere?"

"It was insane. Covered in moss in the middle of nowhere."

"You were up Dunbar, right? So cool, the stuff you can find out dere. Seems a shame to cut it all down."

Something seemed to be slinking into the shadows of what Renée was saying. Details the woman didn't want to disclose. A hippie chick got blamed, Chaz said.

"What about you? Have you spent much time in the woods?" Lily asked.

"I work here, if you want to call dis de woods. But I tell you, no? I lived in a cabin for a time. No running water. No electricity. On the edge of the forest, near the sea."

No, Renée had not told Lily about a cabin. Lily knew next to nothing about her roommate. "Where was that?"

"Pas loin, pas loin, ma chérie." Renée picked up a scarf and started an elaborate procedure of wrapping her head with folds and twists. Eventually she'd contained her hair in a waterfall spray down one of her shoulders. "Well, dat the first one. I live in another one too. Closer to town, but never mind."

"Wait. Where was it?" Lily didn't want to come straight out and ask Renée about the cabin she'd found, because maybe Renée knew something about those totes.

Before her roommate could answer, someone knocked on the door.

"Go away," Renée called out. "We don't want any."

"It's Grayson. Lily needs to come. She has a phone call."

Lily told Renée that she'd be right back, that she wanted to finish the conversation. But Renée just shrugged. This better be some phone call, Lily thought, as she followed Grayson across the compound. Lily hadn't even known she could receive a call. Or make one. She walked into the building and Grayson told her to press the green button on the walkie-talkie-looking satellite phone. She waved Grayson out of the room and held her breath until she heard the caller's voice.

"Ryan? What's the matter? Why are you calling? Is Dad okay?" Lily said.

"Calm down. Dad's fine, but I have to tell you something." Then Ryan took a deep breath. "Remember how I said Dad asked Mom to marry him, but she took off instead? Well, she was pregnant when she came back."

"So?" Lily didn't understand. "She changed her mind. Decided to have a baby and settle down after all."

"You don't get it. She left in the summer and came back at the end of February. You were born eight months later."

Lily could hear her brother's words, but they hadn't reached her yet. His voice beamed into outer space, bounced off an orbiting piece of junk, before flinging back into her head.

"Dad thought you knew. He thought that was why you wanted to go to the Charlottes. To look for him."

"Look for who?" she said.

"Do I have to spell it out, Lily? Your dad."

"My dad isn't..."

Grayson banged on the door. "Hey. New girl. That's enough. It's five bucks a minute. Rick's going to have to take it off your pay."

"Okay, okay." Lily couldn't breathe. "I get it, but I have to go," she said to her brother.

"Wait. Are you okay? Mom wants to come..." Lily only heard the start before she pressed the button to shut down the call. Her brother—correction, half-brother—disappeared into thin air.

Lily tripped as she stumbled away from the desk. *I'm not going there because of her.* She'd said it to Brian, before she drove away from Frontier, but he hadn't listened. He never listened. She'd never wanted to be an accountant. Never wanted any of the things he'd wanted, and now she understood why. She didn't belong to him.

Lily thought of the shadow she'd followed through the maze. She thought of her parents' voices booming through the house and hiding in the bathroom. She used to look in the mirror and wonder where she belonged. Her mother was a thunderstorm and her father didn't know her at all. Because he wasn't her...

"Phone," said Grayson, holding his hand out and making kissy faces at her.

"Eff you, Grayson," she said as she pushed through the door and into the fresh air.

Her mother was pregnant when she came back? The news felt like a sickness rising in her throat. Who the hell was her father? Not Brian. No mother, no father, no baby. No Jeremy. She really knew nothing anymore.

Lily looked at all the metal trailers in the camp and knew she couldn't be inside of one right now, so she started for the beach. Farther down, she saw Chaz pulling an aluminum skiff into the water. She heard the knock of the oar echoing against the side of the boat and saw the vessel rock in a small riffle as he started rowing—and all she wanted was to be on the ocean with him.

"Chaz!" Lily waved her arms over her head.

"What's up?"

"Can I come with you?"

"I guess so." He bumped the rowboat back against the beach. "Get in." She grabbed one side and the other lurched up. "Not like that," he said and braced the other way. "Haven't you ever gotten into a boat before?"

"Not unless you count the ferry. I'm from the Prairies, remember?!"

Chaz jumped out and held the bow steady until she plunked herself onto the stern seat. Nothing matters except this boat, Lily told herself as Chaz sat back down, facing her, and started rowing. She focused on the movements he made as the boat swept forward. Again and again. She saw the pressure on his chest. The stretch across his arms. She looked over the edge and saw her carnival-like reflection slide through the deep green. They sailed past a floating salad of weeds that looked like broccoli and cauliflower. A fried egg jiggled just under the water. Chaz called it a lion's mane jellyfish. She pointed at an angel-like thing and Chaz said it was a hooded nudibranch. Names out of storybooks. This was better than the drama going on in her head. Anything was better than that.

What kind of mother lies about her child's father and then leaves? What kind of father thinks his daughter has snuck away to go look for a real one? Lily started to sink back into the darkness, but Chaz splashed a little water on her. "Cheer up. We can't do anything about that canoe tonight."

In all that had happened, she'd forgotten about the canoe. She reached into the green to flick some of the brine back at him. Rick the prick. She'd looked him in the eye and he'd shook his head coolly and then shrugged. As if the secrets of the forest meant nothing. As if nothing mattered more than the bottom line. She couldn't see anything of Chaz in him.

"What would you do if you found out your father wasn't your father?" Lily hadn't meant to say it, but somehow the words came out.

"Whoa. Where did that come from?" Chaz said.

"Sorry. I don't know. Just forget it."

"No, it's okay. Seriously, I don't think I'd be too surprised."

"Okay. My turn to say whoa. What do you mean?"

"I mean, I was told he's my father, but he's never felt like one. Not just what he says or does, but nothing about me recognizes him."

Lily shivered and rubbed her hands on her arms. Brian tried. She got that. He provided a safe place for her to grow up, but something had always been missing. She'd been chasing her father through mirrors for her entire life.

The distant shore was getting closer and Lily looked back to see how far they'd come. The logging camp looked a long way off. "Shouldn't we head back?" she said.

"You cold?" Chaz asked and she nodded. "Here. You should try rowing."

"Really?" Lily tried to protest, but he insisted, shifting back on the bench.

"Come sit in front of me. So you can feel how the oars grab the water."

Lily looked at him warily, but he patted the spot. "Just for a minute. It's the best way to learn." So she tucked herself in, pushing up against his crotch.

"Hey. Watch the family jewels."

"There isn't a lot of room."

"Yeah, I guess I was pretty little when my granddad taught me this way. Here, put your hands on mine."

Lily pressed her back into his chest as their arms bent together and they pulled through the water. Their hands hit her breasts, just for a second, and then they leaned forward in unison again. After three strokes, a line of sweat dripped down her back and her face was red. Shit, that felt sexy. Lily tried to push the thought away. She did not need any more complications in her life. She and Chaz were too different; or maybe too similar? Each of them missing someone. Searching for something. Not sure of the stories they'd been told.

"Okay, okay. I think I get it," she said.

Chaz pressed against her back with one more stroke and then pulled away. She shuffled her butt back and waited for him to climb around to face her. Instead the weight in the boat shifted and she heard a splash and a snort. Lily almost dropped the oars. She turned to see a dark head bobbing in the water.

"Chaz?"

"Relax, it's a seal," Chaz said from behind her. "Here, boy." He called and the nose and eyes slipped below the surface again.

"Oh my god. I thought it was a dog," she said, but she didn't. She thought it was someone who'd capsized. The man in the forest. A presence who'd been there one minute, and then become lost. She couldn't believe how quickly everything could change. "So, my dad..." All of a sudden, she wanted to blurt everything out, but Chaz stopped her.

"Shh. A few more strokes and we'll be at the headland."

Lily dropped back into the present moment. She saw the sea lighten as they came closer to a crag jutting out from a sandy beach. All the secrets under the surface began to be revealed. Rocky ledges, colourful blobs. Soon Lily was squealing: "Starfish!"

"Sea stars," Chaz corrected her. "They're not fish."

Fine, she thought, but she didn't care. He could tell her anything, because she knew nothing. Not about the stars or the round spiky things or the cucumber-shaped slugs. All of Haida Gwaii was still a mystery to her.

"So good," Chaz said. "We could eat any of this."

"Seriously?" Lily cringed.

"In fact, we're going to eat something in about five minutes."

She wanted to learn about wild food, but she couldn't see how they'd cook on the boat. Did he mean she'd have to eat it raw?

"Don't turn your body," he said. "It pushes us off course. Just keep heading straight. Nice. Now pull with your left and swing us around so we come alongside." When the boat bumped up against the headland, she felt Chaz stand up. "You're a natural. Now hold on to something and keep us against the rocks."

"Like this?" She laughed and grabbed at the bulbous end of a kelp frond, assuming it would just slip out of the sea and she could whip it at him. But the piece of seaweed didn't move.

"That's great. Bull kelp is attached to the bottom," Chaz said. "Don't pull too hard though, the tops can break off."

He scuffled around in the boat grabbing the extra oar and a net bag.

"Now what?" she said, twisting around.

"You'll see."

Just below the water, she could see the round, spiny things. Beyond that: darkness. "Those? You're going to make me eat those?"

He didn't answer, but she watched him lean over the bow and use the oar with one hand to knock one of the creatures off the submerged rocks and into his bag.

"This is crazy," she said.

"Just don't let go." And he leaned farther into the sea.

Lily heard a popping sound and the boat tipped to the side before she realized that the kelp bulb she'd been squeezing had broken off.

"Pull in," Chaz said, but she panicked and rocked the boat even more. Then Chaz, who'd been half out of the boat, toppled overboard.

The force of his body falling pushed the boat back even farther and Lily fumbled with the oars while his head came up from the black water with a hard gasp. He flailed in the seaweed and she saw a line of blood dripping from his temple.

"Lily!" he called, and then he slipped down as a small wave smacked over his head.

She tried rowing toward him but the boat spun in a circle. Finally she bumped against the rocks and sat for a moment, holding her breath. Refusing to become unbalanced, she crawled forward and grabbed onto the bumpy headland. Air bubbled up from below, and in the deep seaweed she thought she saw his arm, maybe some hair.

"Chaz?" Where was he? She scanned the water surface. Was that his oar floating? near the shore? She looked back at the logging camp. Dark clouds, thickening in the sky. Help was a long way off.

When a large gasp broke the surface between her and the sandy beach she spun her head toward the sound. Seal, she thought, but its arms were hauling toward the nearby shoreline in a powerful crawl and she knew it was Chaz. She kept rowing, pulling through the water with a rhythm she'd finally found. When she got near the lost oar she fished it out of the water and then followed him in.

3
Awakenings

15

Chaz, throat thick with ocean water, heaved his chest, then his legs, onto the beach. One minute he'd been with Lily on the boat and the next he'd been... He didn't want to think about where he'd been. He felt cold and broken, as if something inside had snapped. He coughed, not quite half-drowned, and tried to catch his breath. The wind picked up. So cold. A triangle of sun remained on the sand and he crawled toward it, cocooning himself in the light. He turned onto his back and tried to suck the warmth from the ground. He'd seen her. Just as he had in all those dreams.

They always started the same way, in the dugout canoe that his grandad carved. His chinaay, who'd first told him about the Gaagiixiid. Who'd always pronounced Gogeet the Haida way. Who always spoke Haida in Chaz's dreams. But Chinaay was never in the canoe. No, Chaz would be paddling with Uncle or Banger. They'd see the great blue heron at the end of the beach—the old man who warns paddlers about storms. They never heeded the warning. They always went out, twisting their paddles through ropes of kelp as they cut through the swell.

Then, in some dream-like instant, the sky would darken with slashing rain. And no matter what Chaz did to avoid it, the sea monster always came. Ts'amus, his chinaay would have said. The floating log would rise out of the water and transform into a creature—part grizzly bear, part killer whale. Then it would breach and its tall dorsal fin would cut through the middle of the boat like a knife.

Chaz shivered. They were only dreams. Weren't they? He dug his fingers into the sand and felt the warm sun. He remembered losing his balance and falling out of the rowboat. He'd heard Lily's scream as he sunk into the darkness. And *she* was there, as she always was. Dream or no dream, Chaz had floundered and his mother had tried to pull him deeper and deeper into the water.

Heat streamed into Chaz's left eye. He reached to touch it, then pulled his hand back and saw the blood. The ocean salt stung the wound. He still had the net bag around his other wrist and he tugged it off. Four sea urchins. Not a bad haul.

Then he heard Lily calling and felt the boat scratch into the shore. She ran up the beach, straddled his splayed body and pitched her knees into the sand.

"Your clothes." She tore at his shirt. "Get them off."

He tried to rise, but he was so tired.

"Hey, hey!" he said, as she scooched back, unbuttoned his pants and pulled at the bottom of his jeans.

"Shut up. You'll get hypothermia. I have to get you warm."

He let her have her way, but he didn't think he was that far gone.

"Skin on skin, that's what they say you should do." She pulled him up to sitting and then tugged her shirt up, her breasts bound behind a purple sports bra, and pressed up against him. If only Banger could see him now. No way was he going to tell Lily that he was okay. That he'd been wetter and colder before. That Uncle used to make him go swimming even during meat-locker winters. They'd walk barefoot across the road to the dark cauldron of water, shuck their jeans, brace against the wet slap and dive in.

Nope, Chaz let Lily squeeze his shoulders and rub his back. Uncle used to pick up wet ropes of seaweed and whip Chaz's skin. *Make's you strong, like a warrior*, he'd said. This was better. Lily's legs wrapped around his waist, the heat inching its way up. He looked at her. He ought to kiss her. But her eyes weren't even raised.

Uncle always said to have extra clothes on a boat. A towel at least. You never knew when you might need it. He pressed his chest against Lily's and rested his chin on her shoulder. He thought that he could stay like this for a long while, but when he looked past her, he could see the darkness coming.

"We have to get back," he said suddenly.

"You're going to freeze."

"No, I'm going to row."

He grabbed the net bag and they got into the boat. He pushed off, picking a line, and let the work bring the heat back to his body. Lily slid around behind him and held on. A whisper of wind spread through the trees and he could tell by the sky that it would soon turn into a roar. When the rain came, his teeth started chattering, but he was above water and they were both alive and that's how they made it to the other side.

16

Larry stood on the grass behind the cookhouse and watched the gulls fighting over discarded kitchen scraps. They wheeled around in the wind, about two dozen of them. One would dive and the others would swoop to see what had been found. Some would make a play to steal it, while others aimed for the baitfish flashing at the surface of the water instead. He loved the cries of the glaucous-winged gulls. How they hung out in a gang. A pile of kids fighting over popsicles and freezies. Over ball games and girls. He'd been part of a noisier life somewhere deep in his past, but since moving to the Charlottes, he'd become a solitary man.

Larry had seen Chaz and Lily row out an hour before. Larry noticed the storm coming and he'd looked around for another boat to help search, if it came to that. But it wouldn't. Chaz could handle himself. The boy came from a long line of seafarers. None more impressive than Chaz's mother had been.

Larry wondered if Chaz knew that his mother had worked at the logging camp too. Larry never spoke of it and Chaz never asked. Rick might have told him, but he doubted it. They didn't seem to talk about much of anything. Anyway, June had only spent a couple of summers in the woods, mostly in the kitchen. The last being the summer before Chaz was conceived. A fist tightened in Larry's chest when he thought about that.

June sure had a way with a rowboat. She'd said her father had taught her and Larry presumed the old man was the one who taught his grandson too. The wind picked up quickly and Larry felt his hair blow sideways. He looked across the water again. Nothing but whitecaps and foam. How quickly things changed. Finally a glint caught his eye. Movement. Good. He guessed that they'd been on the other shore, possibly at the same beach where June had taken him, all those years before. She'd shown him the sea stars under the riffles and tried to make him touch a sea cucumber.

"History repeats itself." A woman's voice came from behind him.

Larry froze, then drew a breath and turned. Renée. She'd been at camp back then too. Larry had a hard time keeping track of the various hippie girls who'd paraded across the islands over the years. They all looked the same, with their tangled hair and flower skirts. The rank weed they all smoked, their dirty patchouli smell. Renée—had she been called Renée back then? It seemed like everyone had a nickname.

"What history?" A gull hovered, then dropped into a dive, breaking the dark water with a splash.

"A boy and a girl on a boat."

The wind began making a buzzing sound. He could almost hear voices—garbled, maybe a flock of sandhill cranes passing through. Or a trail of ghosts. Larry didn't like ghosts.

If Larry had his memories straight, Renée had disappeared for a long time too. People said she'd gone back to whatever French part of the world she came from. When she returned, she'd started asking questions about what happened to June. Christ, would that have been four or five years later? How old had Chaz been when June left? The timelines remained murky, same as the deep ocean out in the inlet.

"Dat June, she could be dangerous," Renée said.

"You don't say." Had Renée seen him and June in the boat? She must have, or why would she mention it? Those kitchen witches thought they knew so much. But they couldn't know everything. Nobody did.

"You know as well as I do."

"She played games, that's for sure." Larry tried to remain cool. Tried to focus on what Renée was actually saying, not the thoughts swirling around in his head.

"She played you."

Larry held his breath and waited for her to say more. Waited for her to accuse him. Of what? Lying? Had he lied? No. Not to June. Maybe. Or had he just left things out? Lies of omission. But what had June done to him?

When Renée stayed silent, Larry released his breath slowly, like air from a thorn prick in a bicycle tire. He used to ride his bicycle more. He used to be fitter. Healthier. Hopeful. He didn't know what he was anymore.

"And you? What part did you play?" He kicked himself after the words came out. Why stir her? Why not leave well enough alone?

Renée shook her head. "I'm still playing, just like you. Dis is not over..."

Silence again. Larry watched as the boat kept coming closer. He could see Chaz rowing, but Lily? She was not in the front. He wouldn't have left her. Couldn't have. Not if he knew anything about the boy.

"Do you still wonder what happened to her?" Renée said.

"Who?" Larry was getting confused.

"June, who else?"

"Yes. Every day." In the lineup for breakfast, he'd think of her spooning eggs onto his tray. That smile she had. That gaze. He saw it every morning when Chaz crawled into the truck. Every day, Larry wondered what would have happened if he hadn't done what he'd done.

"Franchement! You could go do other tings—work at the grocery store. The post office. Instead of coming here every year. Tu fait le choix," said Renée.

What did she mean? Larry built up his defences again. "I like the work."

"Bullshit. Even you don believe that."

"Someone has to keep an eye on Rick."

"For what? Rick is an imbécile. Why don he come out to worry about his boy?" The rain started and Renée pointed her chin at the little boat slicing through the chop. "Dey will make it. I'm going in."

That was it, then. She didn't know after all. Relief melted over him like the butter on the cinnamon toast June used to prepare. Larry took a deep breath and watched Renée walk away. What part did she play? She hadn't answered. They had both been there, that night of the bar fight. After the day he'd spent with June in the bush. Was that the moment that started everything? Or ended it? Renée and June dancing. Laughing like loons. He had never been sure they weren't laughing at him.

When the rowboat crawled closer to shore, Larry saw that Lily was wrapped around Chaz as he rowed. History repeats itself. Lily and Chaz. Larry and June. Something wasn't right, but Larry didn't want to think anymore. He turned and walked up to the supply room, found two emergency blankets and stuffed them under his thick green raincoat.

17

At the first bump of land, Lily hopped out and ran at Larry, who pushed through sheets of rain toward them.

"He fell in on the other side and hit his head."

Chaz sat in the boat as if frozen, oars still clenched in his hands. Larry pulled the two crinkling silver emergency blankets out from under his coat and wrapped one around him.

"Here," he said, but Lily wouldn't take a blanket.

"Help him. I'm fine."

Larry peeled Chaz's hands from the long handles and picked up the shivering boy, using Chaz's body and his own chin to point Lily in the direction of the right trailer. "His room is on the right," Larry called as Lily ran ahead and pushed open the door.

To her surprise, Grayson stood between the beds, in his boxers, pumping weights. "Whoa, little lady. Your boyfriend isn't here right now. Or maybe you're looking for me?"

"You're roommates? That's weird, but never mind. Chaz needs to get warm quick."

Larry pushed into the room and set Chaz on his feet at the base of one of the beds. Chaz leaned on the old forest tech's sinewy shoulder as Lily ripped the covers back and offered to help him get in.

"No," said Chaz. "I can do it."

Still shaking, he kicked off his shoes and pulled off his socks.

"Hey, he's dripping all over the floor," Grayson snapped at Lily. "So are you."

"Lay off," she said and directed her concern at Chaz. "Are you okay?"

Chaz stumbled forward and crawled under the covers.

"He's fine. Poor soggy little thing." Grayson talked as if he were the mother and they were babies. "Did you get caught in the rain?"

"I could make you some tea." Lily spoke directly to Chaz, ignoring Grayson.

But Chaz waved her away. "I'm fine. Go."

Back in her room, Lily pulled on her pyjamas and sat pulsing on the edge of her bed. Still feeling the back and forth of the oars, the rise and fall of Chaz's back on her chest. Should she go back to see if he was really okay? And do what? Push Grayson out the door? Invite him back here? Look after him in her own bed. Renée wasn't around—wouldn't be around, maybe? But just as Lily had that thought, Renée pushed through the door.

"You made it," Renée said as she blasted into the room. "I saw you out on de water. Crazy."

"Ya, we were lucky, I think," Lily said. "It could have been worse."

"Well, its not the first time dat boy's faced bad weather and it won't be the last." Renée lit up one of her cigarettes.

Lily got up to open the door and let some fresh air in, and found Larry outside with a dripping bag of sea urchins. "Chaz wanted to make sure you ladies got these," Larry said.

"Oh my gosh," said Lily. "What are we supposed to do with them?"

"You don know much, do you, Alberta girl." Renée reached past Lily and grabbed the bag from Larry. "But don worry. I'll show you."

Lily pulled a wool sweater over her head and followed Renée out the door. They tracked mud across Cookie's immaculate kitchen and Renée plunked the bag on the stainless steel counter. A red urchin tumbled out, spines waving in the air. Renée flipped it over and Lily winced as the animal scratched at the metal and tried to escape.

"The first time I taste this was on the fishing boat I took to dese islands." Renée pulled a sharp knife out of the drawer, then cut a circle, starting at the hole on the bottom of the creature. "Get a plate."

The spines kept swaying as she broke it apart. Lily had never seen anything so freshly killed before.

"This is what you want." Renée showed Lily the tongue-like slips of orange and rinsed them gently under the tap. "Those fishermen. Dey were Haida guys, and dey ate dis stuff straight. Me, I like a little lemon and salt."

"You took a fishing boat to the islands?"

"Ya, not so easy to get to here twenty years ago. Me and a guy drove from Quebec in a VW van. We get to Prince Rupert and there was no passenger ship for a week. We stayed a couple of nights in the van. It rained a lot. Den all of a sudden, he don want to wait. Says we should go to Vancouver. But I don know why we came all dis way for not going to de Charlottes. We go to a bar and I get talking with dese fishermen. Dey take a liking to me, but not so much to my boyfriend. When dey offer a ride, my boyfriend and I have a huge fight, and den he took the van with all my stuff and left."

Renée stopped talking and went to the fridge. "Lemon. We need lemon." She squeezed juice and shook a spray of salt over over the orange lumps, then picked one up and slurped it down. "Dis will put hair on your chest."

"So you went back and found the fishermen?" said Lily, avoiding the moment she'd have to try the urchin.

"Ya, de next morning. And de Alberta girl, she came too." Renée pushed the plate at Lily. "Eat."

"What Alberta girl?" Lily drew away and hoped Renée would just keep talking, but Renée inched the plate toward her. "Don be afraid."

Lily finally relented. "Can I at least use a spoon?" Renée smiled and then pulled one from the drawer. Lily shovelled a tiny portion onto it and brought it to her lips. The smell of ocean mixed with lemon was not bad, but when she touched it to her tongue, the texture freaked her out.

"Don think about it. Just do it. It's a good motto," said Renée.

Lily put the spoon into her mouth and let the urchin flavour sit there for a minute. She did not want to chew or move her tongue.

"Asti. Aren't you going to swallow?" Renée chuckled.

Lily swallowed the substance and quickly swirled her tongue around in her mouth. It wasn't so bad. Sort of sweet and creamy with a tingly metallic aftertaste. She ate the rest and took a breath. She felt positively buzzed.

"Dat face." Renée laughed harder. "It's good, no? Gonads are superfood."

"Gonads?" Lily said.

"Like balls. On a guy," Renée's eyes sparkled. "Dose Haida guys, dey eat a few of these and don't need nothing else all day."

"Oh my God. I didn't need to know that." Lily wanted to get the thought of what she'd eaten out of her head, so she went back to the story. "The girl from Alberta. Tell me more."

The urchin seemed to dose Renée with truth serum. "She was wild. First day dey pulled in a giant squid. Bigger dan her. She lay beside it and tell dem to take a picture. Dey try to stop her, but she don't get stopped.

"The squid wrapped a tentacle around de girl's leg and one of de guys had to hack at it, while de other clubbed it between de eyes. De girl keep laughing, and when she was free, she stripped down to her undies and jumped in de ocean. Dat pissed them off. Dey had to haul her up by her arms because dey didn't have a ladder and she couldn't pull herself back into de boat. Den we cooked up de tentacle and drink a lot of rum. Everyone passed out, but we woke up quick when de wind pick up." Renée broke open another urchin and prepared the gonads for the plate. This time Lily took a piece without prompting.

"Scary. Why you make me think of dis? Frigging Alberta girl. She was on de deck, hollering as if she was riding a tabarnac bull. Dose fishermen, dey were steering for der lives. Finally one of dem had to get her below deck and lock her in de cabin. Otherwise she might have been washed away. She wasn't too happy by the time we got to de dock."

Lily squeezed more lemon on the last piece of urchin and popped it into her mouth. Was this story about her mother? She tried to imagine Arlene on a boat, hollering into the waves. Arlene is so much weather. A thunderstorm. A hurricane. The net bag scratched on the counter and Renée cracked another urchin apart.

"Do you have the picture?" Lily asked.

"What picture?"

"Of the girl and the squid."

"No, I don't tink I do."

Damn, thought Lily. "So once you got here where did you live? Did you stay with the Alberta girl?"

"You got me tinking back now. Me and dat girl fought over the fishermen. She liked one. He liked me. I go live wit him for a couple of months in a cabin in de woods."

"A cabin near here?"

"Ya, just up de beach. He wanted to live off de land. Back den some old-timers lived nearby with their vegetable patches."

"What about the Alberta girl. What happened to her?"

"She work in town. Waitress. Came out to visit." Renée slurped up the last of the sea urchin innards. "Mmm, cabin life. We ate a lot of deese..."

"Maybe she was my mom."

"Who?" said Renée.

"The Alberta girl."

"April?"

"Arlene." Lily held the edge of the counter.

"Dat was her name?"

"My mother's, yes."

Renée brushed her hands on her skirt. "No shit? I thought you looked familiar. I guess den the story might be true."

"What story?" But Lily couldn't get anything more out of her roommate.

"Sorry, honey. Urchins make me horny." Renée seemed perplexed as she backed out the door. "I don't know," she kept saying.

"What story might be true?" Lily asked.

"Let me tink before I speak," she said. "Dis was a long time ago."

Hours after Lily had gone back to her room and crawled into bed, the sound of footsteps woke her. Darkness had fallen and whoever it was grunted as they pushed up to the top step. She lay still and wondered about a weapon. Did she have one more lethal than her pillow? How loudly could she scream?

"Asshole. Always was one. Always tink he know everything."

Of course, it was Renée. Drunk, yes, but only Renée. The door flung open and Renée stormed in. She slammed drawers and pulled at clothes. She tossed skirts and silks into the air.

Lily pressed into the covers. Trying to be quiet. Trying to be invisible. Silently imploring Renée to drunkenly finish her story about Arlene.

"Everyone want something. From me. Not demselves. Like I know all the secrets. Like dey are mine to tell. Fuck you, June. You left. Fuck you too, April. Arlene. Whoever you are. You can't build fires and not get burnt. Fuck men. Dey all bastards. Fuck dis Gogeet. He get someone pregnant and then he fucks off..."

Lily peeked out from under the covers and in the dim light she could see Renée holding up the glass ball Blaize had given her. She raised it above her head and closed one eye. Lily thought it was about to come smashing down—that maybe Renée wanted to aim it at her head.

"All dese young ones." She threw the ball in the air and caught it again. "No clue who dere father is. No clue about de lying creatures roaming dis world. Fucking Rick. Fucking Larry. Fucking Stypes. Only Cookie is good. Good for fucking."

She started laughing then. "Right! Fucking. What I come back here for?"

Cigarettes, Lily wanted to say, but Renée pulled the thought out herself, and dug into her drawer.

"Only two left? Dis is bullshit. Somebody is a thief." Lily caught the smoke wafting as Renée scratched at the doorknob and stumbled back out of the trailer. She got up, went to the window and saw Renée stomping down the muddy road. Lily found the glass ball on Renée's jumbled bed and snatched it back. Then she opened the door to be sure that her roommate had rounded the corner by the cookhouse, shut it again and locked it. All the lying men. She thought about them as she pulled open her own little side table drawer. Yes, she'd stolen one from Renée's pack. But only one.

Lily lit it up and thought through all the tidbits she'd just heard. Who doesn't know who their father is? Obviously she didn't, but Renée didn't know that. Did she? What was she saying about fires? And fucking. And the Gogeet getting someone pregnant?

Lily lay back down on her bed. She needed info from this unruly Quebecois woman, but the cigarette might be all she was going to get.

18

Two weeks in and the forest techs finally got the weekend off. Renée, as elusive as the birds flickering around the forest, had not reappeared, so Lily had learned nothing more about whether April and Arlene were the same person or if the guy who got someone pregnant and the Walker were the same person. Could the Walker have anything to do with her?

When Chaz met her at the truck to drive her into town, Lily was just glad to get away. Larry had caught a lift with someone else, so she had Chaz to herself. She told him that all she wanted to do was shove things into her pack and do some exploring. Hike to a destination. Pitch her tent. Start a fire. She didn't mention the unwanted pregnancies or the mysterious man who might be her father. But she wasn't sure about going by herself, so she asked Chaz if he'd like to come along.

"The last thing I want to do on my days off is go out in the bush," he said as they drove past Skidegate. "Besides, there's a dance at the hall. Why don't you stay in town and party instead?"

Nope. Lily did not want to go to any parties. She would be fine on her own.

Chaz told her about a trail to a campsite on the beach at Yakoun Lake and then dropped her by the ferry, where her car still clung to the edge of the road. He said there was a sign at the turnoff on the Queen Charlotte Mainline. She waved at Chaz as he rolled away and then realized that they hadn't made a plan to meet up again. Never mind, she had a couple of days to worry about that.

She stopped at the grocery store for grub. No meat this time, because she didn't want to attract a bear, but in the vegetable section she couldn't find many options.

"What in bejeezus do you do with this?" The cashier poked at the large green globe of kohlrabi she'd found.

"Peel and eat it raw?" Lily had only tried it once. "It's all you had."

"Fresh veg don't come 'til Monday," the cashier said. "Haven't you figured that out by now?"

"What do you mean?"

"I seen you here a few weeks ago. Did you move to the islands or something?"

Lily was surprised this woman would remember her. "I've been in the bush. I work for Totem Timber."

"Figures. Off-islanders always get the best jobs."

Taken aback, Lily tried to defend herself. "Well, I guess I'm kind of from here?"

The cashier leaned in. "Now I want to know what you mean."

Lily wished she hadn't said anything, but what the hell. If she didn't start asking around how would she ever find out?

"My dad, I mean. I'm looking for him. Maybe I can ask you. Have you heard of some guy wandering in the forest?"

"One of the lost ones?"

"What do you mean lost?"

"The otters find them washed up on shore, then take them away."

Here we go, Lily thought. Monsters again. Why can't a man just be a man? "Who says that?"

"Elders, that's who. You're supposed to leave them alone. Once they've gone to the woods, that's where they belong."

"I think he's just a guy. They say he got someone pregnant and then disappeared."

"Who says?"

"Good question. That's what I'm trying to find out."

The cashier just shrugged. "A lot of people do weird shit around here."

"Okay, thanks," Lily said and gathered her kohlrabi, cheese and whole wheat buns and walked out the door. She drove past the campground by the graveyard where she'd stayed her first night and continued up the pitted logging road. As she searched for the hard-to-find mileage markers, she prayed that a loaded truck wouldn't come rumbling toward her. Did Chaz say to turn at 13 or 31? She perked up just after kilometre 13 when she found a crumbling sign with a faded letter Y for Yakoun and a blue blob that looked like a lake. She turned through a grey and white archway of alders and felt her tires sink into the surface. Tracks indicated that a vehicle had been this way before, so she revved through a puddle deep enough to make the underside of her Colt hiss. A minute later, she stopped at a massive tree across the path. Chaz would have had a chainsaw in the back of the truck; she didn't even have an axe.

Lily slammed the car door and inhaled the nutmeg scent—the quiet weight of the place. She took one step and her boots sank into soft ground. Hopscotching through muck to the fallen tree, she climbed over it and found another sign about five metres past the obstruction. The paint was washed out, but Lily could make Y and K out of the smudges. Then she saw a trail. Hallelujah. She rushed back to the car, shouldered her behemoth pack and left her keys in the gas cap. Just in case. Of what she didn't know.

She pushed through spiky branches that spread over the trail. She forded small streams, then pulled out her *Plants of Coastal BC*. She could find things to eat. The red huckleberries were tart and crisp. Young shoots of cow parsnip were edible, but how to be sure that's what they were? She hoped she hadn't tried a poisonous twinberry.

Lily heard a noise as she straddled a tree that crossed the path. A thud and a branch crack. She heaved the weight of her pack to the other side of the tree. "Hello?" she whispered, and then she heard the same kind of footsteps she'd heard in the forest before. A black shadow moved through the trees. A bear? Another branch snapped and blood raced to her cheeks, the way a submerged body rushes back to the surface. She thought of Chaz popping out of the dark cold water in the inlet. She wasn't afraid. Not yet. But she got her bear spray ready.

"Is it you?" She spoke loudly and the movement stopped. "I think I know who you are." For two whole minutes, neither the Gogeet nor the man answered, and she decided that she knew nothing at all.

Maybe it was a bird? A wren could make as much noise in the undergrowth as a deer. That's what Larry would have said. Or was that a towhee?

Lily kept moving forward, trying to focus on the pebble beach she was heading to and the warm fire she would build. Her tent beside a beautiful lake. All would be fine.

An hour later she finally heard water, and Lily scratched through the last few branches to reach the shore. A huge watery expanse spread out before her, but where was the beach? She stood on a tiny corner of woody debris by a creek pulsing out of the dark, black lake. Great campsite, Chaz had said.

    Lily dropped her pack and pulled out her food. She scarfed down a bun with cheese and stared into the dark water. She thought of heading back, then ate another bun and decided to stay. The site was just big enough. She pulled out her tent and unfurled the bottom layer, then added the poles and watched her home in the wildrness pop into shape.

19

Chaz walked up to Banger's garage in Skidegate Heights and found him tapping on the propellor of his 250 hp boat motor. "I think there's a crack in it," he said.

"I thought you were having a party?" said Chaz.

"I am. I gotta get shit done, before I become undone!"

Chaz shook his head. "Dude."

"You da dude. Where's your girlfriend?"

"What girlfriend?" Chaz looked at Banger looking at him. That same expression since childhood. Always thinking he knows everything.

"Don't give me that shit. I've got my eye on you, even when you're out in the bush."

"I wish I felt reassured."

"You should, buddy boy, you should." Banger kept tapping and Chaz knew something was turning around in his mind. His best friend was always crafting ways to get under people's skin.

"So what did your spies say about this girlfriend?" said Chaz.

"Witnesses. I prefer the term witnesses."

"Whatever."

"She sounds cute. Where the hell is she?"

"She went camping." She wasn't his girlfriend, but Chaz felt bad about their last few interactions. The canoe in the forest. Rick's refusal to protect it. Then the boat experience had been too much on so many levels and he'd sucked the parts he'd exposed back into his hermit crab shell.

"Camping? Like at the graveyard? What, she's got some chick friends to hang with?"

"No, she hiked into Yakoun Lake by herself."

"Oh, little bro. You can't be serious."

"What's your deal now?"

"You let some off-island chick drive up the back road and go hiking alone?"

"She didn't want to stay in town. And I didn't want to go with her."

"Too right, too right, brother. WRONG. We are going to have to correct this." Banger threw his wrench onto the workbench and grabbed his jacket.

"What are you on about?"

"Don't you listen to the weather? It's supposed to puke rain tonight." Banger always checked the forecast, always knew the reefs better than Chaz. Always had extra supplies. He knew where the fish were biting. He knew when it was better to give up, rather than keep putting out lines. Chaz hated how much of a know-it-all Banger could be. Trouble was, he was usually right.

"Think about it. The road to Yakoun Lake always gets more rain in a storm. What's she driving?"

"Some little hatchback."

"She might never make it out again."

Lily pushed at a log with with her boot and watched the embers glow. Above her, the clouds started filling in the circle of sky. She wasn't a lonely person, but she did often wonder how she fit in. Not like her mother, who would talk to anyone. Arlene spinning sugar at customers in the furniture store, even if, a minute later, she'd fling crap on them. Or striking up conversations with people in the grocery lineup. Asking a lady buying a roast if she was having a fancy family dinner. Meanwhile, Arlene never bought a roast. Never did anything that other mothers did.

Lily stirred her fire and thought of what might have happened if she'd followed in her mother's footsteps. If she'd had a child too young, by a man who was no longer in the picture. She sure as hell wouldn't be at a beautiful lake on an island in the northern Pacific Ocean. No, Jeremy had taken off and Lily had dealt with the problem instead. She couldn't fathom anything else. But if her mother had chosen the same path, Lily wouldn't be around.

Sounds of wood cracking behind her in the forest. Or had it been the fire? She pictured paths among the trees. The drainages and creek beds. The moss and the devil's club. How many turns could lead between two distant places? A ghost-like figure slipping through the forest by the logging camp. A shadow near a lake, closer to town. *The monster*, Blaize had called her on the Ancient Forest Trail. There are no monsters here.

She threw another stick on the fire and the hiss merged into a different sound. People looking so hard they couldn't see what was right in front of their faces. Had Larry or Renée said that? Not a legend, but a man, who couldn't own up to what he brought into the world. She could feel the wind picking up and the light changing. A chill coming on.

Lily heard a splash and saw the ripples moving away from the beach as if something had been tossed into the water from behind her, from the forest, where Walker might be. The Walker. She squinted and thought she saw a ball-shaped object floating on the surface. A small blue globe or a trick of the light? She turned to look into the darkening landscape and heard a call.

"Lily!" A man's voice, but not lonely and not behind her. The sound echoed across the water and she could just make out a red canoe. As the boat got closer, she knew it was Chaz.

"Hey." Chaz spoke casually from the bow seat, as if showing up in a canoe in the middle of nowhere was the natural progression of things. He stowed his paddle, hopped out and a guy in the back tiptoed to the front in his leather shoes.

"That's Banger," Chaz said.

"What the...? What are you guys doing here?" Lily scampered to her feet.

"That's what we wanted to ask you," said Banger.

"Well, it's pretty obvious. I'm camping."

"Ya. But why here?" said Banger.

Lily raised her eyebrows at Chaz. "You're the one who suggested Yakoun Lake."

"But this isn't where people usually come when they go to Yakoun Lake." Chaz pointed into the distance. "That's the camping beach."

Lily looked at the dark line and shrugged. "So, you guys are camped over there?"

"No. We came to get you," Chaz said.

"Get me?"

"Get you outta here. There's a system moving in. It's going to blow rain on your parade," said Banger.

"I'm not afraid of a bit of rain," she said

"This is going to be deluge." Banger started kicking dirt onto the fire. "Let's go. Time's a-wastin'."

Chaz touched her arm. "So, Banger's also the one having a party. People will start showing up in a bit. We've got to get going."

Lily pulled away from him. What did these guys think? That she would just jump up and do what they say? But before she could protest, water started spraying in dart-like drops. Banger started pulling up her tent pegs and Chaz nudged her with his shoulder.

"Come on. We came all this way. It'll suck being out here in the rain."

"I can't believe this," Lily said.

"Believe it. It'll be great. You can meet all our friends."

Lily scowled at Banger and then pushed him aside and crawled into her tent to pack up.

"Whoa, okay little lady," he said. "Just trying to help."

"Stuff this." She handed Chaz her sleeping bag and then rolled up her mat.

With the camp dismantled and the fire out, Chaz held the boat as Banger and Lily got in. The canoe was tippier than the rowboat, but she held the side rails this time, scrunched into the middle with her pack while the boys paddled toward the elusive perfect-for-camping beach. When they pulled up, Lily could see the wide expanse. Flat at the top for tents and a gentle slope to the water. Much better. But she didn't have much time to think about how she ended up in such a different place, because the guys had already stashed the canoe and were diving through the trees as the rain gushed down. Ten minutes later they were back at Banger's truck, soaked but safe. She got shuffled into the sideways back seat and as they bumped down the gravel road she saw a huge sign at kilometre 31. YAKOUN LAKE. The words thick and black on a white sign.

Chaz turned back to her. "I can't believe you got lost."

"I wasn't lost."

"You had no idea where you were," said Banger.

"Yes, I did! I was at the end of a trail."

"Not the right one," said Chaz.

"Whatever." She might have gone to a different place, but she wasn't lost.

Five minutes later, they passed an archway through the alders that she recognized.

"My car," she yelled. "It's down there."

"We're not going down there tonight," said Banger. "It's probably a mud pit."

"But..." She tried to object.

"Don't worry." Chaz piped up. "We'll come back for it tomorrow."

20

By the time Lily and the boys got back to town, the rain had slowed and Banger wasn't even using the windshield wipers anymore. Chaz kept turning to her and smiling. She tried to smile back, but she wasn't happy about this turn of events. A party and a dance. On the reserve? The village, Banger called it. He'd been talking non-stop as if giving a tour. Apparently five kilometres separated the two towns: one housed government workers, teachers and forest techs —Larry lived in Queen Charlotte City, like most of the white people, Banger said—and Haidas lived in the other place. Skidegate *Village*.

"I thought it was supposed to be pouring." Lily peered out the window as the road opened up by the bay with the lone totem pole. Clouds lingered above the hills, but faded rays of light shone on the grey water.

"It rains different in Skidegate," Banger said.

He turned onto Front Street and Lily took in the house-lined sweep of beach again. Banger pointed out the takeout burger place, the postal kiosk and the band office. A raven perched atop a dorsal fin on a totem pole in front of a wood building. She could see the huge beams sticking out from under the roof and she thought of the longhouses and canoes. The silver poles. Sissy said she knew nothing back in Prince George. What more did she know now?

She knew Chaz. She'd seen a canoe in the forest. She would always have that.

Finally Banger stopped the truck in front of the same small white house where Larry had first picked up Chaz. Chaz fumbled with the door while Lily looked out at the water. A low mist hung over an island and birds circled in the fading light. The beach stretched for a kilometre and she pictured walking along the sand. Maybe being in town wasn't so bad after all. She could do this.

Inside Chaz went straight for the pot simmering on the stove. "Mmm. Chowder." He opened a cupboard to find a bowl and scooped some into it. "You want some?"

She reluctantly took the bowl and poked the spoon at something thin and green sandwiched between two layers of tiny white bumps.

"It's k'aaw. Herring roe on kelp. There's salmon in there too."

She fished past whatever he said, not completely understanding most of the words he used, and found the pink flesh. Salmon she could do. She broke the chunk into two, took the smaller piece in her spoon and let it slide apart in her mouth. The fish had a silky sea flavour that felt fine.

Who was she kidding? She'd eaten urchin gonads already. Emboldened, she took the k'aaw between her teeth. Tiny blasts sprayed her tongue as she bit down, the flavour sharp like a paper cut. She pulled her teeth apart slowly, so the explosive material wouldn't squeeze out again. The next spoonful, salmon only, she used like sugar to help the medicine go down. She looked over at Chaz, hoping he hadn't been paying attention, but his eyebrows rose.

"Good, eh?" He slurped the last of the broth from the side of his bowl, while Lily abandoned hers on the counter and looked around the room. A card table pushed against the window with a red-checked tablecloth. A vase with a single flower made of cedar bark. A small brown couch with a crocheted afghan folded over the back. She moved across the floor toward a wall of photos and pointed at a grade one class. "Which one is you?"

He looked at it briefly, then shrugged.

She stared at the image. The toothless smiles, the scrunched noses, the closed eyes. She looked for Chaz's broad nose. There he was in the middle of the third row. Wasn't he?

"This one?" She pointed, but he would not come to look.

Next Lily saw an image of a woman in a high school grad getup. Her black '70s-style hair—straight, with a middle part—and large round glasses. Beside that a shot, same era, of a young man sporting a pizza-slice-sized collar on a paisley shirt.

Lily pointed at the adults on the wall. "Your mom and uncle?"

"Mmm."

She looked at him, hunched over the pot, scooping as much k'aaw as he could into his bowl. He lifted it to his nose and breathed in.

He turned back to her. "You want some more?"

"No, thanks."

Chaz came over with his steaming bowl and she thought he was going to explain the pictures to her, but he just pointed at a door.

"That's Nanaay's room."

"Nanaay?" she said.

"I mean Gran." He frowned.

"Is that the Haida language? I've heard you use it a couple of times. How much do you know?"

He seemed to ignore her question. "My room's downstairs. You'll stay there tonight and I'll sleep on the couch."

The rain had started up again. Lily could feel it pounding at the roof like a waterfall. A stream snaked off the front porch as Chaz's grandmother walked in. He introduced them and Gran took Lily's hand for a millisecond and then slipped hers away.

"Are you two hungry?" she said.

"Thank you, but I already..." Lily started to object, but Gran got another bowl and scooped chowder into it. Lily's eyes widened as Chaz smirked and she had to crunch the stuff down again.

Gran sat across the table, turning the salt shaker around, watching them eat. She didn't ask where Lily came from or how she liked it on the islands. She didn't question where she'd be spending the night. Lily hoped Chaz would initiate some conversation, but he just picked up the empty bowls and whisked them over to the sink. Gran started her knitting and Lily fidgeted in her chair. "What are you making?" Lily finally said.

Gran held up the small opalescent shape. "It's for the baby."

"Hey, we've got to get ready," Chaz said. Rescuing her? Oblivious? He tugged at Lily's sleeve. Lily looked at Gran and felt as if she had to explain.

"We're going to Banger's." Gran nodded, eyes focused on her needles.

She looked at Chaz and bugged out her eyes again, but he pulled her downstairs. Once in his room, he dove at the bed and propped himself against the pillows. Lily stayed just inside the door.

"I thought we had to get ready?"

Chaz grabbed a Nerf ball and tossed it at a Canucks flag hanging from the ceiling.

"In a minute. Sit down. Take a load off." He patted the bed. "Don't worry, I won't try anything." He hucked the soft ball at her and Lily caught it, then she came over to the end of the bed and slid her butt past his sock feet to lean against the wall.

"What baby?" She volleyed the ball back to him, but Chaz didn't know what she was talking about.

"The one your Gran is knitting for?"

"Oh." He shrugged. "Probably an aunty?"

"Your uncle is having a baby?"

"What? No. Not that I know of anyway."

"You said it was for your aunty."

"Almost every lady in town is my aunty. Who knows? Maybe it's a younger girl? I think Trina's sister might be pregnant."

"Who is Trina? Your girlfriend?"

"She's just a friend. I've known her my entire life."

"Okay. Sure. Her older sister?"

"What?"

"Is pregnant?"

"Sheesh. Nosy. It's her younger sister."

"Younger than you?

"Yeah, still in high school. Why so many questions?" Chaz lifted himself up on one elbow and looked at Lily.

"Do girls ever take care of things here?" He scrunched his eyes and she could see that she would have to spell it out. "Like if a girl gets pregnant and she doesn't want it, could she do anything about it?"

"Like what?"

"Oh my god, Chaz. Are you that clueless? Like abortion." Lily could not believe she'd even started this conversation, but she'd have to finish it.

"Holy shit. Are you in trouble?"

"No. No. Not me. I'm just asking."

"Right, for a friend."

"Shut up." She hit him on the shoulder. "It's just such a small place."

"I haven't heard of that, but I'm no expert. I think her mom will probably help raise the kid, or an aunty. That's what usually happens." He paused. "Or a grandparent."

"Oh shit, Chaz. I wasn't even thinking about your mom."

"Yeah, but I guess that's what she did. She had a baby and couldn't handle it. Maybe she'd rather have done it your way."

"Don't talk like that."

He flopped back down on the bed. "You started it."

Lily missed the next Nerf shot and the ball bounced off the back wall of the room, landing next to a pile of dirty clothes on the floor.

"So how did you end up on that side of Yakoun Lake anyway?" Chaz said.

"Don't we have to get to Banger's?"

"In a minute. Tell me your story first."

So Lily wove a tale about how she'd forgotten the kilometre number. The tree down along the back road and the winding trail through the woods. "And I think I saw that guy again."

"What guy?"

"The mystery man."

"*Riiight.* You think you saw the same guy wandering in the woods down here as the one you think you saw way out on the cutblock the other day?" Chaz pushed himself up again and looked at her. "That's insane."

She did feel strange seeing the same man in the bush everywhere she went. Or evidence of him anyway. She thought about telling Chaz about the cabin and the tote box full of flagging tape. But he spoke again first.

"That settles it. You're not going out there alone again."

"Out where?"

"The forest."

Lily watched his eyes search hers. For what, she did not know. Then he lay back down. Neither of them spoke. Neither of them moved.

She didn't think much of his ultimatum. Or his hockey flags and bad cologne. She couldn't help how her body reacted to him, but it was none of his business what she did with her life.

Lily decided there and then that she wasn't going to the party. She would pitch her tent in the backyard and spend the evening with his gran. She would do what she liked, including go into the forest to look for the Gogeet. But when she finally pushed herself up to tell him, Chaz was asleep.

21

"No one gets to a dance before midnight," Chaz said with a groan after Lily poked him awake. How long had he been snoozing? Somehow she was beside him instead of sitting on the end of his bed. He saw drool dried at the corner of her mouth. She must have fallen asleep too. Chaz rolled over to look at the clock: 10:15 p.m. He stretched and sighed. It felt good to be in his own bed. Not so bad to have a woman in it either. Even if she was some white girl from away who could barely choke down a bowl of chowder.

Never trust the white ones, Chinaay always said. *They'll sell anything, even their own land*. But my dad is white, Chaz had tried to argue, and his grandfather had gone quiet for a long time.

You're Haida, Chinaay finally said.

Lily was rustling around and Chaz felt her arm against his. He thought of them rowing the boat back to shore and took a deep breath. He pressed his thumbs against each of his fingertips and they still felt numb. That was the coldest he'd ever been. The closest he'd ever been to just giving up. And then there was Lily, asking questions. Always asking questions. *Stick to your own kind*. Chaz could hear his nanaay saying it too. He didn't think she was being mean—just stating the truth. Look what happens when you get involved with a white one. He thought of his mom. Her hair billowing out of the kelp. The troubles a young woman could get into and how a moment could change a life. Lily asking about abortion. Jeez. What makes a girl think of something like that? Not sexy.

Still, Chaz couldn't help wondering how it would feel to curl up with her instead of getting dressed to go to Banger's. He'd let her go off on her own and he wouldn't do it again. Bunch of crazies on these islands. The long-haired man in leather pants who sharpened his handmade hunting knife in front of the bar. Or the hippie who'd been busted while crawling through the soccer field looking for shrooms. The guy with his homemade bicycle that looked like a Harley-Davidson. Anything could have happened to her. He closed his eyes and when he opened them again, she was staring at him.

"Okay, seriously," she said.

A beam of light from the bare bulb in the hall cut through the dust and lingered on her face. He could kiss her right now.

"Chaz?"

"What?"

"What are we doing?" Lily got up on one elbow and blinked at him for ten seconds or more, then flopped back down.

The moment was over, but the evening wasn't. Chaz jumped out of bed. "Now we *partay*," he said.

It was almost eleven by the time they trudged up the hill to Banger's.

"Bro. Thought you might not show," Banger shouted over "Roxanne" by the Police. He offered them a Pimm's and when Lily asked what that was, he said it was the cocktail of choice at Wimbledon. She looked at Chaz and he shrugged. Lily agreed to try one, so Banger poured 7-Up and the spicy crimson liquor over ice and added a cucumber spear. Chaz declined and pulled a mickey of Wiser's from his coat pocket instead.

"Got any Coke?"

"Cocaine? Whoa, with an uncle like yours, you've probably got better sources," said Banger.

"Coca-Cola, asshole."

"Dude, you know my mom won't let that crap in the house. Too much sugar."

"What about that shit?" Chaz pointed at the Pimm's.

"Trina likes it. She calls it panty remover," said Banger.

They both laughed.

"It's not bad, actually," Lily said after taking a sip.

"Drink up," said Banger.

The door opened again and three young women strode in like a blast from an aerosol can. One of them shot Banger a look and all three of them squealed and came over to hug Chaz.

"You're back."

"You survived."

"No spirits took you in forest. I don't know how you can spend so many days out there."

Lily heard their names, Trina, Penny and Sue, as a stream of chatter flowed out, but she couldn't keep track of who was who.

The women said nothing to Lily and Chaz didn't introduce her, so she took her cocktail across the room and sank into the couch.

Soon the room filled with other partiers and everyone but Lily got loaded. She nursed her Pimm's until the ice melted but no one seemed too interested in the stranger in the house. A tall guy with short hair shaved extra thin around his ears came toward her and she said hi. But then he realized she wasn't who he thought she was and he looked embarrassed before he got swept away by a group comparing high scores in the hockey pool. A bunch of others played darts, barely ever hitting the target. Lily cringed every time the projectiles plunged into the wall.

Banger stayed in the kitchen mixing drinks for his guests and Chaz stood over the stove inhaling blue smoke off two knives he'd put under the burner. When it came to Banger's turn for a hit, he sucked in the smoke, threw his head back, and blew a column of haze to the ceiling. He howled, spun in a circle and banged his fist on the cupboard door. The door popped open and without missing a beat, Banger pulled five shot glasses out and thwacked them onto the counter. Straight tequila flowed into each one.

Banger swallowed his shot fast. Then the three girls followed suit. He turned to Chaz with the last one. "This one's yours."

"I'm good."

"Drink," Banger said, but Chaz stuck to his rye.

Banger snatched the shot glass back and downed it. Then he grabbed the tequila bottle and filled five more. "How about your girlfriend?" he said.

"Leave her alone," Chaz said.

"*You* sure are," said Banger. He grabbed a shot in each hand, stumbled across the living room and flopped onto the couch as Lily tried to leap out of it. He downed one half-spilled shot and shoved the other at her. Chaz came over and smacked the tiny glass out of Banger's hand. Lily watched the wet stain spread on the creamy rug.

"I'll get a rag," she said, sliding away from Banger. By the time she came back, Banger was gone.

"Don't mind him," said Chaz. "He gets a little crazy when his parents are away."

They arrived at the big community hall after midnight and a live band was rocking on the stage. It must have been a gymnasium too, because the bleachers were pushed back and the basketball hoops raised. Chaz started dancing to "Sweet Home Alabama" and gestured for her to join in, but then he got distracted by more buddies. Banger lunged onto the dance floor in the middle of "New Orleans is Sinking," his pale yellow shirt wet-stained from the left shoulder to his chest. When Fleetwood Mac's "Go Your Own Way" came on, Lily closed her eyes and drifted around the dance floor by herself. She opened them again as the drummer sprayed sweat during a big solo and saw Larry lumbering around on the sidelines. She waved but he turned away, so she kept spinning, Stevie Nicks–style. Was he avoiding her? So what? As if she missed Larry and his maps and chatter about birds and plants. Then there was the thing about her boots! She was still pissed about that, but frankly, at this moment, in the middle of a crowd of strangers, Lily was happy to see his familiar face.

"Flashback," he said, wandering over at the end of the song.

"For me too. That was my favourite song in high school," she said.

"You're not that old. That album came out in, what, '77?"

"Classic rock radio," she said. "It's all we got in Frontier."

"Frontier? What's that? Time travel?"

"Small-town Alberta. Might as well be a different century."

"Well, I didn't expect to see you here," said Larry.

"Or me you."

"There aren't a lot of places to hide in a town this size."

"Skidegate?"

"Skidegate, Queen Charlotte. It all kind of melds into one when there's a do."

"A do?"

"A dance. At the hall," said Larry. "Where everyone knows everyone."

"I don't know anyone, except you and Chaz. So who are all these people?"

"Cripes. You want a bloody list?"

Lily laughed. "A taxonomy."

"Fine." He nodded toward a table covered in empty booze cups: "Those are the Career-Drinkers." Around the room he went with a name for all of them. The Spend-All-Their-Money-On-Druggies. The New-Age-Healers, in their baggy pants. The Bake-Salers at the treat table with their cling-wrapped lemon loaves.

Lily laughed at his naming convention. "Come on. What do these people really do?"

"Those are the nurses," Larry continued. "You never see doctors out at these things. The teachers are over there. They bring their own booze and make it look like they aren't pounding as hard as the fallers and fishermen. Most of those guys haven't shown up yet. Still doing lines at so and so's house. You never see the social workers either. Too many clients around. Skidegate band councillors over there. The ones from Queen Charlotte never come. Funny that, as they were all partiers back in the day. You want any other classifications? Like who's slept with who?"

Lily held up her hand. "I'm good." Who slept with who in the present didn't matter to her, but twenty years ago? She looked at all the people Larry pointed out and wondered if she wanted to know any of them. "How about this Walker guy that Renée keeps talking about?"

"Who?"

"The guy I saw in the woods."

"The sasquatch?"

"No. It was a guy. Some guy Renée used to know?"

A scowl came over Larry's face. "I wouldn't put much stock in anything Renée says."

"How so?"

"That lady has done a lot of psychedelic drugs. Used to sell the stuff. She *sees* things, if you know what I mean."

"But I've seen him too. Twice."

"Who?"

"The Walker. Didn't that Cradle Logging guy say you knew him?" Lily nodded toward Fletcher, who had just walked up to the bar. Which corner did he fit into?

Larry went silent, his lips pressed together until he took a slow inhale. "Lotta weirdos show up around here. I've seen guys barefoot in winter with sticks pierced into their noses. Yahoos wheeling around the streets on kids' ride-on toys..." He stopped mid-sentence and she watched his face contort as his gaze trailed behind her. "Speaking of crazy..."

Lily recognized a familiar odour mixed with incense before she felt the bark-thick hands on her shoulders. "Monster," Blaize whispered into her ear. "We meet again."

Lily turned and looked around for Sissy. There she was writhing on the dance floor. Trina and the others had already caught sight of her dreadlocks. Lily's pulse quickened watching Trina and the others sneer. Banger looked interested, as if he might move in for a strike.

"What are you doing here?" Lily said to Blaize. "I thought you were tree planting."

"Yeah, bit of a screw up. The seedlings didn't arrive. Or they didn't order them? I don't know, but we don't start up for a couple of weeks. So we came here."

Larry cleared his throat.

"Oh, Blaize, this is my—"

"Boss," said Blaize. "Logger man. Got it."

"He's my co-worker. A forest tech. We're laying out blocks."

"Yeah, dude. I can't condone that. I mean this is Haida land."

"Tree hugger are ya?" said Larry. "Whaddya use to wipe your ass? Leaves?"

"Hanky," said Blaize, reaching into his pocket and waving a bandana at Larry. "Wanna borrow it?"

"Disgusting," said Larry.

Lily laughed as Blaize held the rag up to his nose and blew. "You don't really use that as toilet paper?"

Blaize shrugged.

"There you are." Sissy sidled up to Blaize. "And our logging nymph. Wasn't hard to find you."

"Cripes. Patchouli now. Hippie soap substitute," said Larry, plugging his nose.

Sissy shook her dreads at Larry and Lily waited for another nasty comment to escape out of him, but he'd already turned away. When Sissy flounced off to the bar again, Lily, like most others in the hall, couldn't take her eyes off the girl.

"So who's this?" Chaz sauntered up and stepped between Blaize and Lily.

Lily was surprised by his tone. "A friend."

"What kind of friend?"

What was up with Chaz? Lily couldn't keep up with any of it. When she tried to introduce the two guys, Blaize raised his fist as if to bump a greeting, but Chaz just glared at him.

Sissy returned from the bar and interrupted the tension with three tequila shots, one of which she passed to Lily. Lily had seen enough booze consumed at Banger's, but found she couldn't refuse an offering from Sissy. When she reached out to clink glasses, Sissy had already zoned in on Chaz. "Who are you?" The way she said it made Lily's chest rise with jealousy.

"We work together," said Chaz.

"A logger too?" Blaize had ambled away, so Sissy offered him one of the tequila shots.

"We're the layout crew." Chaz took the small glass without pause, clinked it against Sissy's and knocked it back.

"Trippy," Sissy said. "And who's the old guy? Someone's dad?"

Larry turned toward them again, shaking his head. "Not unless they breed in Kleenex."

Sissy laughed. "Blaize uses handkerchiefs."

"Okay, that's it. I'm outta here." Larry addressed Lily as he started away. "You good? Or do you need a ride somewhere?"

"No thanks, I'm okay," said Lily, vaguely honoured that he'd asked.

"Good riddance, logger man," Sissy called after him.

Lily felt put off by her snark, but when the twang of Ann and Nancy started up, Lily was pulled back in as Sissy led her onto the dance floor.

"It's our song," she said.

"What are you even doing here?" Lily asked as they twisted around each other.

"Helping find the answers you seek."

"Come off it," said Lily.

"Seriously. You came here for a reason. Did you figure it out?"

"Maybe," Lily said, cautiously.

Sissy led Lily through the same octopus-like dance moves they'd performed half a province away. "Do tell!"

Lily needed to tell someone about this whole mess. It might as well be Sissy. "My mom came here before I was born and was pregnant when she went back to Alberta," she said.

"So..."

"So. My dad is not my dad. Apparently my whole life has been a lie." Just saying it made Lily feel stronger. She took the lead and initiated the next twirl. Sissy flung out dramatically, her arms and legs splayed like a sea star.

"Whoa. That's next level. Did your dad-who-is-not-your-dad know?"

"I think so. How could he not? I mean... I don't actually know." Lily dipped Sissy, like they'd done in Prince George, and Sissy giggled.

"So who is this guy that your mom slept with? Someone from here?"

"I've got a lead," Lily said.

"You lead, I'll follow." Sissy pressed closer.

"Seriously. My roommate at camp. I think she knew my mom."

"A lady logger?"

"She works in the kitchen—an old hippie. You'd like her."

"If you like her, I like her," said Sissy, her whisper tangling into Lily's ear.

When the music stopped, it was as if the spell was broken. Lily dropped Sissy's hands and tried to squirm away. Were the Bake-Sale ladies shaking their heads? The Career-Drinkers were getting louder. "You guys never said what you're doing here," she said.

Sissy shrugged. The music started up again. "Mustang Sally."

"You know how Blaize keeps going on about Haida Gwaii. Besides, if all goes well, it won't be long before you find out."

Sissy wandered off and Lily went out to get some fresh air. When she came back inside no one she knew was around. Not even Chaz. She couldn't keep up with him, even in the dance hall.

Soon she was looking around for the bathroom. She spotted the ladies' room at the back of the building and, as the Rolling Stones came on, she made her way through the dim light. Was that Banger on the dance floor pulling knees-high, elbows-up Jagger moves? She saw Chaz and Sissy walk through the back door together as she reached the ladies' room. They split and Chaz headed for the bar, while Sissy aimed for the can.

Lily barricaded herself into a stall and did her business as Sissy shuffled in. The door next to hers slammed and Lily heard Sissy exhale a deep sigh.

"That you, logger girl?" Sissy said.

"Yeah," said Lily.

"Thought so. So tell me, how much logging gore is really on your hands?"

"What?"

"You heard me."

Lily wiped her hands on her jeans and thought of all the beauty she'd seen. Skirting amber-coloured streams and mounds of moss. The criss-crossed cedar boughs at the base of some giants. Then she thought of the clearcut where Larry had gone into the ditch. The size of it. The pitch-blood smell. She couldn't deny that it felt violent to be in such a freshly cut place. Those stumps oozing gum, which in normal circumstances a tree would use to heal itself. The fuel stink and sweat of the fallers. But she felt defensive and didn't want to answer Sissy. She also had a question of her own.

"What were you doing with Chaz?" Lily tried to sound casual, not jealous or proprietorial or any of those things. She had no hold over him.

"Not too much. Don't you worry," Sissy said. Her voice had changed, as if she was choking on the words, and Lily flinched. Then Sissy started retching.

"Find Blaize," she croaked.

"Will do."

When Blaize arrived, he tried to help her up. "No, no," she said. "I want to stay in here."

"Come on," he said. "Our stuff's out on the beach." Sissy's body slid out of his arms as if she were made of Jell-O.

"God. How much did she drink?" said Lily.

"I don't know. Not that much? Nothing until we got here." Blaize looked worried as he rubbed Sissy's back.

"Can I do anything?" Lily said.

"Help me get her outside. She's always happier in the fresh air."

Sissy leaned on the two of them and once they got outside, Blaize turned down a back street toward the water.

"Where are we going?"

"I built us a shelter."

"Out of what?"

"Driftwood. I'll show you."

On the beach below the longhouse with the totem pole, he'd rigged a canvas tarp between upright silver logs and even created a makeshift table and chairs.

"I don't know if you're allowed to stay here," Lily said, following Blaize into the shelter.

Lily sat down on the sand as Blaize got Sissy under a sleeping bag and stroked her cheek. "We'll be okay until morning."

Sissy stirred. "Blaize! Blaize. Our stash. Did you get it?" She rambled on. Her head was cold, did he have any crackers? Something to calm her stomach?

"Don't worry. I'll take care of it. I'll take care of you. Of everything," Blaize said in a singsong voice. He started rummaging in his pack and pulled out a small glass bottle. He dripped some of the liquid onto his fingers and then massaged Sissy's temples. "Lavender to soothe you, my dear," he said, and then he pulled a spliff out from behind his ear and lit up.

When Blaize tried to pass her the joint, Lily pushed herself up out of the sand. "I should get back."

"Okay," said Blaize, who was now shaking granola into a small wooden bowl that he'd wiped out with his sleeve. "This is all we have, Sissy." He passed it to her and she picked at a cluster, took a nibble and then tossed it back into the bowl and groaned. Blaize turned back to Lily, "Hey, maybe you can give us a ride tomorrow..."

"I don't have my car," she said.

"Aw. No way. The little Colt. What happened to it?"

"It's up a side road at kilometre 13 on the Queen Charlotte Mainline."

"Whoa. That's a weird parking spot."

"Yeah. It's a long story. Where are you guys trying to go?"

"Up island a-ways. You know, to the old growth."

"What for?"

"Um... nothing much. Just to spend some time in the forest."

"Sounds nice. I've got to go get it tomorrow. I'll come look for you guys after."

"That would be awesome, Lily." He touched her arm and she backed away.

"Okay, okay. Hey. Tell Sissy this is the beach from the photo."

"What photo?"

"She'll know."

When she got back to the hall, the band was packing up and Chaz was nowhere to be seen. She looked at the clock: two a.m. Maybe she'd be staying with Blaize and Sissy after all.

Out in the parking lot, Lily saw Trina slip into the powdery orange light at side of the building. She followed and found a whole group in a huddle. Then the circle closed and she heard a crack and a thud, and the girl she thought was Penny spilled out one end, dragging Chaz by the arm. He rubbed at his chin with his other hand.

"There you are," Penny said when she saw Lily. Penny shoved Chaz in her direction. "Just make sure he gets home."

"Fucking Banger," Chaz slurred. "Always thinks he knows best."

"What's going on?"

Instead of answering, Chaz slithered into her arms and Lily struggled to hold him up. She looked to Penny for help, but she was long gone. Lily stumbled, then Chaz jumped out of the fall, landing as if he wanted to take another swing.

"Watch it," said Lily. "You just about plowed me."

"I'd like to…" he said. His fingers dug into her upper arm, but she twisted away.

Lily looked back to the huddle and saw Banger on his knees, pushing himself up off the ground. Trina brushing the hair out of his eyes.

"You were fighting with Banger?"

"That guy talks so much shit sometimes."

"About what?"

"Just people. People I care about. Never mind."

22

The next morning, Lily felt trapped in Chaz's basement room. A half bathroom downstairs gave one form of relief, but she could hear Chaz snoring on the couch upstairs. She was too shy to go up so she flipped through UFC magazines on the ancient martial art of kicking ass, and *Men's Health*, featuring exercises to boost your sex stamina, buff bodies and protein supplement ads. She dozed in and out a dozen times between eight and nine a.m.

What was she doing in Chaz's basement? She was still a million miles from anywhere she'd ever wanted to be. Lily flopped back down onto his pillow and the fake lemon cologne smell poofed out. Ugh! If she'd been camping, she'd be out exploring the lake right now. Practising her survival skills. Chatting up this Walker guy. Finding out who he really was. Or maybe she'd be huddled in her tent in the rain. At least she wouldn't have had to go to that party. What a scene. And Banger? Chaz's best friend? Trouble. And what were Blaize and Sissy up to? Lily moaned and rolled over. Good band though. The smell of old socks wafted up from the floor and her head throbbed.

At 9:20, Lily couldn't stand the silence in Chaz's room any longer, so she tiptoed upstairs. Gran was sitting at the kitchen table in the exact spot she'd been in the night before. She put a finger to her lips, gesturing at her snuffling grandson on the couch. Without a sound, she stood and reached for a restaurant-sized mayonnaise jar filled with long green leaves, grabbed a handful and tossed them in the teapot. Then she went to the coffee maker and held up a huge green tin of Edwards fine grind. She gestured to Lily, who nodded and mouthed a thank you. Maybe the smell would rouse Chaz? The coffee gurgled in the machine and when it was done Gran brought her a cup, along with a shaker of Coffee Mate. Lily wanted to ask for the leaves.

Instead, Lily drank her coffee and watched Gran knit four perfect rows. When her empty cup touched the table, Gran stood up, got the pot and refilled it.

"Thank you," she whispered and Gran put her finger to her lips. Lily felt more than awkward. She flipped through a newsletter-like newspaper on the table. *The Observer*. Someone wrote a letter to the editor warning of the Y2K disaster to come. Ferries cancelled. Fuel supplies running out. Blaize said Haida Gwaii would be the perfect place to be during the crisis. She cradled the warm mug in her hands and thought about telling Gran that she had to meet some friends. Then she could escape to find Blaize and Sissy and they could hitch up the back road to get her car.

Four refills later, Chaz finally rose.

"Morning!" He jumped up, kissed Gran on the cheek and fist-bumped Lily's shoulder. "I'm starving. Let's go get some grub."

Whoa. Lily had wanted action, but all of a sudden things were moving too fast. "Can we stop to say hi to my friends on the beach?"

"After breakfast, sure!" he said. "Anything you want."

At the Sea Raven, they found half the party crowded at a table as if they'd all made a plan to meet.

"Chaz!" the girls shouted as they approached. "Hey," they added, nodding at her.

Chaz didn't say anything to Banger. Did he or didn't he punch his best friend? Lily waved at the tall guy she'd sort of met at Banger's house and he widened his eyes, nodded vaguely and then turned away. The others were busy chatting and barely looked up. They grabbed the last two seats and Chaz ordered a logger's breakfast with extra bacon. Lily asked for French toast and mint tea. She'd had too much coffee already.

"Mint tea?" Banger said. "You drink that shit?" Everyone laughed and continued comparing notes about the night out.

"We'd just put out that joint when the cops drove in," said Trina.

"Those moves? Looked like he was humping her while standing," said Sue.

"Did you catch little brother? Not even nineteen and he's already showing up wasted," said Penny, shaking her head. Each comment brought a round of repartee from the revellers, as if they'd all witnessed the exact same things. No one mentioned the fight or how gooned Banger and Chaz had been.

By the time they got the bill, Chaz's friends had stabbed and slurped every bit of jam and peanut butter out of the packets in the holder, built towers out of empty creamers and shaken the last of the sugar packets into half-drunk coffee cups. Then the girls had to pee and the boys descended the front steps into the parking lot and lit up their smokes. Lily followed them out.

A kingfisher chattered and landed on a branch by the water. The clouds spread apart and Lily wondered if Banger's forecasted rain had ended for good. Banger passed a joint around with some of the guys and the Trina trio still hadn't emerged from the toilets. Lily looked for Larry's crow friend.

Chaz finally came over to her. "Hey. We have a basketball game. You want to come?"

"Wait? What? You said we could do anything I want and I want to go get my car."

"Right! We'll get it later. It's still pretty wet out there."

"Maybe we could go to the museum, then?"

"Nothing but dead things," he said.

"The museum is so *borrring*," said Trina, who had waltzed up behind them. "Basketball is great and besides, you can hang out with us."

Banger was trying to do a handstand on the rail. The girls egged him on. Chaz laughed and Lily turned away. Basketball is boring, she thought. At least to her.

But for some reason, she agreed to go with them.

The next thing Lily knew they were back inside the hall. The place stank like booze and people were still stacking chairs in the corner where the Career-Drinkers once sat. Lily did not want to spend another several hours of her life in the gymnasium, but it was too late. The boys all gravitated to a spot under the basketball hoop and the girls aimed for the bleachers. Trina grabbed her arm.

"Up here," she said. "They're waiting for the rest of the intermediates to show up."

A gang of younger teenagers amassed at the far end of the floor waiting for the game to start. Boys with hip bones jutting out the tops of their long shorts. A group of girls, long black hair pulled back, darted in and out trying to snatch the balls away. When a tug-of-war over a ball ensued, all the girls flocked and the one boy waved them off. The other boys stood by, acting uninterested, until another reached out and bonked one of the girls on the head. The girls were startled and surrounded their new prey. Lily felt as if she were watching a slapstick movie. Beside her, Trina, Penny and Sue laughed non-stop, but they weren't even watching the teens.

Banger's whistle stopped the action and the young ones scattered as the intermediate men took the floor. Only six older guys had shown up in total, so they played three-on-three with Chaz and Banger on different teams. Sneakers squeaked like bird sounds as they ran in and out of their play. On the sidelines, the Trina trio planned a trip to Prince Rupert the following February for the All Native Basketball Tournament.

"It's going to be a party," said Penny. They'd get one hotel room between six to cut down on costs. Trina, who had a new job at the bank, didn't know if they'd let her take the time off.

"That's bullshit. They can't stop you. That's like telling someone they can't take Christmas off," said Penny.

"Just call in sick," said Sue.

"Maybe I'll quit by then," said Trina.

"Are you going?" Penny turned to Lily just as Chaz took the ball.

"Me?" said Lily. "I don't even know if I'll be here."

"Where else would you be?"

A shout from the gym floor turned all eyes back to the play. Banger had jumped in front of Chaz, blocking him from a run at the hoop. Chaz pivoted looking for a place to pass, but his teammates were both covered. Banger stepped forward and slammed his heel down on Chaz's foot. Chaz swore as he dropped the ball and Banger grabbed it with a vampire laugh. He bounced it across the floor and Chaz's teammates tried to stop him, but they were too late. Banger strode into a layup, slamming the ball into the hoop.

"Bullshit," a guy on Chaz's team cried. "Foul." But Chaz said nothing. Banger threw him the ball.

"Take a shot, then," he said.

Chaz shook his head. He stood at the end line and threw the ball to a teammate, ran in, the guy passed it back and Chaz made for the basket, stepping wide as Banger moved in. He leapt into the air just as Banger's arms went up to block him and took the shot. The ball hooked into the hoop. All the girls, even Lily, let out a cheer.

"I wouldn't miss the All Native if I were you. Chaz is the captain," said Penny.

"The intermediates are going to kick ass," said Sue.

"Chaz, Chaz, Chaz!" the Trina trio chanted.

After the game, Chaz and Lily walked down Front Street together. She watched his chest heave in wave-like crests. They crossed the grass, passed the swings and an old teeter-totter, and stepped down onto the driftwood-lined sand.

Crap, she'd forgotten all about Sissy and Blaize. She looked down the beach and saw that the sticks from their lean-to were still standing, but the tarps and the tree planters were nowhere to be seen. Chaz opened his jacket as the wind picked up and the waves splattered a foamy spray. Two ravens somersaulted in the breeze.

"Where to now?" he said, bumping against her. "Anywhere you say."

A white-hooded eagle banked on the current, its yellow talons lowering like landing gear. Shrieking seagulls made plays at some rotting thing left by the tide, then scattered at the eagle's descent. The huge bird landed with a little shake and hopped over to claim its prize. Lily bent to pick up a green-and-white-striped pebble, still shiny from the wet. She breathed salt water and wind and leaned into Chaz's shoulder. She was tired and hungover, but he was a good basketball player. By the end of the game, even she could appreciate that.

"I don't know," she said, but she meant that she wanted to stay right there. For the first time in a long time, she wanted nothing more. The beach curving to the other side of the village. The seaweed spread like strands of hair. Tide pools lurking in the rocks at the corner. Maybe they could go look in those. Or she'd be just as happy to keep strolling and pick at the shells scattered across the sand.

"Okay," he said. "Fight's on at Banger's. I'll have a quick shower and we can head up there. He's got pizza in the freezer."

He clutched her hand and twirled her into him, like Sissy had done. She spun against him, and then he pushed her away, dropped her arm, walked backward and smiled. She was about to say something, but he turned and ran, whooping and leaping at a raven perched on the edge of a picnic table. The bird squawked as it raised its wings, then the draft caught it and lifted it into the air.

23

Lily felt a whole new level of bad watching the UFC fight. Knockout, surrender, doctor's intervention or death. Those were the rules. Two guys going medieval on each other and everyone—Banger, Chaz, Trina, Penny and Sue—enjoying every minute. They shouted and rooted for a bare-chested champion who'd set out to kick ass once more. Lily thought he looked like a psychopath. The girls thought he looked hot.

Lily pressed against the back of the couch, her shoulder leaning into Chaz. She slid deeper against him when he raised his arms to shout. With one hand braced in front of her eyes, she peered between her fingers. The weaker guy, the one she wanted to win, was getting slammed.

After the first round she couldn't stand it anymore. She stood up, slipped on her boots and opened the door. Outside, the wind roared like the fight crowd. She walked on a new road in the upper village where they were claiming more house-building land from the forest. The pavement wound up the hillside into empty lots and she could see across the inlet to Moresby Island. She wanted to go there. Chaz had talked about his granddad's fish camp while they'd walked up to Banger's. Soon the sockeye salmon would run, he said, and they'd all be out setting nets across the wide-mouthed channel by the sea. He said the bears come and scoop fish out with their claws. She'd like to see that. Maybe he'd take her on their next days off, but not with Banger. Or the girls. She wanted to be alone with him. She wanted to go out in a rowboat with him again. She liked him better that way.

A gust of wind pushed at her back and she heard footsteps clattering up from behind. She turned, hoping Chaz had come to find her, but she couldn't see anyone. A cracking noise came from the forest and she held her breath to keep the supernaturals at bay.

"Hello? Anybody there?" she called. Was it him? How could the Walker turn up everywhere she went? Something scurried up behind her and Lily jumped around to face him. She wanted to know if he knew her mother. If she had any connection to him. But she saw nothing more than dry leaves rattling on the road. She looked into the wall of brambles at the back of the lots. The thin arms of spruce trees reaching out. She thought of how quickly the houses fade to wilderness. How easy it would be to walk into that blackness and get lost.

By the time she made it back to Banger's, Chaz was at the door.

"Hey, what happened to you?" Chaz pressed the palm of his hand against her cheek as she walked back inside. "You're cold." She bent to take off her shoes, her face burning. Chaz continued to confound her. He did all these things she had no interest in. Stuff that repelled her, really. But the feel of his hand on her cheek made her want more.

"Is it over yet?"

"You don't like scrapping, do you?" But before she could answer he said "I love it," and did a little boxer dance in the hall—jab, jab, uppercut.

If anyone looked sexy, she thought, it was Chaz.

"PS: Your guy lost."

When they got back to the lower village, Chaz saw Nanaay standing at the top of the steps under the porch light. He looked at the hour, but it wasn't too late. Not past her bedtime anyway. He thought of how tiny she was. And grey. It wasn't the first time he'd considered her age. He'd noticed her back curving and her head curling into her shoulders—the beginnings of that hump old ladies get. It made her even shorter, he thought.

He turned to look for Lily again. She had fallen behind. Surprise. He stopped in front of the white house with the picture window next door to Nanaay's and contemplated the grass almost as tall as the front porch, the same old pink plastic tricycle under the stairs, the falling-over boards of the short white fence.

Lily caught up with him and her voice snapped him back to the present. "Whose place is this?"

"We used to live here. All of us. My mom, Chinaay and Nanaay. We moved to the smaller house next door after Chinaay died."

He thought of mentioning the man who had come to the door the morning of that long-ago storm. The rain sideways at the window. Chaz had been in the living room with his toy cars. He'd heard his gran speaking quietly in the front hall: *She's not here anymore.* Who's not, Chaz had wanted to know. He'd skittered around the corner in his sock feet and saw the man on the porch, drenched and sullen. Gran told him to leave. He'd seen the stranger's hand at his forehead, then rubbing his eyes. They'd been talking about his mother, Chaz was sure of that.

Lily stopped at the salmonberry bush in the yard and popped a few of the berries into her mouth. He wanted to tell her to hold off, they weren't quite ready, but Nanaay was at the top of the steps and Chaz could see by the firm line of her mouth that she had something to say. Lily would have to figure out the ripeness of the berries on her own.

"You're up late." Chaz kissed his nanaay on the cheek.

"Your uncle called. He wants you to go fishing."

"I've got a job, Gran." He looked back and saw Lily pulling at another berry.

"He's family."

"Rick is family too."

"Not the same." Gran crossed her arms and went inside and Chaz looked at the planter where she grew marigolds. The rubber boots—always covered in mud, dog shit, seaweed or sand—that were never allowed inside. Chaz thought of the time he'd pushed his toes into one of those boots and something had pushed his foot out. He'd reached in and found an orb made of glass as pale as a cloud-filled sky. Over the years, he'd found glass fishing floats in different places in the yard. Sitting on top of a stump, like a gift. Tucked into a corner by the back fence. When he was little, he'd connected them to the man at the door. Something about the way the man had looked at him. As if he'd recognized him. Chaz looked into the boots as Lily climbed up onto the porch, but they were empty. He hadn't found a glass ball in a long time.

As they started down the stairs to his room he stopped, wondering if he should explain everything to her, about his mother. His sadness. His fear. His out-of-control uncle and his goddamned boat. But she looked at him as if there were no problems in the world, other than a slowdown on the staircase. As if things could just continue on. No one would die or get hurt or disappear. They could just move through each day, and he felt that could all be true if he stuck with her. He might really be able to start again.

Lily felt wiped, even if she wasn't in as rough of shape as Chaz the night before. How could he not be hungover? The guy had been hammered at the dance. Then all that basketball? Hardcore. She watched him putter around in his room for a bit, hemming and hawing, making Lily wonder if there was something he wanted to talk about. She didn't really want to get into any of it. They'd hung out in the village just like he'd wanted. She couldn't wait to get back to work in the woods.

Finally he grabbed some pyjamas and asked if she needed anything else. She shrugged. What was she supposed to say? I need to know who my father is? When he trudged back upstairs, she curled into his bed and immediately fell asleep. But sometime in the night she awoke to banging and clattering; feet shuffling in and out of the house. An axe chopping. Muffled voices. She could smell cloves and chilies and the sea. She saw the light on in the backyard and smoke from burning wood. She saw Chaz's feet through the window and another man's boots. She wondered who it was, but sleep pulled at her and she rolled back into it again.

She woke again when Chaz lifted the covers and curled up beside her. It was four a.m. They had to leave for work in two hours.

"What are you doing?" she said.

He smelled like forest and flames—the darkness that puffs up when you step through campfire remains.

"Shh. Uncle's passed out on the couch. I've got nowhere else to go."

"You're freezing."

His nose was right beside her hair. "You smell so good."

"You do too."

"Heh, really? I thought I reeked. Uncle and his buddy brought in a load of fish. Had to fillet them for the smokehouse."

She turned to face him. "You should have come and got me. I could have helped."

"This is good. You're helping now."

The beginnings of the day leaked into the basement window. Pale light so soft she could feel it brushing her face. Lily felt something different in the way Chaz looked at her. Like he'd come back from somewhere dark and was ready for a fresh beginning. This time he did reach for that kiss and Lily couldn't help herself. She crawled right in.

24

Chaz revved the work truck up to 120 on a straight stretch of the coastal highway and then pulled his foot back to slow and sail around the curve. They'd woken late and he'd had to sneak past Uncle snoring on the couch. Then Lily had a freak-out when she remembered her car still parked out in the bush. She wanted to go back for it, to drive up the back road from Charlotte to camp. Who told her about that route? A grind at the best of times, but washboard hell if you were in a rush. Besides, Rick hated when workers were late, especially him, and what would Lily do once they got to her hatchback? Drive it all the way back to camp too? Hard on the chassis, Mac would say. He had to triple promise that they'd go get it the next time they had days off.

At St. Mary's Spring, the truck hit the fault line that breaks the pavement every year and they bounced in their seats. Chaz told Lily about the water at the spring and how drinking it made people come back to the islands. She wanted to stop but Chaz distracted her by telling her about the supernatural Haida chief whose sexual exploits rumbled under the sea.

"He and his wife are at it all night. Explains why the earth keeps cracking open."

She laughed. Maybe she'd forgiven him about the car. Offshore, the waves crashed as they rolled in and the cormorants spread their wings on the craggy battered rock. He couldn't stop thinking about what happened last night. Well, this morning. He was giddy with lack of sleep. He wished they could just pull over and make it all happen again.

At Tlell, several large spruce trees leaned over the crumbling banks. A road crew blocked their passage while a dump truck released a load of rip-rap over the edge. Futile attempts to armour the highway for the winter's storms. He'd seen the results—ten metres of waterfront disintegrated a few winters ago.

"I went to high school with a guy who lived at this place." Chaz held the wheel around another corner. "Their house used to be thirty metres back from the water, but now there's only five metres left. Until..."

"Until what?"

"Until it all collapses into the sea. One way to get rid of the colonizers."

He hadn't meant to say that. That was something Uncle would say. Damn. He didn't want to think about Uncle. Not now. Not with Lily here beside him.

"So you want to get rid of me?" She punched his shoulder and he laughed.

"Not you. People like you." He blushed. That wasn't the right thing to say either. Maybe he could just leave with her instead? Uncle had warned Chaz not to go back to the logging camp. *Shit's going down*, he'd said. *You don't want to be there when it does.* Chaz tried to ignore him, but they had so many fish to get into the smokehouse that he couldn't get away from the older man. *You're better off with me*, Uncle said. He talked about the salmon openings and how they'd max it out and bring money home for Nanaay. About how Chaz would earn enough to buy a truck in a couple of weeks. Then he could piss off into the sunset if that's what he wanted. But Chaz didn't know what he wanted anymore.

He slowed near the clearing where he'd seen a bear look up from the meadow grass once. He always thought that seeing the bear again would be a sign. Of what, he didn't know. Anyway, the glade was empty.

Chaz looked over at Lily, sorry already that she'd be leaving. That, by the looks of things, even after fishing, he'd continue on as always, and after her summer here, she'd be gone. That was the fact of it all. Haida Gwaii held him, no matter how much he wanted to get away.

After the turnoff near the goose-hunting grounds, the landscape shifted again. The road veered straight through boggy forest toward the centre of the island and the logging town of Port Clements. He had fifteen minutes before they hit gravel. Chaz slid in a CD to make up for the silence.

After less than ten seconds, she made him take it out.

"Pimps, drugs and guns. Is that supposed to be cool?" she said. The expression on her face was stiff and judgy, like so many of his teachers had been. Or the lady that ran the convenience store in

Charlotte. The one at the bank. As if she really did think she was better than him. "I like it better when you talk about Haida chiefs fucking," Lily said.

Chaz chuckled. Okay, not as prim as Uncle warned him about. "Why don't you tell *me* a story," he said.

"About what?"

"Somewhere far away. I don't know. Where you come from?"

"There's nothing interesting about that place."

"Must be."

"Nope. I never want to go back."

"Jeez. Don't you have family there?"

"My brother, I guess. Mom's long gone. And the guy I thought was my dad? Turns out he wasn't."

He hit the bump at the first timber bridge over Geikie Creek with too much gas and they bounced. "What? Holy shit. You just drop that like a bomb?"

"Take it easy." Lily braced against the dash.

"Just trying to get us to work," he said.

The second bridge came quick and he slowed the truck in time. Chinaay helped build this bridge back when he was on the road crew. Weeks of work in the boggy slop. The whole road made of planks before that, laid out lengthwise, one lane only. If two vehicles met, one would have to back up to the nearest pullout so the other could pass.

"Okay, so what's the deal about your dad?" Chaz remembered her asking what he'd do if he found out his dad wasn't his dad. He thought she'd been talking about Rick.

"Nothing. I mean, I don't know anything about my real father except, well, apparently my mom met him out here."

"Here?"

"On the islands."

"Your mom is from here? Jeez, Lily, why didn't you say?"

"She isn't from here. She left Brian—my so-called dad—and came here twenty years ago. Got pregnant. Went back to Alberta. Got back together with Brian and had me."

"Okay. What? Slow down. Your mom came here? Then went back to Alberta? So she never mentioned who the dad was?"

"She left again, remember? She's in Costa Rica or something. I didn't even know about any of this until my brother called the other day."

"Serious?"

"Never been more serious about anything in my life."

"Well, what does your dad, Brian, or whoever he is, say?"

"I haven't talked to him either. Not since I left home. We kind of had a fight. He thought I was staying to work at the family business for the summer. But that was the last thing I wanted to do."

"I hear you on that." Chaz thought of his uncle again. "But wait, you didn't know about your dad until after you left home. So why did you even come here?"

"It's like a fricking movie plot, Chaz. I saw pictures of this place in a magazine and I wanted to see the giant trees for myself. My dad saw the photos over my shoulder, then realized it was the Queen Charlotte Islands. I mean Haida Gwaii. He muttered something about how my mom had been here. Then I saw the job posting months after that. I didn't know that she'd left him before coming here. I didn't know she got pregnant here. I didn't know I'd meet you or who the Haida were. All I knew is that I wanted to walk through these forests and I don't know what I want anymore…"

Chaz glanced over at the end of her rant. Lily's chest was heaving and Chaz thought she might be crying. Or was about to.

He slowed the vehicle as they entered Port Clements.

"Okay, calm down. Let me buy you a drink."

"It's a little early for that, and besides, I thought we were late?"

"A can of soda. That's all I'm offering. We've got time."

He pulled up in front of the Port grocery store. The dock where the crew boats used to take loggers in to camp was just around the side. Before the logging road had been punched in, Chaz and Chinaay would drive Uncle up to catch the boat. Afterward the old man would always buy Chaz a pop for the way home.

Chaz hopped out and Lily stayed in the truck. He wasn't sorry. He needed a break. Too many troubles of his own to worry about. Besides, he liked to wander the bulk food aisle and look at the weird powders and grains in their see-through bags. Basmati rice. Mung beans. Chick pea flour. What did people do with them? He meant to find out someday. When he was living his other life.

At the checkout, Chaz dropped two cans, lemon and cherry, on the belt and the woman whisked them through the scanner. She looked up at him as he handed over a fiver and tilted her head.

"Whoa." She scrunched her eyebrows together.

"What?" he said.

"Déjà vu."

Chaz held out his hand to receive the change, but she wouldn't let it go. He glanced at her name tag.

"Uh, Connie. Earth to Connie."

She took a step back. "You know my name?"

He pointed at her chest and she slapped her hand to the plastic rectangle above her heart.

"Oh, right... It's just that you look like someone who used to live around here."

Chaz shrugged.

"Where are you from?" she said.

"Skidegate." She still had his change and he did not want this conversation to continue. Maybe he didn't need it back.

"Who's your dad?"

What's it to you? he wanted to say. Instead he reached for his drinks and then, after a moment's hesitation, he dropped the name like a defensive strike.

"Rick Reckless."

"Totem Timber." She nodded, but her face looked disappointed, as if he'd gotten the answer wrong.

"And your mom. It's June, isn't it?"

"Look. Can I just get my change?"

"You don't know, do you?" She spilled a toonie and a few extra coins into his hand.

He ignored her comment and walked away. Then remembered to throw a thanks over his shoulder, his voice rising to the height of a six-year-old who was talking to a stranger.

Outside Chaz's mind raced. What didn't he know? It was Lily who didn't know who her father was.

He handed Lily a can of cherry-flavoured fizzy water and popped the lemon one. Downed it. After he started the truck, Chaz looked out the rearview mirror and shoulder checked, then pulled onto the road. The sun peeked through a cloud and hit him on the forehead. He started to sweat. He put in a new CD before they hit the back road gravel. Public Enemy fast forwarded to "Fight the Power." The whole song started off in chaos, but he liked when the title kept repeating.

He looked at Lily to see if she liked it too, but apparently not. "*This* music?" she said and shook her head.

You know nothing, he wanted to say. At least she grew up with some kind of father, even if he wasn't the real deal.

25

When they got to camp, Lily dropped her backpack in her room and noticed the chaos on Renée's side. Brown ends of cigarettes scrunched onto greasy plates, more butts floating in coffee mugs. A tipped over bottle of wine. Piles of soggy tissue. Scarves, jeans, socks exploded all over. Lily opened the window and shook her head. The breeze moved the yeasty smell around. Had Renée been on a bender?

Chaz had gone all gallant and offered to go to the mess hall to grab lunch bags. God. Those kisses in the night? The adrenalin after waking up beside him and realizing how late they were. The rush into the truck. Then Lily had to bring up all that stuff about her dad. She'd almost cried. Maybe she should've just gone all dramatic, traumatic, and had a weeping fit. Maybe then she wouldn't feel any of these messed-up emotions anymore. Let the liquid spill, then soak it up with paper towels and toss it all into a Port grocery store bag.

She needed to know who this Walker really was. She wrote a quick note to Renée—*Talk tonight?*—and threw it on her roommate's bed. Then she grabbed her gear and scuttled out.

Lily nodded up at the sky as she stood by the truck. Beautiful—bluer than the orbs she'd seen in the net bag at the cabin, or the glass ball Blaize had given her. So weird to see Blaize and Sissy. So much had happened since she'd left them in their driftwood shanty after the dance. What were they doing here? Right, they'd asked for a ride. She thought of her car again, still alone out there, in the forest. Poor baby Colt. How would she get it now?

She looked at her caulk boots, safely tucked in the back of the truck. She would not let Larry and his strangeness bother her. As if on cue, he walked up shaking the keys in her general direction. As if he was taunting her. As if he wanted her to make a big deal about something that he had done.

She barely listened as Larry heaved out instructions for the day. Something about coordinates and a new direction for the survey.

Blah, blah, blah. She looked past him to the inlet and saw something moving by the water. Then she heard a toggling cry.

Larry stopped talking immediately and stood still, searching. Then he pointed at the marsh grass at the edge of the bay.

"Get the binoculars, quick," he said.

Lily pulled them out from under the driver's seat and handed them over.

"Sandhill cranes," he said. Even without the binos, Lily could see a body with wings waving, head bobbing, flipping and spinning. Then another. Two birds with long necks dipping and swirling around each other.

"Mating dance," Larry said. "Lucky guy. If she chooses him, he's got a partner for life."

Larry handed Lily the binoculars. "Check it out. They're grey birds, but sometimes they stain their feathers with rusty soil. No one knows why."

"To make themselves more attractive, you said."

"I did? When?" Never mind, Lily thought, but he just kept talking anyway.

"Maybe it's to blend in better on the nest? Who knows what motivates birds? Who knows what motivates anyone," he said.

"Freaking Larry. You've always got to take topics to the next level," said Chaz, thumping his fingers on the truck hood.

Lily watched the birds dancing for a moment longer, until Chaz called out, "Let's go."

"Okay, okay," she said. But really, she wanted to get closer to the birds and hear them call again. Never mind Chaz either. She would come back later to scan the ground where the pair pirouetted. She wanted to find another feather.

f

Once they piled out of the truck, Chaz pulled out his map and checked the compass bearing. He'd brought Lily a ham sandwich, but she'd barely thanked him, just pushed ahead. She hadn't said two words since they got back to camp. He thought about turning and pressing her into a tree. Falling puddled together in the moss. But he could hear her grumbling about birds and Larry. Or was it Brian? Her not-dad. She had a few things going on. But she had her caulk boots, so that was a bonus. Best to leave her alone. Everything kept shifting anyway, like the beach logs after a storm.

Chaz started into the forest and heard the typewriter chatter of the winter wren. He could picture the movement of fingers on an old machine. The ding when the cartridge got to the end. He must have seen it in a movie, because he didn't know anyone with a typewriter on the islands. Superman and Lois Lane writing up the news.

When Chaz heard a snap, he looked back. There was Lily, charging up and over a fallen tree. He watched her gouge her caulk boots into a log bridge and stomp across. Nothing could stop her. She seemed pissed, though. Made her sexy.

Chaz clicked his Walkman on, hoping the music would keep his mind off Lily. Uncle. Rick. Gran. The choices he would have to make. The batteries on the player were almost dead, but "Fight for Your Right" scratched through the foam. He liked the fight songs. Chaz did a few lunges as he walked, a vague attempt to keep his muscles working for basketball. He should be doing sprints. Banger could always beat him down the court. He didn't always make the shot, but the bugger could run.

Fucking Banger. He didn't know anything about forestry. Chaz had been slogging in the bush since he was sixteen. Told Rick he'd already graduated when really he had a whole year of high school left. And the jerk never checked. Or even counted back the years. Not like Larry, who paid too much attention. Damn him. Larry had always known Chaz was too young.

Where the hell was Larry anyhow? Chaz looked through a run of trees and imagined they'd been planted in a row. Like a corn row. He pictured the thick-stalked grass. The kind that grew above your head and sprouted ears of bright yellow seeds. Maybe Lily came from some corn-growing region? Some prairie farm somewhere. *Children of the Corn.* Freaking creepy. The children murdering all the adults in some small town. That stupid blond guy who wouldn't leave, even when his wife begged him to. And then there she was, strung up with a crown of thorns around her head. It still gave him the shivers.

Banger and his horror movies. Chaz was the one who had to walk home at three a.m. The swish of wind in the overgrown grass by the beach; the tall stalks rising above the rusted body of an abandoned fire truck. The time the door slammed and Uncle had bashed his way into the night. He'd shouted out as the screen rebounded and whacked him from behind. Chaz frozen, pressed against the trunk of a cedar tree, hoping his uncle, who'd been drinking again, wouldn't notice him.

Chaz thought of that big tree as he turned to look back for Lily and Larry again. He couldn't see either of them. As if they'd vanished into the gloom. That cedar tree had gone too. It had stood by Chinaay and Nanaay's house for most of his childhood, but when the top snapped off in a storm, the village decided the whole thing had to come down.

Chaz pushed through a dry creek bed and almost grabbed a prickly devil's club stem to steady himself. He snatched his hand back, and pressed his elbows tight to his sides. A mittful of devil's club would be humiliating. He'd had those little spikes embedded in his hand before. Puss-filled and swollen in the night.

He bounced his knees up and down and wished he had a ball. He put his arm out as if he was making a run for the basket. Screw fishing. He had to get away. Living in a town with so many relatives. Uncle's temper. Nanaay's sorrow. Everything felt so intense.

Chaz circled another tree and the wind picked up. The Beastie Boys gave way to "Hell Bent for Leather" and the forest started to darken. He looked to see what the sky might be doing, but he couldn't see past the trees. If he'd been on the ocean, he'd know whether rain was on the way. But if he was on the ocean, he'd be on Uncle's boat. Not his favourite option. Chaz cracked his neck to the left and then to the right, as the music built. Guitar rage needed to complete the survey line.

A second later he stopped and pushed his headphones off. Had he heard something? A goshawk about to rip his brains out? A raven cackle? What would one of those big black birds be doing this far back in the forest? He thought of them as village birds, hanging around the clans, keeping an eye on the people. Chaz heard the raven sound again and scanned the ridge he'd just come down. He was glad to see the orange of Lily's hard hat.

"Hey, kid," Larry called down to him. "Gogeet might get you if get too far ahead."

"Piss off, old man," he muttered, then bumped his headphones back over his ears and continued along the compass line.

That's when Lily leapt at him, knocking Rob Halford out of his head.

"Come." She pulled on his sleeve and dragged him back up the hill.

"Whoa, whoa. Slow down."

She stopped in front of an ancient tree with a big gash in the trunk. He looked at it, then reached forward to touch the edge.

"It's a test hole." Lily grinned as if she'd just discovered a pot of fish stew. Ha. As if.

"You sure about that?" Chaz looked at the hole and wanted to say that it could have been made by a bird or an animal, but he knew it hadn't. He could already see the wedge-shaped cuts that dug into the centre.

"They would chip in to see if the tree was sound before felling it for a canoe or something," she said.

"Really? Good to know." He rolled his eyes at her.

"Sorry. I guess you knew that." Lily blushed and ran her hands along the texture of the cuts. She'd run her hands along his biceps the night before. He had to look away.

"Do you think they used stone or iron tools?"

"It's stone," said Larry, who'd wafted up behind them like a ghoul. Of course. Larry always had an explanation for everything.

"You can see by the irregular marks," Larry went on. "An iron blade would have left uniform gouges. Could be this was done pre-contact. But you can't know for sure, because iron tools would have taken a while to disperse. Mind you, we are on the tip-top of the islands, near where Haidas first saw Juan Perez come sailing in, so why wouldn't they have iron, if there was iron to be had."

"Okay. Okay," said Chaz. "Jeez, Larry, you want a Ph.D. for your time here? Don't we have trees to measure or something?"

"Maybe we can tell it was made with a stone tool from this?" Lily pulled a long wedge of rock out of the hole. The adze was thin, almost bevelled on the blade end, but thick and round on the other. She wrapped her hand around the handle and matched it to one of the marks. A perfect fit. "It's still sharp." She dug the stone into the edge of the cut wood and Chaz wanted to grab it away from her.

"Put it back," he said.

"Are you crazy? Let me see that thing," said Larry. Lily hesitated, but then handed it to Larry and Chaz took a deep inhale. "This is a major find. We should take it to the museum." Larry held the tool in one hand and thwapped it against his open palm.

"Stop it." Chaz's face fired to red. He pictured the men finding the tree without a compass or maps. The water that led back to the inlet. He didn't know why, but he couldn't stop himself from shouting: "It stays here. Put it back."

Lily looked surprised. "But what if something happens to it?"

"What's going to happen to it? It's been here for ages." Chaz checked the compass and the map. "We're not even in the chart area. Leave it."

"Come on," said Larry. "Do you know how rare it is to find something like this? People are going to want to see it."

"Then they'll have to find it, like we did," said Chaz.

Larry kept turning the adze over and over in his hands. He looked as if he wanted to pocket it. As if he might bonk someone on the head with it and run. Chaz primed himself, ready to fight like hell if the old man tried anything.

"Chaz..." Lily looked as if she wanted to say more. Like she knew better than him, even though she knew nothing about this place or his people. The forest was like some sort of game to her. A stream of challenges that she would try and get through before her turn ran out.

She didn't belong here. Larry didn't belong here. Chaz felt himself cracking.

Lily finally broke the silence. "Okay. Okay. We're not going to tell anyone where it is. Are we?" She moved toward Larry as the two men stared each other down.

"I'm not," said Chaz. Something ancient and buried had been uncovered. All of a sudden he didn't know if he trusted Larry. Maybe he never did.

"Okay then." Lily reached for the adze. Chaz watched Larry bristle, saw his paw curl around the tool—but Lily's small hand slipped it out of Larry's tightening grip. She turned it over once more, cradling the weight for two or three deep breaths, before offering it to Chaz.

"Here, if that's what you think is best," she said, but he shook his head. He couldn't touch it. Something told him that.

"Put it back and let's go."

26

When they got back to camp at the end of the day and unloaded their gear, Chaz waded around, his legs unsteady as if he'd come ashore after a month at sea. He couldn't believe how much this job took out of him. Or what they'd seen out there. What he'd made them leave. He thought of all the secrets that the forest held. All the ghosts. *Haidas don't belong in the forest*, Uncle always said. Exactly. He'd rather be anywhere else. The village. With the Canucks at BC Place Stadium. Better yet, a basketball game in Dallas. Or Los Angeles? The NBA live! Huge rooms filled with waving fans. The squeak of shoes on the courts. People running their asses off. Making moves. Getting shit done.

Larry and Lily went to get changed for supper and Chaz took the truck to the machine shed. Mud caked the bottom and he wanted to spray it down.

That adze had thrown him off. Now that he was back in camp, he wanted to have it in his hands so badly that he almost jumped in the truck and drove back. What an idiot. He wished Chinaay could have seen it. Uncle too. He pictured it on Nanaay's mantle below all the family photos. All those people, each in their own frame. Lily and her questions. Is this you? Is this your mother? Chaz too embarrassed to admit how he always avoided raising his eyes in that part of the living room. He didn't want to confront any of those people. His mother, his uncle, his younger self.

The machine shed had the only concrete floor in the camp and Chaz felt solid in there. Tools. Diagnostic machines. Everything had a purpose. Things might fall apart, but a blueprint for how to rebuild them could be found.

He pulled out the undercarriage pressure washer and found a can of degreaser. Chaz put on a pair of safety goggles and sprayed the shit out of the chassis.

When the water shut off unexpectantly, Chaz turned and saw Mac. "Are you making a mess of my shop again, you little shit?" Chaz didn't know how anyone so short could have fathered someone as tall as Banger.

"I don't know why you waste your time washing these damn trucks. Dirt's what holds them together." Mac got out the mop and started pushing water out the door.

"We saw Banger in town on the weekend," Chaz said.

"We?"

"Me and Lily."

"You and Lily," Mac reiterated in that annoying way adults had, when they thought they knew something but they didn't.

Lily went to her room and changed into a sweatshirt and jeans. Renée still wasn't there, but she had been. Cigarette butts gone, clothes folded, wine bottle cleaned up. Maybe things were falling into place. Lily had her questions lined up about Arlene being April. About May and June. The Walker. She looked to see if Renée might have written back but all she found was her own scribbled note in the bin. Never mind. It was time for supper anyway.

She turned to leave and bumped an oversized green book off Renée's bedside table. Lily bent to collect the pages that scattered out: a diagram showing the difference between a male and female crab; a recipe for pickled bull kelp; a newspaper report about locals busted while collecting hallucinogenic mushrooms. Was this the thin green book she'd seen at the cabin? The pebbled cover felt the same, like some kind of visitor book. Lily skimmed past missives from kayakers who'd stayed a night; hunters who'd cut up fifteen deer; biologists studying grouse. Dates and temperatures. Card games: Rummy, Hearts, Asshole. When she got to an entry near the front, she had to catch her breath:

I didn't know why I left until I got here.
Now I don't know how I'll ever find my way home.
A., August 1979

Her mother's writing. Lily hadn't meant to chase her mother's ghost. She'd just wanted a job and a different sort of life. But here was Arlene, demanding all the attention as always. Setting the tone. The rest of the pages spilled through her fingers like a river, then closer to the centre of the book she found another note, in a different hand:

She's gone. I didn't know there was a baby. I'm lost.

No signature, not even an initial, but Lily knew who it was. Walker. He got someone pregnant and disappeared. That's what Renée said. He could be anyone, but Lily was now convinced that he was her dad.

Lily stood to put the book back on the bedside table, but picked it up again when she realized what had been underneath. Laminated sheets. What the heck? She turned one over and saw the tops of trees. The shape of the cutblock they'd laid out. What was Renée doing with aerial photos of the block where they'd found the canoe?

Lily backed away from whatever this meant. She was hungry and exhausted by all the secrets that the forest held.

27

The next morning, Larry drove, Chaz pouted and Lily, for once, stayed quiet. She expected to head back to the area by the adze, but Larry chose a new route yet again and she wondered if they would ever get a full survey done. This time, he pulled off by an old skid road, the ruts smoothed with fine gravel. When they started walking, Larry started yakking as usual.

"They used to dig the pebbles out of the salmon streams. Run the backhoe into the creek, dig a few scoops, and spread 'em on the road. Carved out some of the Yakoun's best fishing holes that way."

"Jesus," said Chaz.

"Doesn't happen anymore. Too many fish biologists got pissed," said Larry. "But I've seen them out fly-fishing in those pools like everyone else. Best chance for a steelhead by a long shot."

Lily wished Larry would shut up. She couldn't tell if he was full of shit half the time or all of the time. She hung back a couple of paces whispering at the plants: false Solomon's seal, bunchberry, phlox. Larry switched to rumours of protests as they passed an old landing with a rusted machine covered in moss.

"How many more trees can one island protect?" he said, as Lily looked through the forest and thought she saw a small hump of red. And a tent. Was that smoke? She had been wondering how to start looking for the Walker. Could he be that easily found?

Lily heard a cracking sound, then a low moan, and a crash. Larry and Chaz veered off into the labyrinth of second growth and motioned for her to follow.

"Shh," Chaz said as he nodded toward a big brown form on the side of the track.

"A bear?" she whispered.

"Maybe it's your Gogeet," said Carl.

The creature snarled again and pulled a tree out by its roots. The trunk wasn't big, just a spike of a thing, but still.

"Holy shit," Lily said.

"It's dead. Real easy to rip out," said Chaz, but nevertheless he got into a defensive position between her and the shaggy being.

"To hell with you too," the thing yelled and Lily immediately knew who it was.

"Blaize," she said. Lily stopped and Chaz hung back too, but Larry plugged his nose and swatted toward the hippies before he kept going.

Lily could see Sissy now, stumbling and yelling from the direction of the tent. "Stop it," she said. "We can do this together."

"Do what together?" he yelled. "You do everything on your own."

"I don't mean to."

"You never mean to, you just do whatever the hell you want."

"That's not fair. I don't do everything I want. I came here for you. Now we can stay," Sissy said.

Blaize ripped another spear-thin snag from the moss. "Why do I fall for this every time?"

"You fall for me. Because you love me and we're going to have a baby."

"You're going to have a baby. Not me."

"We're going to save the forest. Just like you wanted."

"We're not going to do that. The people who live here are with or without us."

"We're going to live here too, like elves. We'll use moss for pillows and eat berries and deer and we're going to do it together, because being a father will be the most important thing you've ever done."

"It's not my baby, Sissy."

"It *is* yours."

"You can't keep changing the story."

"That's all we are," she said.

"What?" He kicked at a rotting log on the forest floor.

"Stories. Our lives. Just event after event until a plot is formed," she said.

"You just read that the other day."

"It doesn't matter. What I'm saying is that you can tell yourself anything you want."

"It doesn't make it true," he said.

"It does if you want it to be." Sissy grabbed his hand and twirled herself in and Lily knew where that could lead. Blaize looked at Sissy and she reached up to kiss him, but he jerked away and roared.

If resolve, torn asunder, had a sound, this was it. Lily watched him reach around and grab her ass and Lily grabbed Chaz by the sleeve and they continued on.

"Did they even notice us standing there," asked Chaz.

Lily shrugged. Larry was long gone and Chaz was getting ahead now too, but she couldn't help looking back. She'd seen a flash of metal through the trees. She didn't really care about Sissy and Blaize. They would figure it out. But that metal thing behind the tent? The blistered red. It couldn't have been. But she was pretty sure that it was her car.

Larry couldn't believe the drivel that took place between hippies. Weren't they the same stinky couple he'd seen with Lily at the dance? The snake-haired girl. The barefoot boy. Larry pulled out his hankie and wiped his nose. Not unless they breed in Kleenex. Ha. That had shut her up.

Sweet, sweet, I'm so sweet. He heard the brown creeper but couldn't see the small bird bouncing up the tree trunks, searching for bugs to ferret out of the smallest holes. Larry looked around the beautiful forest. He had pushed past the old clearcut and now he was into the old growth on the other side of the creek from the adze. Everyone does what they have to do to survive. Wasn't Lily yapping about looming disasters the other day? How to survive Y2K? One breath at a time kid, one breath at a time.

Larry didn't know why he stayed in this job or on the islands. But where else could he go? Back in town, he had a rented trailer with a garden. Sometimes he told himself that it was all the perennials that made him stay. Four different types of clematis winding along the fence. They'd cost forty bucks a pop. And the girl at the grocery store always said hi. Laughed and sent him back to the shelf when he forgot to grab eggs. At the liquor store, they knew about his penchant for Baileys. The manager suggested he try the cheaper brand, just to see. But he didn't like it as much.

Years ago, another forest tech had moved to a creamier job in Dease Lake—benefits, housing. Larry had kept in touch and thought about moving there himself. More action, different women and the town was close enough to Whitehorse if he got too bushed. Jim sent a photo once, as if to prove how much fun he was having. He'd been wearing a New Year's paper hat. Someone pouring Baby Duck. Larry missed those party hat days. Bands every night at the bar. Fishing boats tied up five against each other on the dock. Until the good times collapsed.

Yep, he'd thought about leaving back then. Jim's letters from Dease were pretty tempting. But he remembered how he'd gotten the chills after looking at the photo more carefully. The party swirling around a makeshift dance floor, Jim smiling like a fool. Streamers raining down from the ceiling and in the background he could swear he saw someone had a gun pointed at Jim's head.

To hell with this job. He could go back and get that adze. Bring it to a private collector—and then what? They'd give him a million bucks and he'd be set for life. Yeah. Right.

Larry stomped forward and realized that he'd stepped on a single delight. His favourite flower. The one the Haida used to eat to gain supernatural strength. June must have told him that. He needed to smarten up. Get on with measuring tree widths and heights. That was what they were here for, damn it. He did not need to consider the results of his actions all those years ago. Not while he was out here in the indulgent moss.

Larry could hear Lily and Chaz coming along behind him and called out. He pulled out the terrain map and double-checked he was nowhere near the canoe or the adze. Fucking Rick. Always seemed to have a reason to yell at him these days. Rick wanted any problems to just go away, but so did Larry. That's why he'd suggested signing the canoe block over to Cradle. For using their damn access road. Then Fletcher could deal with it. Brilliant, really.

Yep. I still got it, he thought, as he walked into a thick grove of impressively massive trees. Larry stood back for a second and checked his maps again. Maybe this would work out in his favour after all. A longer route, but if he could get these pumpkins into the road, Rick wouldn't have to pay stumpage.

Everything always came too easy for that guy. Money. Power. June. He had her and didn't even appreciate it. At least he didn't have her for long.

Larry hooked his d-tape into the textured bark of a huge hemlock and started to pull. Winding it around the tree, the tape already read four metres and he was only three-quarters of the way back to the start. He started to feel better. The more fibre he could squeeze into the road, the happier everyone would be.

Then Larry looked up at the giant and felt a moment of regret. Nobody wanted hemlock. Wasn't worth shit in the market. A tree like this could be turned into an entire house, but likely as not it would be pulped. He pulled at the tape again, but the metal band wouldn't move any farther. Why did he keep using this rusted old bobbin? There were way more flexible kinds of tape. He tugged again, then stumbled and in the second it took him to recover, the sharp thin ribbon of his d-tape came spinning at him like a snake.

He tried to block the bite with his hand, but the tape ripped through the space between his thumb and forefinger, and then twirled back into the case.

"Shit," he said quietly. More delays. Larry slipped the d-tape into his front pocket and rummaged for a hankie. It was just a paper cut. He took the cloth and wrapped it between his thumb and fingers, then tied it off.

Larry pushed off from the tree and walked over to the next giant trunk. "It's nothing," he whispered aloud. But as he moved, he could feel the muscles in his hand starting to pulse.

Lily found Larry lying on the forest floor, his face mottled and white like an old alder trunk, and his hand bleeding through a handkerchief.

"She danced with him," he said.

"Holy shit, Larry." Lily crouched down beside him and yelled out to Chaz. Lily tried to think of the steps in first aid. Ensure safety. Assess consciousness. Call for help.

"I'm sorry," Larry said when Chaz skidded up.

"About what?" he said.

"About June."

"My mom?"

Lily shook her head. What the heck? April, May, June. April was the Alberta girl. Who was May? Never mind. She couldn't think about that now. "Let me see." She lifted Larry's hand as if it were an injured bird. She could feel it throbbing and when she untied the handkerchief, his thumb flopped.

"I think he's cut it right through the tendon." Lily pulled a dressing out of the first aid kit she'd been carrying on her belt and wound it around and around, clamping his fingers back together. "What's he sorry for?" she asked Chaz.

"I have no idea."

"We should get him to the hospital."

Chaz crouched under Larry's bad arm and Lily got under the other. They hobbled that way through the forest, past Blaize and Sissy's camp, and back to the truck. When they finally got to the road, the two of them shoved Larry into the middle and strapped him in. Lily held him up on one side and Chaz sandwiched him on the left. Larry's head sagged and he started to drool. Chaz peeled out and raced back to the logging camp.

When he pulled up to the office, he looked over at Lily. "Go tell Rick what's happened and I'll get Larry into town."

"Let me come with you," she said. "Then after we can get my car." If it's still there. Or had she really seen it where Blaize and Sissy were camped?

"No, Lily. I promise we'll get it later."

"Don't wait," Larry moaned. "If you want something. Do it now."

"He's delirious," said Lily.

Chaz reached across Larry, who was babbling about fungus, and put his hand on hers. "I'll see you when I get back. I promise."

28

The next morning, Lily walked into the mess hall and grabbed a tray. Renée was there shovelling the scrambled eggs. She tried to catch her roommate's eye, but Stypes was right behind her pushing his way along the line. Lily got a cup of coffee and moved through the tables looking for Chaz and Larry. But of course they weren't at their usual table. Obviously they weren't back yet. Or maybe the forest had swallowed them whole.

When Lily saw Rick walking toward her, his solid shoulders upright and stiff, she tried to turn away—but he caught hold of her. She flinched and searched his face for Chaz. But she couldn't find him there either.

"Today, you'll go out with Grayson," Rick said. He held a stack of aerial photos very similar to the ones she'd seen on Renée's side of the room. Like the ones she'd seen in the cabin.

"Why not Chaz?"

"He's still with Larry. They're getting in to see the doctor today."

"Is he okay?"

"Chaz? He's fine. He's costing me money though. They both are."

"I meant Larry."

"Larry always has something going on. I'm sure it will work out. Meanwhile, let's keep you out of trouble."

"What does that mean?

"I mean, you three have been causing a lot of problems. First goshawks and then canoes. And now what?"

"We're just following the maps," said Lily, glad he hadn't mentioned the adze.

"Yes, but somehow everyone seems to know what's out there," Rick said.

"You're the one who said it's not easy keeping secrets around here."

"Right, well, maybe goshawk nests will be less obvious from the air. We've got some helicopter work booked. Just check in with Grayson and try to stay out of trouble. "

Lily looked over at Chaz's roommate, sitting at Rick's table. He smiled and shoved a sausage into his mouth.

"Grayson and who?"

Rick had already walked away, but he turned back. "Just the two of you. And the pilot, of course."

Grayson gestured for her to come sit down. She sighed and complied. What else could she do?

"Too bad about your boyfriend," Grayson said.

"He'll be back." Lily looked at the yellow slab of eggs oozing salty water on her toast. She didn't feel like eating anymore.

"That's not what I heard," he said.

"What's that supposed to mean?"

Grayson flipped through a field book. When he tossed it at her, Lily could see that it was Chaz's. "Seems like you guys didn't get that much work done out there. When you're with me, you're going to have to perform."

Ten minutes later, Lily spotted Grayson standing by the helipad in a "We came, we sawed, we conquered" t-shirt and his hard hat. Her horror at being stuck with him for the day was drowned out by the noise that took over the sky. A helicopter appeared from behind the trees like a giant moth, then it hovered as if it might land on top of him. She hoped, meanly, that it would. Instead it set down alongside him and Grayson stood tall and walked toward the moving blades. She was amazed he kept his head.

He turned and looked back at her and gestured with his arm.

She had her pack and work vest. She didn't know if she needed her caulk boots. Were they getting out of this thing and walking? The instructions had been unclear. She contemplated the shuddering machine and wanted to ask more, but instead she just sucked in her breath, crouched and kept moving forward, as she'd done so many times before.

As she approached, Grayson grabbed her gear, put it in the compartment at the back and carefully closed the door. Then he hopped into the bug-like body and held out his hand. She didn't need his help but she couldn't get past him. She reached to push his arm aside and he clutched her fist, pulling her up, right between his legs. Lily struggled to untangle herself from his arms as the pilot turned around and shook his head at them.

Lily smacked Grayson and got into her seat. The pilot pointed to their headsets and mimicked putting them on. He pointed at the small chin mike and opened and closed his mouth to show her how to talk. Lily followed Grayson's movements and strapped in. She'd never been in a helicopter before. She heard the pilot say "Ready?" through the headset and Grayson said "Ready" and the machine rose. Her stomach lagged behind but it soon caught up. Lily tried to follow the roads she, Chaz and Larry had driven, but the chopper moved too fast and the lines trickled into the green. Grayson told the pilot that Lily was a newbie, so he hammed it up—strafing the ridge-top trees as if they were in *Apocalypse Now*. Jeremy would have loved it. Would Chaz? Lily looked out the window, as they flew beyond all the territory she had covered before.

She already felt as if things had changed irrevocably. As if she had so many things she wished she'd said to Chaz, to Larry. They'd be back tonight. Wouldn't they?

Meanwhile, Grayson shuffled through the aerial photos, passing them to her, pointing at the shapes. "We're keeping an eye out for high-value stands. The dark patches are cedar and spruce." The pilot stayed low along a valley. From the air all the trees looked the same to Lily, but Grayson kept a tally. Circled them on the image. Barked out dollar values: $600,000 worth of cedar, $1 million in spruce. Lily wrote the numbers down but couldn't imagine how he knew.

"How can you tell the spruce from the cedar?" she said.

"The round, conical tops are spruce. The cedars are broader." He leaned over to her side of the machine. "The spruce are taller too."

Lily could feel the change in the helicopter, how it dipped with Grayson's weight.

"Hey," she said and slapped him away. Grayson lurched back to the other side of the chopper.

"What are you two doing back there?" the pilot said. "You want us all to make it back, right?"

Lily didn't want to think about that and kept her focus on the trees. So insane to see them from the sky, crowns billowing and bending. Shaking their heads in the breeze.

"Imagine climbing one," she said. "Rising from forest floor into the sky."

"We're here to cut 'em. Why would we climb them?"

"For the view."

The helicopter rose above the ridge and a vista straight to the ocean spread out before them.

"I've got a better idea," Grayson said. "Raze them to the water so we can see the whales from the road." If Chaz had said that, she would have punched him, but Grayson could go to hell.

The helicopter dropped away from the trees and banked toward the beach. She looked out at the matte grey water—how calm it looked. Maybe the ocean was a more soothing place than the forest after all.

When the pilot leaned into a turn to head north, Lily spotted movement by the trees.

A man, in dark blue, skittered for cover.

"Did you see...?" she started to say into her mic.

"Who the heck...?" the pilot spat.

"The enemy! Anyone got a gun?" Grayson hunched at the window pretending to spray bullets at the sand. Ugh, Lily thought. Where did Rick find this guy? The pilot, no better, spun back to the small bay and stayed low, as if seeking quarry. The wind from the blades shook the tree branches and Lily imagined the man hunkered down trying to stay camouflaged by the green.

"Who is he and what the hell is he doing out here?" said the pilot.

"Must be some crazy backpacker," said Grayson.

"Too old for a backpacker," said the pilot.

Lily didn't say anything, but she knew exactly who it was.

"Do you think he needs help?" shouted the pilot.

"Forget about him," Grayson said as he emptied his imaginary semi-automatic weapon at the forest's edge. "We've got to finish surveying. There are at least two good blocks on that ridge, good enough to justify the cost of the hauling."

Lily, glad to distract them away from the man, started asking forestry questions. "How do you get the trees out of a place like that? That's a long road to put in."

"Same way everyone'll get here. By helicopter," said Grayson.

Not everyone, she thought, looking back for other signs of the Walker. Not a myth, but a real man. "That must be crazy expensive," she said.

"You know it. That's why we only take the high value, baby."

"Isn't that high grading?" said Lily.

"Hell yeah, do you think anyone wants most of the crap we cut down?"

"Seems like a waste then, if no one even wants the wood."

"Where there's money to be made there's business to be done."

Lily sighed, but no one heard over the helicopter's roar. They continued criss-crossing over virgin forest with Grayson circling and adding up revenue. They'd flown back too far to see the beach in between their passes. Lily kept straining to catch a glimpse of sand, but Grayson finally determined that he'd found enough and told the pilot to head to camp.

The radio crackled as they veered south again. Lily could make out one side of the conversation through her headphones. The pilot confirmed a location and she thought he said something about whether to bring the cops in.

"What's happening?" she asked.

"Slight detour. We've got to go pick up your boss," the pilot said.

29

The chopper set down on the road by the block where they'd found the canoe. One of the Totem Timber trucks was parked and several other vehicles had created a wall blocking it, along with access to the new branch road. Smoke curled from wood in a fire ring. Lily watched a line of fifteen or twenty men and women converge in front of the vehicles, their faces painted with black lines and smudges. They came forward, no drumming or chanting, just walking hand in hand in the direction of the helicopter.

Rick, chin raised in defiance, stood behind the line where all the tents and tarps were, arguing with a tall heavy man in a jean jacket. Lily recognized him as one of the guys she'd seen with Chaz's uncle in the forest. Rick's hands leapt into the air as he talked, his body twisted. The rotor whine slowed to a stop, and the pilot opened the helicopter door.

"One of you, go get Rick. I'll stand by and be ready to lift if this mob tries anything."

"Is this a blockade?" said Lily.

"What's it look like?" said Grayson.

Lily couldn't believe it. She'd seen news stories. She had the pictures in the magazine, but this was real. "I'll go," she said.

"Probably best," said Grayson. "If I went, I'd probably want to kick the shit out of someone."

"More like you'd get your shit kicked," the pilot said. "Tell Rick the police won't be out until tomorrow."

"Police?"

"Injunction baby. These hooligans are out of line," said Grayson.

Lily saw a woman around her age carrying a small boy, an elderly man wrapped in a black blanket with red trim, and young men in t-shirts with black smudge lines crossing their cheeks. Some scruffy white people milled around in the camp. Larry would have called them hippies, but no one looked unruly. Even the man that Rick was flaring at stood calmly with his arms crossed over his chest. All these people were soon to be arrested? She tried to keep a neutral face, but as she got closer to Rick, the comments started.

"I see they've sent in the big guns."

"Are you the National Guard, honey?"

"I'm just picking up Rick," she said to the line of faces.

"Yeah, well we might just keep him."

"And his truck."

She scanned the group, looking for Chaz's uncle. Did she see Sissy and Blaize?

Rick pushed through the barricade of bodies when he spotted Lily and grabbed her arm. "Did you know about this?"

"Hey, let go of her," said someone in the crowd.

"Me? What? How would I know?"

"The canoe tree. That's why they're here. People are telling me that Chaz showed it to his uncle."

"Whoa. That's not how it happened. They were looking for goshawk nests and we bumped into Chaz's uncle and two other guys. We were standing right beside the canoe at the time."

"Great. So you showed them the goshawk nest too?"

"No. They didn't find that, as far as I know," said Lily.

"Well, they're blockading a month's worth of layout work. We have permits, but they've barricaded my truck. I'm just lucky the chopper was in the air or they'd have held me captive too."

Lily heard someone swear at Rick. She turned and saw Chaz's uncle push his way through the crowd. "Leave her alone, you prick. This has been coming a long time and you know it. Another barge of cedar went out today—our ancestors, on a floating grave, heading where? And for whose benefit?"

"Oh for Christ's sake, Chuck, stop being so dramatic. They're trees. They'll grow back. You can't even stop shit from growing around here. You know that." Lily backed away from the two men as some of the protesters started booing and hissing.

"Give your head a shake, man. Not at this rate. Not in this place. I watched it all happen. I never thought we could wipe out the valley we started on when I was eighteen. We logged it all before I was twenty-five. And for what?" said Chuck.

"Multiple family's lives," said Rick. He leaned back and folded his arms across his chest. "You got a big truck and a salmon troller out of it, if I recall."

"Fuck you, Rick." Chaz's uncle stepped forward and a clipped cheer rose from the group. Lily looked at the helicopter for backup, but Grayson and the pilot were just sitting inside.

"Ha! Can't take the truth?" Rick uncrossed his arms and leaned in too. Lily pictured the crowd circling and the chants starting as they had when Chaz and Banger fought after the dance.

"Don't talk to me about truth. You wouldn't know truth if it hit you in the face." Lily gasped as Chuck's fist shot out and she heard Rick's nose crack.

"What the hell?" Rick's hands went up to catch the blood.

"That's for my sister," Chaz's uncle said, shaking out his hand.

"Your sister?" Rick spat. "That's the biggest truth that you and the rest of your family never want to face!" As the men shifted to more personal matters, the crowd seemed to loosen instead of tightening around them.

"Right. You screwed her, then left, and now you barely talk to her son."

"Exactly. Her son."

"Your son," Chuck corrected him.

"That's what you all like to think." Rick was bent over by then, his words barely audible. Chuck ignored him and walked away, but Lily had heard.

She came up beside her boss and put her hand on his back. "Squeeze your nostrils," she said.

Murmuring sounds spread as people in the crowd turned to talk among themselves. Then the elderly man in the blanket robe spoke up. "I'd like us all to remember why we are here. We demand that Rick Reckless of Totem Timber cease and desist his current logging plans in the Canoe Tree area. This land provides transportation, housing materials and food. It is home to the great black bear, taan, and the wily goshawk, stads k'un. It was used by our shamans as a place of healing. More than twenty culturally modified trees have been identified in the area. We hereby declare this a Haida Heritage Site."

"This is bullshit. Where are the cops?" said Rick as he straightened up.

"The pilot said they're not coming until tomorrow," said Lily. "Are you okay?"

Rick looked around. Chaz's uncle had disappeared. "I'll survive," he said.

"Come on then, let's get out of here," Lily said. She scanned the faces as they made their way back to the helicopter. Was Chaz here? That was really all Lily wanted to know.

At the mess hall that evening, the heavy-duty mechanics circled the forest tech table.

"Where's your boyfriend?"

"Gone to the other side, I heard."

"Selling all his daddy's secrets."

"Maybe the Gogeet got to him out there?"

"Maybe he's gotten to you too?"

She thought of what Rick had implied about Chaz not being his son. She didn't know what to think, so she waved her arms around her head as if she were scattering flies. The big men chuckled as they walked away.

30

Chaz woke with a start. She'd come to him with a raven t-shirt on. Thick black lines forming the outside edge—its curved beak pointing to the right, its outstretched wings, the folded tail feathers and the claws coiled on each side. A circle to represent the sun in its mouth.

"What are you wearing that for," he'd said.

"For you," Lily replied.

"You can't."

She did not look pleased.

"I'm a Raven. You can't be one too."

"It's just a t-shirt."

"You don't understand." He wished he'd stopped then, but he moved toward her. "No, really," he whispered. "I'm a Raven, my gran is a Raven, even my uncle is a Raven. You have to be an Eagle. I have to be with someone of the opposite clan."

"But I'm not even Haida. What difference does it make?"

"It wouldn't make any difference if you weren't with me."

"I'm not with you," she'd said, ripping the t-shirt off and tossing it onto the floor.

Chaz reached out to touch her but instead woke up with moonlight hitting his face. He looked around and remembered where he was. On watch, outside on the deck of *Haida Slayer*, Uncle's fishing boat.

That night Lily awoke to the sound of tapping. Her heart still raced from a dream. They'd been in a boat and Chaz had asked the old man at the end of the beach whether it was a good day to go out. *Not good*, he'd said, but they pushed off anyway. She turned around and the old man had become a blue heron and a storm of black clouds streamed over the tops of the trees. The rowboat transformed into a canoe and the waves bumped it as they tried to head back. She could still feel their fear. If they turned, they would topple, if they kept going they'd disappear. Chaz had braced in the chop, the large blade of his paddle cutting into the waves and knocking on the bottom of the canoe. Then that became the sound of knuckles on the windowpane and Lily opened her eyes to see Chaz's face.

He hadn't been at dinner. He must have come back in the night. He waved and knocked again, beckoning for her to come outside. She looked at Renée's bed but, of course, her roommate wasn't there. Half asleep in the darkness, Lily couldn't understand what he was doing there. She found her sweatshirt on the floor, pulled it on and moved toward the window. Chaz held his hands open wide, waving at her to stop. He pointed at the door. He wanted her to come outside. Lily, about to turn, took one last look at him. Had his face changed? He looked older, and tired. Had she seen hair between his fingers? She started to move closer but he dropped out of sight. She hurried to the window and looked out. In the darkness, she saw something slip into the forest, but she couldn't be sure.

She must have crawled back into bed and slept, because when she woke again, the morning light filled the room and Renée sighed and rolled over on her bed.

"Renée. You're back?" Lily rubbed at her eyes.

"Merde. I guess so."

"When did you get in?"

"A little before midnight."

"But I woke up in the middle of the night and you weren't here."

"You must have been dreaming. I haven't even turned over. I tink my right arm is still asleep."

"Did you hear the tapping?" said Lily.

"I didn't hear nothing," she said.

"Chaz was at the window. He wanted me to come outside."

"I thought Chaz went to town."

"That's what I thought too, but there he was. It was so creepy though, and his hands looked kind of hairy."

"Hairy?"

"I don't know. That sounds crazy. Anyway, I went to the window and he was gone."

"Mon dieu. Dat wasn't Chaz. Dat was an otter. Dey're shape shifters."

"Come on," said Lily. "What are you talking about?"

"I'm not joking. One of the nanaays in Skidegate warned me

about dem. Dey dress up like the one you love and try to entice you into the night. Den dey take you to der village and steal your soul."

Lily pulled on her jeans and her boots. "Yeah, right." She still had so much to ask Renée, but at this moment finding Chaz seemed more important. "For one thing, I'm not in love with him. And for another, he's probably at breakfast."

Her boots sucked into the mud as she hopped off the stoop. She looked at her watch. Too early for breakfast, so she turned to look along the side of the trailer, by the window near her bed. She would see his prints, wouldn't she? But she looked down at the ground and saw nothing except her own feet. She looked toward the forest and back at the windowsill. The opening was well above her head. Above Chaz's. She thought of how his face had changed into someone old enough to be her father, but she must have imagined that. And his look of fear as she came over to the window. Too weird. Anyway, whoever it was would have needed a stepladder to see into her room.

Rick was standing outside the cookhouse, blocking the door. "Just so you know, they're not coming back."

"Who?" said Lily. She was hungry and freaked out and didn't want to talk to her uptight boss.

"Larry and Chaz." He folded his arms over his plaid shirt and frowned as if Lily had done something wrong.

"What? Is Larry alright?"

"He's been medevaced to Terrace. The tendon between his thumb and finger was severed. He'll need surgery. They said his hand might never work the same way again."

"Oh my god. But Chaz is back now, isn't he?"

"No."

Of course he was. She'd seen him, hadn't she? Or had she still been dreaming?

"Did he go with Larry to Terrace?" she said.

"No."

"So he'll be back to work tomorrow?"

"No."

"The next day?"

"No. Look, I told you. He's not coming back."

"I don't understand."

"There's not much more to say."

She pushed past Rick and walked into the mess hall. Stypes and his gang looked at her and looked away. Mac nodded. She scanned the room and didn't see Chaz. But Grayson sat at the forest tech table—the place that belonged to Larry, Chaz and her. He waved her over, smiling some kind of shit-eating grin. They were supposed to go out in the helicopter again. Lily looked at the counter where Renée was serving up the food. She thought of the Walker and her father and all the things Renée had said. Through a small window by the door, she could see the edge of the forest—where an otter could have come from. The opening where footsteps could either lead into the brush, or move away from it. She felt the urge to run. Instead, she made herself a couple of sandwiches, packed them in a brown paper bag with an apple and went back out the door.

f

The morning light streamed into the wheelhouse on Uncle's boat and Chaz looked at the radio. He wanted to call Lily. But even if the repeaters could relay a message from Skidegate Inlet to camp, he couldn't talk to Lily on this thing. Everyone on the islands would hear him. And what could he say? Sorry. My uncle had a mess of reasons for why I had to leave. The chinook salmon opening. Getting fish into the hold because the processors won't wait and he owes money to everyone. Plus, he didn't want me around for the blockade.

Chaz didn't want to think about Rick—how mad he must be. Uncle had come back to Nanaay's in a fury. He said that Haidas weren't going to take it anymore. No more wood would leave these islands for some corporation's gain. Those monumental cedars, with all their evidence of Haida cultural use, were sacred. Uncle had laughed and admitted that Totem Timber had done them a favour by finding one of the best examples of a canoe tree that anyone had ever seen. Chaz knew how it looked. First the goshawk nest. Then Lily confronted Rick about the canoe and got nowhere. Next they found an adze in a test hole and quit surveying the area, and the Haida set up a blockade. Convenient.

He picked up the satellite phone and went onto the deck for a better shot at the orbit. It was unlikely, but maybe Lily would be passing by the office? Or if Mac was ordering parts, he might answer. Anyone but Rick. He powered up the phone and waited for it to scan the skies. When the line opened, Chaz felt like he could reach anyone. 1-800-HEY-MOM? If only he knew the right number to call.

He knew Totem's digits though. The beep from each button echoed like a taunt. Why had he agreed to go fishing? What if Lily left before he got back? How would he ever find her again? The phone started ringing and he held his breath. Maybe no one would answer and he could say that he tried—but of course, a familiar voice picked up.

"Chaz!" said Grayson. "What's your deal? Looking for Rick? Calling to fess up?"

"Is Lily around?"

"Lily? Are you kidding?"

"Never been more serious. I need to talk to her." Chaz tried to sound strong instead of desperate.

"She won't want to talk to you. She's with me now. Thanks bro."

"What's that supposed to mean?"

"You just enjoy your time on the boat. We've got trees to survey up here."

"What do you know about me and boats?"

"Everyone knows you've gone fishing with your uncle."

"Does Lily?"

"Not unless you told her." Grayson chuckled.

"Just tell her I called."

"Good luck with that," Grayson said and the phone went dead.

Chaz stared at it and wanted to push the numbers again. This was all Larry's fault. If Chaz hadn't had to drive Larry into town with his bloody hand, he'd still be in the forest for a few more days—the last place he ever thought he wanted to be. Everything was so mixed up.

Christ, Larry. Chaz thought of how he'd been babbling in the truck. Why the hell had Larry been talking about his mom? Kept saying her name: *June. June.* And apologizing to someone named Walker.

31

Lily was in the air with Grayson again and they had three more blocks to identify. These would eventually need ground truthing, but Lily didn't know if she'd be around long enough to be involved. Seeing the man at the edge of the forest had amped her up. She needed to know if he had anything to do with her life. Someone was her father. Renée was no help. She'd tried to ask Larry about him at the dance. She would never ask Rick. Arlene was useless. She'd have to go and find out for herself.

She looked out at the patchwork landscape as the helicopter flew. She thought about the time it would take to bring a tree down in the old way. Chipping at the edges and lighting small fires. Slowly working their way around. She'd been reading about Haida ways in a book called *Cedar* that she'd found in the rec hall. She had no idea that cedar could be used in so many ways. Boards and beams, sure, but also baskets and mats. Ropes. Even clothes. Why were logging companies in such a rush to get so much down? Money, obviously. Always the prime motivator. Jobs. For people like you, Larry would say. Then there's all the suburbanites who want cedar decks so they can look out over their domain. And cedar fences to keep everyone else out. That would be Larry again. His practical perspective. Then, to cinch it, he'd say that if Canadians don't supply the wood, it'll be some other country with less environmental protections.

When they touched down on a beach for lunch, Grayson acted all civil and pointed out the pilings from an old whaling station. He described the slipway they used to haul the whales out of the water. She could see the old boilers rusting in the sunshine.

"Almost ten thousand whales were carved up for oil, shoe polish, perfumes or transmission fluid. Blues, finbacks, humpbacks and sperms," Grayson said, almost gleefully.

"Christ, Grayson, just when I think you're human."

"You want sympathy, it's in the dictionary between shit and syphilis."

The pilot snorted. "A lot of weird stories came out of this territory. I heard they pulled a sea serpent with a horse's head out of a whale they were gutting once. Some Loch Ness type thing. Made the news back in Victoria."

"Cadborosaurus," said Grayson. "The fishermen had conniptions when they caught one of those babies in their nets. Like the thing might contaminate their fish. Best to do away with freaks right away. Like the Gogeet. You know they killed one of your wild men out here back in the day. The thing was nosing around, stealing stuff and then, *blam!*"

"What?" said Lily.

"You heard me."

Lily couldn't believe what he said or that he meant some of these things. Didn't want to believe it, so she just picked up her lunch bag and walked away.

"Hey, where you going?" Grayson said.

"As far as I can get away from you."

"You see dat Gogeet again?" Renée asked when Lily got back to their room after supper.

"I thought you called him Walker."

"Maybe dey are the same," she said.

Renée had reappeared and was talking to her again, but Lily was wary of saying the wrong thing and having her bounce out the door. So she started with the whaling station instead. Renée corroborated the story about a worker who'd shot a wild man back in the old days. Supplies had been stolen and a hairy figure had been snooping around the big-barrel boilers at the rendering plant.

"So some guy set a trap. He left a bucket of whale trimmings at the edge of de forest and when a shadow moved, the guy took a shot. The monster went down. Den the men at the plant waited until daylight to go to find him. His skin was blue, dey said, and his hair had grown over his forehead and into his face."

"He was a man?"

"Mais no. He was a Gogeet. They packed him off to Masset on the next boat and de local doctor got a look at him. His chest had spread and his fingernails had grown but de Masset Haida knew right away what he was. The doctor didn't know what to say. But during his examination, he found that one of the creature's teeth had a silver filling in it."

"Weird."

"De people thought back and remembered a travelling dentist who'd brought a big chair wit him. Dey thought it was some sort of torture chamber. The dentist convinced one or two Haidas to get work done. A while later one of dose men had been out hunting seals and den dey never see him again… Until then."

"So you're saying the Gogeet was the hunter."

"Yep."

"Is this true?"

"As true as any ting I tell you," said Renée.

"But where is it written?"

"Nowhere, so far as I know."

"Then how do you know someone didn't just invent it?" Lily said.

"Why would dey?"

"To fool people? There must be something. A doctor's report or a newspaper story."

"Peut être."

"But it needs to be written down. Or how will anyone really know?"

"Ah chérie. Stories come. If you are ready to hear dem, den dere dey are." Renée lit a cigarette and the sweet smoke curled into the room.

"Fine. What about Arlene?" Lily ventured. "What can you tell me about her? You said you needed to think. Did you have something more to say about the Alberta girl?"

"Would you look at dat. I've got to go." As if she'd been tugged off the stage with a cane, she picked up her stuff and left. Just like that. Renée had a secret and she wouldn't let it rise to the surface.

Lily lay on her bed, counting the holes in the ceiling tiles. When she got to 158, she knew it was time to get out of the logging camp. She thought of her mother and her father and whatever happened that led to her beginnings on these islands. Then she thought of the man wandering around in the forest.

She could picture the map showing the trail to the west coast she'd seen at the cabin and she knew exactly where to find a set of truck keys. Lily looked at her watch. She still couldn't believe how much light was in the sky at ten p.m. But better to wait. She would be ready when the sun started to rise again.

4

A Room in the Forest

32

The rings, peeps and chimes of the songbirds broke into Lily's dream. Swainson's thrush, yellow-throated warbler. She squinted at the sky between the branches, at the darker and lighter shades between the leaves. Larry and his birds. Townsend's warbler. Pine grosbeak. Cedar waxwing. Lily remembered their names, but she had no idea what they looked like. Except the Steller's jay. His constant screech outside the window left her with no chance of falling back to sleep. She looked at her watch: four a.m. Renée had come back late that evening, but she'd been drinking. You knew my mother, Lily had said. So who is my father? Renée babbled, but most of what she said came out in a drunken mess. Her nickname was May, to fit between April and June. Larry. Rick. Walker. Who loved who? Lily tried for clarity, but Renée just flopped onto the bed and started, almost immediately, to snore. In the end it didn't matter what Renée said, Lily already knew who she needed to ask.

She had packed her tent, her plant book and as many granola bars as she could find in the boxes littered around the room. Bags of tea and a couple of packs of instant noodles. The last of the beef jerky she'd bought in Jasper. Her glass ball from Blaize. She hoped to find Walker before she ran out of food. Wondering was getting her nowhere. Lily listened to the birds flitting around the tangled forest for a moment longer. Then she took a deep breath and walked out of the trailer.

She geared down as the truck tires crunched past the protest camp at the new branch road. If she'd been walking, she would have been on tiptoes. She'd taken the total beater. A truck that no one would miss, she hoped. Lily begged the vehicle not to sputter in low and conk out. A fire smouldered in the early morning mist and although tents poked out of the moss, the blockaders were nowhere to be seen. Would they leap out of the woods at any moment and force her back? To what? A job that her heart wasn't in anymore?

As she inched past the final clutch of tarps, Lily saw something move through the trees. A figure behind a veil of trunks? She pressed on the gas and the truck hiccupped. When she came to a Y in the road, she had to choose fast. Lily thought of the roads leading to the coast she'd seen from the air and picked the left fork. The truck fishtailed as she gunned it, and she steered into the skid, pulling herself out of the slide. She could see Chaz and Brian nodding. Impressive recovery. Larry would have shook his head. *Shouldn't have let the girlie drive.* When the tires gained purchase on the gravel, she charged forward with the same fury she felt for her mother. For her father. For Chaz.

She drove west for another thirty minutes. When the road ended abruptly, she could imagine its builders looking into the impenetrable glades of the dark forest and deciding they'd pushed far enough. She pictured the protesters getting out markers and ripping apart a cardboard box to make their signs. LEAVE THE REST ALONE, they'd write. Lily wished it were true. Or possible. Anything was possible. She turned off the ignition and got out.

A howl careened around her as she changed into her caulk boots. This was not the sound of a working forest. No loaders grabbing tree trunks and piling them onto trucks. No future lumber, decks or guitars. Just branches waving and thick clouds cruising across the sky. The sound deepened and Lily felt the wind picking up. She stuffed her hikers into her pack and shouldered the bag and took one last look in the truck.

She didn't have cardboard or a marker, but she wrote a note on the back of a napkin and left it on the dash in the truck: *Gone west.* Lily signed it, threw the keys on the seat and closed the door.

She hooked the hip chain onto her belt and flicked the switch to let the string run. Colour pulsed into her cheeks and she felt like a window had opened in a long-forgotten room. When she was little, she used to walk to calm her night fears. Arlene said she could pace the cobwebs right out of her bedroom. Lily thought of her mother sitting at the table in the back office, managing the furniture store's affairs. She and Ryan would be leaping from armrests to seat cushions in an attempt to circumnavigate the room. Keep moving. Even then, the words had run like a mantra through every thought. *You're just like her*, Brian always said.

Ha! Her mother hadn't been able to handle these islands and Lily was diving right in. There was no sign of an overgrown trail, but Lily set a compass bearing based on her memory of the hand-drawn map and her reckoning of where she'd seen the Walker on the beach. Then she stepped into the forest.

She tumbled down a slope, trying to dig her boots in—but skidded on a tree root instead. From the helicopter, it had looked like a straight, easy line to the sea, but after half an hour in the tangled undergrowth, the whole adventure began to seem like a really bad idea.

Her bandana slid off as she tripped through the criss-crossed branches of salal. A twig slapped her in the face. The forest had become a musty attic and her back was crusted with dry needles and debris. She couldn't even feel the wind anymore. Where were the wide open, deer-browsed spaces they'd been walking through at work? Chaz hated the deer. Said they mowed the cedar, the huckleberry bushes and even the devil's club.

Had it really been that easy for him to leave? She thought of how he'd pressed his nose into her hair and inhaled. She thought of how he said he'd come back, and his face at the window in her dream.

On she went as the soft twine unfurled from her belt. Her shin was stick-ripped with long red scratches and the back of her left thigh surged with a darkening bruise from a bad move that she could no longer remember. Another jagged branch nearly missed her eye. Maybe she should have worn her hard hat. She tapped the little container on her belt and looked back. Lily could barely see the line, but she could feel it following her through the trees.

By nightfall, she stood at the top of a steep cliff. She could smell the sea and hear the rush of it, but she couldn't see her way down, so she curled up in a mossy hollow. The wind had calmed and she was too tired to set up her tent. Too conscious of her meagre supplies to eat. She wondered if she was crazy. Would finding this man provide any relief? Or would that just make everything worse? *There's good bullshit and bad bullshit*, Larry would have chimed in.

Lily smelled smoke on the breeze and thought she could see the sparkle of a fire on the beach. She hoped that when she found him, he'd be happy for the company, if nothing else.

By noon the next day, Lily had reached the beach she'd seen from the helicopter, but she had not found him. She saw a small grey pile from his doused fire and she noticed the divots his feet made in the sand. He was on the move, but she could not tell how far ahead he might be.

When the wind picked up again, it slapped at her with gusts. She lost count of the changes along the twisting coastline. Every bend opened to a different beach. Some were covered in fine white sand, some peppered with jagged black rocks. On one beach she marched across crumbly layers of red shale, on another her feet sank into multi-hued pebbles. She had thought she was in love with the forest, but she wondered if Chaz was right. Maybe the in-between space was better. Maybe she'd finally find what she was looking for on the edge, sandwiched between the ocean and the trees.

33

On his third night at sea, Chaz heard the wind breaking through the grove of trees covering the low dip between east and west. Uncle had motored the boat around the corner and tucked into the cove, thinking they'd be safe. But the ocean always had surprises.

Chaz knew the smacking slap of the southeaster like he knew his own breath. He used to tuck himself under the steps in front of his grandparents' house to feel the blasts. He'd stick his face out and the gale would push back, tightening his eyes and pulling at the corners of his lips. He and Banger would try to see themselves like that in front of the floor-to-ceiling mirrors in Banger's fancy new place in Skidegate Heights. Two boys, their cheeks pressed back by the palms of their own hands, trying to see the tension take over their eyes. Chaz had no idea if it looked similar, but it didn't feel the same. Nothing tugged like the wind.

Southeasters he could handle, but winds from the west worried him. They're just different, Uncle would say. But Chaz saw them as erratic and strong, more like a cornered animal than pure air.

When the sun rose after Chaz had been awake most of the night listening, he could have been upside down for all the difference he could see between the grey of its reflection and the grey of the actual sky. He thought of the stories underneath the surface, of Lily and her lips smooth as a porcelain cup. The sweet scent of her neck. She'd thrown her head back when they'd been in his bed, and he'd marvelled at the whiteness she'd exposed.

She'd told him that day about some Y2K computer bug and how power was going to fail worldwide after midnight next New Year's Eve. Communications and transportation systems would go down. People were squirrelling away supplies and chopping firewood in preparation. She wanted to be ready. That's probably why she kept asking about edible plants and which leaf was used for which medicine, as if the woods of Haida Gwaii would be a good place to ride out the chaotic storm.

He'd tried to tell her that the ocean was where it was at, if she wanted to survive. Catching fish. That's how his people fed themselves for generations. Cripes. Chaz would never head into the woods to stay alive.

He untangled the blanket that had wrapped itself around his torso and pulled himself up from the corner of the deck. Yep, the boat was swinging on the anchor, but as the sky brightened he could tell that they'd hardly moved.

Uncle came out of the lower cabin, rubbing his eyes.

"Where's the coffee?"

"In the cupboard."

"You little shit. You haven't made any yet? What am I paying you for?"

"You haven't paid me a dime and I've been on watch, dude. Making sure your precious boat didn't drag itself into the rocks."

"This spot was bomber. Mud bottom. You think I've never set an anchor before?"

"Not in a southwester."

"Shit. I've been out here in everything. Now make some coffee."

"Fine," Chaz said. He couldn't argue with his uncle. There was no point.

Later that afternoon, Chaz could hear a motor coming from a long way off. Uncle was down in his bunk again. At least they'd gotten the lines out and had done several passes that morning. They'd even put a decent load of salmon in the hold. Uncle had been on his game, unhooking the fish and pulling the lures and weights off the line, while Chaz stood in the bouncing back of the boat, gutting the salmon. Head and tail on, empty bellies, the way the packers liked them.

They'd anchored and Chaz had battered and fried a feed of herring for lunch. After that, Uncle disappeared. Chaz emptied the rest of his bottle of vodka into the ocean. Banger would say it's because of residential schools. That's why so many of Uncle's generation drink. Chaz's mom had been taken away to school too. Not for as long, Gran had said, but there hadn't been a high school on the islands then, so there hadn't been much of a choice. Not that he'd asked her. He'd only heard Uncle yelling—looking for someone to blame.

The motor's whine kept coming and he could now see a boat bouncing across the chop, heading into the bay. Tourists, probably. Chaz poked his head down into Uncle's bunk and heard him snoring. He could try to do another run on his own, but maybe a leg stretch was a better idea. Chaz pulled the skiff up and hopped in. He untied, yanked the outboard to life, then aimed for shore.

Chaz looked out at the horizon line, then south toward all the inlets shaping the coast. He thought about just motoring away. There were cabins out in some of these coves left over from when people used to fish regularly on the west coast. Chaz wondered if he could just set up shop in one. Become a hermit. Hadn't he heard of men going wild like that? Not Gogeets, but by choice, when they wanted to be completely alone.

He bumped the boat into the beach and jumped above the pulse of an incoming wave. The carrot-nosed oystercatchers whistled as he pulled the bow rope into the trees. He did a couple of jumping jacks and tried to think of the other calisthenics the basketball team did to train. Lunges. The beach was a bit jagged for burpees. He was out of shape. He tried some deep knee bends and heard voices. Chattering laughter sprayed across the breeze. His uncle had told him he'd heard the sounds of children at an old village site. But these sounds came from the Zodiac aiming straight for him. The boat pushed onto the sand and Banger hopped out.

"What the hell?" Chaz said.

"Hitched a ride." Banger nodded at the Goretex-wearing driver, as the guy popped the motor into reverse. There were five other people aboard, kitted out in thick green raingear.

Chaz watched the tourists buzz away before turning to his friend. They'd barely spoken since he'd bloodied Banger's nose. For what? A fight over a girl? Chaz had won and then they'd gone for breakfast. Watched mixed martial arts on TV. Played basketball. Left everything unsaid.

"I decided that I couldn't desert you with your uncle." Banger threw a false punch at Chaz, who didn't flinch. "How's it been?"

"It's been crazy."

"I bet. Your uncle's crazy." Banger set his duffel bag down, picked up a big rock and handed it to Chaz.

"Yep." The dark grey rock was smooth, with a few sharp edges, just like his friend.

"In a good way," Banger said. He found a similar rock for himself and started doing weighted squats.

"You think?" Chaz followed suit, but instead of rising and falling like Banger, he let his hips deepen into the stretch.

"Chuck's a superhero, man. He's raging against the machine." Banger quit the squats and lifted the rock above his head a few times.

"What the hell are you talking about?" Chaz stayed low, barely tolerating the strain on his knees and watching his buddy, wondering what chaos he'd get up to next.

"The man is gonna tear things down." Banger tossed his rock to the ground, then went for a whip-like piece of bull kelp. The bulb on the end still streamed with thick, hair-like blades. The type of kelp Lily held onto when they'd been out on the rowboat. The type of kelp he'd seen his mother in. Chaz knew better than to be near Banger when he grabbed a weapon.

"Tear what down?" Chaz let go of his rock and got ready to spring out of Banger's way.

"The system. The bullshit white man telling us what to do all the time."

Banger lifted his arm to snap the rope of kelp and Chaz made the last minute decision to grab the end before it could rise. They both laughed as the game turned into a tug-o-war.

"He's not gonna get far passed out in the hold," Chaz said.

"He has his demons," said Banger, dropping the kelp.

"What if I just want to get out of this place? A fresh start. Find a place where no one knows me," said Chaz.

"What the hell for? We need you, brother. On the islands. Besides, who would I play basketball with?"

"It's all a little too much sometimes."

"Leaving is not going to make that go away," Banger said.

Banger went back to his calisthenics, first lunges, then jumping jacks. He boxed at the air. Then boxed Chaz's shoulder and laughed. "Looks like you could do with some training. Getting flabby."

34

Larry lay on the operating table as the anaesthetist lowered the mask. "When I start, we'll count backward from ten," she said. The surgeon looked at Larry's injury and asked when the accident had taken place.

"I might have left it too long," Larry said.

Larry's hand was clamped onto a stand and his body strapped in. He felt as if he was about to be tortured and he probably deserved it. If they asked for a confession, he would give one.

The anaesthetist's palm cupped his forehead. "Ten." Larry wished he could take it all back. He'd known, even then, that she wasn't really interested. But she'd worked in the logging camp kitchen and each meal she'd made was the best he'd ever tasted. Wild mushrooms and fresh fish. Hot fried bannock sifted with cinnamon sugar.

She'd gone back to the cabin with him to smoke a joint after their afternoon on the boat. There'd been friendly chatter and he'd made a move, and then she'd gotten up and left. Tossed his advance out the back window of whatever high-speed car she'd been racing through life. He should have kept moving too, but instead he'd hoped to change her mind. That whatever he'd felt could be salvageable, like old tire treads with enough depth to squeeze another season in.

The anaesthetist had gotten to six. "Are you counting?"

He nodded.

June hadn't been avoiding him. That's what she said afterward. But she didn't stay long in any room he was in. The next time he'd been around her was that day in the bush and that night at the bar when he'd taken a swing at Rick. The brawl had started after that. June had left with someone else and he couldn't think about the rest. What he'd done. Everything changed then. Even she had changed. That was the worst of it. He'd watched her fading into a shadow.

When he finally told her that he knew where the loner from Port Clements had gone, he was heartened to see how she'd perked up.

He could still see the sharp gulp she'd taken. As if she had stopped breathing and then finally inhaled.

He's in Vancouver, Larry said. But he didn't really know. He only knew the guy had gone home—wherever that was.

"Four, three, two," said the anaesthetist. Larry nodded. He thought he could rescue her. If he sent her away, then he could swoop in after a few days and bring her back home. He'd planned to let her search around for a bit, get disheartened. Bloody stupid, whatever that thought was. Because by the time he went to the city to look for her, she was already gone.

35

Walker had been moving so long that he wondered which parts of his life had been real and which were just a dream. He felt as if he'd been stuck in a different dimension. A murky distortion between beach and forest. Twisted branches and waxy leaves. A screen of salal.

He could understand his journey back to the islands, but he couldn't quite put the rest of it together. Like why he'd left.

He thought of her singing in the car as they drove to her home after the bar that long ago night. They'd worked in the forest together that day and she sang as they'd walked through the trees. Again after they made love. He'd heard it ringing through his head ever since. A puzzle of rhythm and heat. A Haida song, she'd said.

He thought of how dark it had been on the deck of the ferry the night he came back. The vessel had been moving like a black slug through calm water and the trip was taking too long. A week's worth of hitchhiking to get back to Prince Rupert and three days to wait for the ferry. He'd slept in ditches and done dishes for meals at truck stops. He'd promised himself he would not stop until he got to the islands. It had been five years, but he could not wait to see her again.

He paced the deck, like he'd done the night he left. Circling, circling. Past the inflatable rescue rafts, the empty bench seating and the low lockers filled with life jackets. Past the wafts of burning oil, the rumble of engines and the salt-puke ocean smell.

Over the loudspeaker, the purser warned passengers about the coming storm. Walker was used to rough nights. He'd been facing them since he'd left. Stupid man. Why had he gone back to his parents' place? They'd never forgiven him anyway.

At some point, he must have curled into a corner. He dreamed of her hair spread across the pillow, black as a raven's wing. The sour of her drink-studded breath. The bar, the fight and their escape. The improbability that he'd ended up in her bed.

When he awoke, he could just make out Skidegate's lights in the distance. He was almost there. Between gusts, two women with hoods cinched tight had pressed up against the rail. They lit cigarettes and cracked open beers and their cackling voices crested and fell as he let the noise wash over him. One had been in Vancouver. The other had been back in Quebec, where her mother had died. She'd been glad her mother was finally gone, and he wished that his was too.

Between snippets of their conversation, his mind travelled back to the brawl, when chairs were broken and he'd hidden under the table with two women. He wondered if the town would still be the same. Would his shack be the way he'd left it?

The women cracked opened two more beers and he curled his knees to his chest. As the French woman laughed and clicked her can to the other's, he knew.

"May?"

The woman turned. She had the dangly gold earrings he remembered. Under her hood, she wore a scarf. She narrowed her eyes. He was tucked up on the bulkhead and they hadn't known he was there.

"Mister?"

"I know you. From the bar."

"Asti tabarnac," said Renée. "I remember you too."

36

After a night on the beach, Lily ate another of her precious granola bars and found water spilling down a cliff. Most of the wide-mouthed creeks cutting through the sand were brown and mixed with salt. The first water she'd tried had made her retch. Chaz had told her that drinking water must be collected from above the high-tide mark, but when she walked back toward the forest, driftwood and debris blocked the streams.

She missed Chaz. She even missed Larry. Her bed in the ATCO trailer camp. What had compelled her on to this quest? A brief sighting of a mysterious man. A few footprints along stretches of beach. Every minute she moved forward, the idea of turning back consumed her. She pictured the truck parked at the end of that road. She imagined pulling herself up the cliffs, clutching at roots, slipping in mud. But would she ever find the spot where she'd spilled out of the forest onto the beach? She'd tied a small piece of flagging tape to a branch, so she could find her string line again, but it could have blown off. Or what if the truck was gone? Surely Rick would have retrieved it. He would have looked at the note and thought good riddance.

Lily would have nothing more than she had now. No answers. No clarity. No peace. So she kept going. She saw a deer eating seaweed on the shore and shook her head. They ate everything. If things got bad enough, she might try some too. Deer were survivors. The few huckleberry bushes she'd found among the Sitka spruce were browsed into tall zombie stalks, but even the unripe berries went into her mouth.

She heard a rolling echo of rocks being lifted and dropped—squinting, she saw a man-shaped movement. Her heart stopped. When she actually found him, what would she say? Are you my father? What did you know about me? Who left first?

But it wasn't him. It was a big black bear trolling the shore, lifting and scooping at rocks. She imagined the small purple crabs trying to hide from its thick, wide paw. Lily stayed far back in fear, but she also envied this bear. His paw at his mouth, his primeval chewing. She knew she would need to find something more to eat soon.

Another headland, another half-moon beach filled with sand, another body. This one round with spindly legs. A smaller, stranger deer? It looked sick, somehow all wrong, and she wondered if she could find a way to kill it with her bare hands, like Blaize said. But the creature jolted at the sound of her step and its long neck came up from the grass it had been probing. The crimson top of its head, its beak, its now-obvious feathers on an ostrich-like body. Not a deer, but a sandhill crane. It hopped forward with one wing hanging, and made a gargling noise. As she moved, another noise emerged. A different crane rushed out of the grass and started another limping show. The two adult birds danced and rattled and she realized they were trying to send her back the way she'd come. Larry said they mate for life. They protect their children by faking injuries to distract the predator. She finally saw the small one, its dark silhouette bobbing out among the tide pools.

Lily hurried past the family. When she looked back, the baby was still there, but the couple had gone. They'd stopped their dance and lifted into the air, flying away from her and the nest.

"Please come back for your child," Lily called to them, but she could do nothing about it, so she continued on.

Chaz woke the next morning and everything had changed again. According to Uncle, the salmon buyers had screwed them, so they were getting some urchin instead. If they could bring a good haul back to the village Uncle could trade to pay off some of his debts. So Chaz cleaned out one of the giant fish boxes as Uncle and Banger called directions to him. To the left. You missed that spot of slime. The water had to be perfectly pure to keep the sea urchins at top quality. Guuding.ngaay, Gran called them. Uni to the Japanese. Chaz had never seen so many before. The area had once been a kelp bed, one of his chinaay's favourite spots, but the urchins had taken over.

"They munch through like an army," Uncle said, as if convincing himself of this change in plan. "Wiping out everything in their way."

"Good for us though," said Banger.

Next, Chaz took stock of the gear. Regulator functioning. Check. Oxygen tank full. Check. Weights. Wetsuit. Gloves. Net bag. He felt relieved that he got to be the one to dive. Where it's quiet. Where he could be alone.

He put everything on and the regulator in his mouth, jumped off the side and let his body sink. He checked his knife and his air again, then he looked up and saw the hull. They were drifting in the current between the islands, and Banger held the rope that was tied around his waist like an umbilical cord. Uncle had the troller in low reverse and Chaz had his net bag ready. The red spiny creatures were everywhere.

The fact that you could get money for these things amazed him. Maybe that's what he'd do in the city. Distribute the catch from the islands to fancy restaurants. How much would they pay for an urchin? Maybe he'd open his own restaurant. Urchins right out of the sea. Crabs, sea cucumbers and lots of fish. Uncle would insist on rice too. Not potatoes, unless they were in soup. And soy sauce. None of the Japanese stuff. China Lily. That was the Haida way.

Chaz exhaled and watched the bubbles float upward. He descended toward the moonscape at the edge of the rocks and started reaching for the spiky creatures. His breath echoed in his head. The last time he'd collected urchins had been when he fell in and saw his mother in the darkness. But there was no kelp to hide in here and the white sand gave the water a soft, blue glow. He filled his bag, then heard something. He looked up, but the boat still hung above him like a cloud.

He turned back to the urchins, and out of the corner of his eye noticed a different movement. A giant octopus. A naaw. His nanaay would always remind him to use its Haida name. The naaw was camouflaged the same colour as the rocks as it leapt toward him. Chaz backed away. Respectful. Fearful. He worked to keep his breath even. Checked his regulator. Checked his tank. Checked the naaw.

The octopus moved again. He remembered an early tide with Nanaay a few years ago. She'd whispered a thank you to Low Tide Woman and wriggled a stick under the rock. After waiting and waiting, a tentacle finally reached into the dim light of their headlamp. Chaz had grabbed it and pulled. Two more red tentacles emerged and wrapped themselves around his arm. It pulled with such strength that Chaz had felt as if he might be sucked into the creature's lair.

Chaz took in some air and saw that his urchin sack was full. He looked back at the octopus, but it had become a rock again. He tugged at the line. On the beach, he'd had to fight the octopus. His nanaay clutched at him, her small hands pulling each sucker off; each release like a tongue popping out of a cheek. When they'd finally gotten the upper hand and pulled the gangly creature from its cave, it stared with disdain out of its cat-like eyes. Nanaay whispered more thanks, then grabbed a rock and smashed its sac-like head. Chaz had turned the naaw inside out to gut it, just like she'd shown him, then he'd dropped it in the bucket. Chaz hadn't liked watching it die.

The bubbles streamed out of his regulator as he rose up to the boat. Chaz looked back at the octopus, shimmering in some kind of half-life between rock and mythical beast. He thought about his mother's black hair swirling around his wrists in the water near the logging camp. The deep quiet he'd felt. How he'd almost stayed down. He took another breath and his exhale drifted out of the regulator like a sparkle of light. When he broke surface, Banger was hanging over the edge.

"Grayson was just on the horn from camp. Lily took off a couple of days ago. They found the truck she used and some kind of note."

Chaz's face streamed sea water and he pulled the regulator from his lips. "What?"

"Your girlfriend, dude. Grayson says she's out chasing some wild man in the woods."

Banger hooked the bag out of Chaz's outstretched arm and pulled it up. Chaz manoeuvred around to the ladder at the back and climbed up onto the deck. He shivered, as if he was cold, although the sun beamed down.

"What does she think this is? A movie?"

"What are you talking about, bro?"

"You can't just wander off and survive." People don't come back, Chaz thought. He could prove it. His mother hadn't. Neither had that man who'd come to Nanaay's door.

"We're going to find her," Banger said.

"How are we going to do that? She could be anywhere," said Chaz.

Uncle came out of the wheelhouse. "What are you two ladies whining about and why are those urchins still scratching around on the floor of my boat?"

"Chaz's girlfriend," said Banger. "She's lost in the woods and he wants to go find her."

"Does he now?"

"She's up coast. They say she's gone to look for the Gogeet. We should go," said Banger.

"What are we going to do with all these guuding.ngaay?" said Uncle.

But Banger was already releasing the urchins, and Uncle turned to haul in the skiff. Chaz watched the spiny creatures fall like stars toward the moon's surface. He looked for the octopus and remembered the force of that other one pulling at his arm. How his gran had jerked and wrenched him free. How she'd smashed the flesh with a mallet and rolled it into nuggets to fry for dinner. Chaz remembered Lily trying to hide her gagging as she tried his nanaay's soup. He wondered if she'd like naaw.

"She's not my girlfriend," he whispered, but it didn't matter, he couldn't leave her out there all alone.

37

Larry climbed onto the bus in Terrace and chose an aisle seat. He put his coat and newspaper down so no one could take the window, then leaned back and focused on his throbbing fingers. The nurse told him to keep his hand raised, when she discharged him. He'd stood on the hospital steps and wondered what to do. Cripes, they medevac you off the island, then just send you off with a wave. Lucky he'd found $100 in his wallet. Even luckier if Chaz left one of the trucks at the ferry terminal for him like he said he'd do. The bus station was nearby, thank Christ. He pushed his seat into recline and tried to relax as the aisle filled with grimy tree planters, a granny with her knitting needles, a solid man with a Western Forest Products baseball cap.

The engine rumbled to life and the air brakes sighed. He closed his eyes and felt calm. Calmer than he had in days. His fingers might actually heal, the doctor said. They might move again. Maybe things would work out and he could go back to work as if nothing happened.

As the bus lurched forward, Larry could feel sleep taking him, but then a banging and a woman's voice brought everything to a stop.

The driver swore as he opened the door. "You two could have been killed, running out in front of me like that."

"We need to get to Prince Rupert and then to the islands." Larry cracked one eye open and saw the woman, vaguely familiar, with a toque pulled over her forehead and curls spilling out below the wool. She and a teenage boy, blonder and taller than her, elbowed their way down the aisle, then stopped at the row behind his and plunked down.

In an instant, the whole vibe of the trip changed. Cripes, Larry knew that he talked a lot—annoyed the hell out of some people, Rick included—but this woman was something else. Why were so many logs piled there? That's a mill? What kind of mill? Where does the lumber go? Have you ever seen so many eagles? And the crows.

"Those are ravens," the Western Forest Products man across the aisle finally said.

"Same difference, no?" she said.

Larry stopped himself from turning around. In another life, he would have been drawn to her questions. He would have told her that ravens were bigger with thicker throats. He would have cited the difference in their calls. But he stayed quiet.

When they got past the straight stretch, the road followed the river and she started up again, talking to her boy this time. See the blue of it? So wide it looks like the ocean. See the ice in the mountains? The sun glinting off the waterfall?

"What's the name of the river again?" Larry could feel the movement behind him, knew that she had reached across the aisle to touch the logger's elbow.

"Skeena," he said, short and cropped.

"It runs all the way to Rupert, right?"

"Yeah."

Larry could picture him shaking his head.

"We're going to see my daughter. On the Charlottes." She paused and Larry waited for the man to grunt or acknowledge her. But he didn't and she continued on. "Her name is Lily. She's working in the woods."

Larry's eyes jerked open and, again, he forced himself to not turn around. No wonder she'd looked so familiar. Larry turned his head to look at the river and noticed how high the water was. He saw a log moving back in the direction of Terrace as the bus continued toward the ocean. The tide must have turned. Things weren't going the way he'd thought. Maybe some of his secrets would rise to the surface after all.

38

The drops started falling like dimes, so Lily stopped before the headland and pulled on her raincoat. As she assessed the jagged cliff between her and the next beach, a stench filled her nose. The water pushed at the divots between boulders just off shore. Gravel rolled and logs churned.

His footprints had led to this jagged outcrop. Wind grasped at her hood as she peered around the cliff to a line of white sand. A splash hit the bottom of her boots and soaked her laces. If she squinted, she could see his steps marching up and out of the trough below. But how did he get from this knife edge to the land? The rocks barely formed a ramp. His path must have been eaten by the tide. She should turn back. She did not belong here. But she had come so far.

Up on the wet sand above the gravel, she watched three ravens rise off a mass piled on the beach. A soup of seaweed and salt water rattled back through the pebbles. She recognized the shape as a dead thing. Not big enough for whale. A walrus? What did she know?

Another wave darted up to her rock and then another. She could see more waves building in the dark shadow of the sea. The rocky white knob she clutched at popped off as she scrambled to regain purchase. When she touched another, a tiny tip popped out of the shell. She held her breath and could hear a small clicking inside. The knobs were alive.

Lily shifted her feet and crushed the tiny hats. She felt her barbs scrape the slick rock—the worst possible surface for caulk boots. She took a sharp breath and inched out farther along the ledge. A wider chunk of rock at a lower level beckoned. If she could just step across space. The wind hit her like a slap in the face. She closed her eyes and leapt.

The next thing Lily felt was a burning sensation along the tips of her right hand. She remembered the scraping and heard the splash.

Someone yelling. Lily felt tumbled and raw, as if she'd rolled down the hill at the schoolyard in Frontier. Ryan and her giggling, with no toboggan, only the gravity of some thrift store fabric on snow, ice crystals pouring in.

She felt so cold.

The yelling again and Lily was not in Frontier. She could see a woman on the death mound on the beach, holding up a baby-shaped bundle. What was she tossing into the rotting pile? Then Jeremy walked over, put his arms around the woman and led her away. Lily was so happy to see him. She tried to yell, but nothing came. Then she was in a forest again, by a sunlit pond, and Arlene was gone. Someone breathed beside her. She turned to comfort her brother, to tell him everything would be alright, but it was Larry, holding his bleeding hand.

Lily opened her eyes and groaned. She felt sore all over. In the dim light coming through a clouded sheet of Plexiglas, she could see the tiny space around her. A small wood stove crackled with fire. Silvery cedar-plank walls. She rose and her forehead clocked a small shelf. A glass ball rolled off and landed in her lap. It was bigger than the one Blaize gave her.

How did she get into this room in the forest? Her sleeping bag had been pulled from its stuff sac and covered her. Her backpack, t-shirt, jeans and jacket dried by the wood stove. Somehow she was in her underpants with a scrape up the side of her right arm. She remembered the cliff and the tide. Had she rolled into the sea?

Lily crawled over to feel her pants pockets for her fishing float. But it was gone. She checked the floor of the cabin and then opened the small wooden door to look outside. She could see the sweep of the bay and to her left, the headland that she'd tried to manoeuvre. The black rotten mound, just a bump above the incoming tide. To her right, the sand continued toward another high cliff. The small A-frame, covered with thick cedar slabs, stood tucked under the boughs of a giant Sitka spruce. She pulled her head back inside like one of the sea creatures she'd ripped her fingertips on. He must be nearby. He must have gotten her out of her wet things. She'd been trying so hard to find him and he'd found her. Her chest surged with alarm. She slammed the door shut and locked it from the inside.

The noise that woke her was as soft as breath. She wasn't sure if she'd been asleep for an hour or a minute, but when her eyes opened, the room was pitch black. The air curled around her like an overturning wave. Was someone inside the room? She fumbled for her headlamp and the bright beam swung from wall to wall. Nothing. She aimed the light at the door, but instead of the silver grey of the aging cedar, she only saw black. The door—hadn't she latched it from the inside? Somehow it was open and pushed out toward the sky.

39

The *Haida Slayer*'s engine chugged in the wind. Uncle said they'd have to run overnight to get up the west coast where Lily might be. Banger had been on the horn with his dad and found out the full story. Mac told him about the protest camp at the blockade and that a Totem Timber truck had been abandoned at the height of land on the new road. Grayson and Lily had seen a man on the beach a couple of days before and Renée was telling everyone that Lily had gone to look for the Gogeet.

"If that's where she started, she might be at the bluffs by now." Uncle looked at the charts and cross-referenced with a topographic map. His finger traced a line from the hills to the beach, and then up the coast.

"How do you know so much about where the new logging roads are?" asked Chaz.

"Haida Gwaii is my business, kid."

Banger held the wheel and stared straight into the mist. "How about a coffee?"

Chaz was happy to keep his hands busy while he thought all this through. Why would Lily take off? He hoped it didn't have anything to do with him. He pulled the Edwards out of the cupboard, filled the pot with water, measured six scoops and set it on the stove. The flame hit metal and sizzled. He loved how quickly a gas stove brought water to a boil. Something a person could count on. He watched for the first sign of bubbles and then he snapped off the heat, just like Chinaay always said. He finished the coffee in the old man's way, stirring once and splashing a bit of cold water to let the grounds fall.

Chaz opened the cooler and looked at the tin of evaporated milk. A yellow crust coated the rim, closing over the puncture hole like a scab. He would have preferred getting a new can, but he could feel the last drops sloshing at the bottom. No waste. Uncle had cuffed him upside the head over less.

"Why the hell is Lily chasing this guy up the west coast?" Chaz finally said once the coffee prep was complete.

"I think I know, but there's a couple of things I should tell you first," said Uncle.

The mugs hung on pegs, their mouths facing out to the sea. Chaz took down Uncle's favourite and two others and split the milk between them. Banger and Uncle liked two scoops of sugar. Chaz preferred his coffee bitter.

"Things like what?" said Chaz.

"Like your mom was in love with someone before she got together with Rick."

The coffee grounds hadn't sunk yet. They tumbled across his tongue as Chaz took his first sip and he stood over the sink to spit them out. "What would you know?" Chaz demanded.

"I know you fucked up the coffee. You've got to let it sit. Patience, nephew. Anyway, your mother told me, okay?"

Chaz's stomach lurched as the boat rolled over a wave. "So what are you trying to say?"

"He was some loner from Port who'd taken off. Good riddance I'd thought when she first told me about it. One white guy's as bad as another. But she wouldn't let it go. She wanted to find him."

"So what happened?"

"I don't know. She started asking around and no one knew where he went."

Chaz stared at his coffee mug as the boat dropped into the waves with more force.

"Hang on," yelled Banger. Chaz lunged sideways as a wave crashed over the deck. Uncle grabbed the mugs before they spilled and then held them high, dancing with the contents. He dropped them into the sink as another wave hit.

"Jesus. While you two crap on about loves lost, we've all of a sudden got some serious weather to contend with," said Banger.

"Turn into the waves—forty-five degrees," Uncle yelled. "Doesn't anyone around here know how to ride out a storm?"

The boat pitched down the slope of a wave and rumbled toward another building crest. Uncle pushed out onto the deck to batten down the gear. Chaz couldn't focus. Why was his uncle telling him about some loner guy? Why was Lily looking for the Gogeet? He's just a man, she'd said. He thought about their conversation in the truck.

How she didn't know who her dad was. Fletcher had yelled at Larry about some loner. Oh god. Chaz wasn't sure he wanted to know more. He felt everything churning and looked out the window and realized the boat was turning the wrong way. Banger was changing course and heading toward the shore.

"What are you doing? We need to go north," Chaz yelled.

"We do not want to be out on this water. If we don't take cover now, we'll go around that point and there'll be nothing between us and Japan," Banger said.

Chaz looked at the chart and at the narrow neck between rock walls that led into a nearby cove. Once inside they might be okay, but a lot depended on whether the seas would let them through. Then, in the face of a full northwester, it could take days before they'd get out past the breakers again.

The cabin door pushed open and Uncle grabbed at the wheel.

"Who gave you the order to switch course?"

"This is nuts," Banger said. Uncle pushed him out of the way and he fell back against the cabin door, clutching his stomach. "I'm not going to die for the sake of some hermit and a white girl."

"Nobody's going to die on my watch," said Uncle. The boat plunged through a trough and shuddered as Uncle tried to force it around. The wind had them and Chaz saw that between the current and the bounce back from the headland they were in trouble. Banger had waited too long to change direction and the *Haida Slayer* was heading straight for a wall of rock.

"You thought you were going in there?" shouted Uncle. He cranked the steering south, back in the direction they'd come, to flow with the wind. "We've got to let her spin us around."

The boat groaned on the axis and Uncle backed off on the engine as the following sea walloped them from behind. The coffee pot fell and a hot mess sprayed all over the floor. Banger heaved forward and pushed open the door, then his guts flung onto the deck.

"Go out and hang onto him," Uncle said.

Chaz grabbed the back of Banger's jeans with one hand and the freezer box with the other while his friend lost it again and again. Chaz watched as the stern lifted into the air and he felt Uncle cut the speed even more to let the breaker roll under them.

Slowly, with each wave, Uncle got the boat around. Chaz braced himself between the side of the boat and the freezer box until they were well away from shore and the seas turned relatively calm again.

"We were too close to the rocks in that wind, buddy," Chaz said as Banger collapsed onto the deck. Chaz had never known his friend to be so wrong. Banger wiped his mouth with the back of his hand and shook his head. Chaz pulled an old floater coat off the hook. "Put this on. I'll check on you in a bit."

Inside the cabin, Uncle was blasting AC/DC through the boat speakers.

"Banger okay?" he said.

"He's good."

"He just about killed us."

"Yah, but you knew exactly what to do. Nice work, Uncle."

"Deep water. Heading into the wind. It's the safest place to be in that kind of situation. Lesson learned for Banger, I hope."

"Okay, then back to Mom. What were you saying about some guy?"

"I didn't know what to do about it back then. The guy just disappeared. I think she wanted me to help. But I wasn't much good to anyone in those days. I asked people, sure. But no one seemed to know. Besides, Rick was sniffing around and next thing I knew she was with him. I thought that was the end of it. Then Rick, the prick, left too—and she told us she was pregnant."

They were past the headland and Chaz could see a flowerpot-shaped island in the distance. Bulbous and round at the bottom; gnarled trees busting out of the flat top. He pictured a marigold growing out of the middle, like the one on Nanaay's deck. He thought of the glass balls he used to find and tried to imagine how many might be hiding in a place like that.

"Is that why she left?" said Chaz.

"She tried, Chaz. She really did. But she wasn't doing so great. Your mother had demons. Eventually, Rick sent some money. And the next thing we knew she was gone."

40

Ryan and Arlene walked off the ferry into the light of a new day, still a bit shaken from the storm that had bashed at the boat overnight. When they got to the corner of the ferry parking lot, Ryan looked at his mother and thought, not for the first time, that she didn't seem particularly well-equipped for life.

"So what's the plan?" he said. They had no vehicle. No knowledge of where Lily might be. Arlene had arrived back from Costa Rica and after one conversation with Brian, which hadn't gone well, decided to hit the road. She heard where Lily had gone and that was it. Ryan couldn't remember whether he'd been dragged along or if he'd agreed to go. It didn't really matter. She always seemed to get what she wanted.

They'd snagged a ride with someone who'd been heading to Prince George. Then they'd stayed in some crappy motel and waited a day for the bus. Then almost missed the connection in Terrace, and now what?

He was about to say more. Something whiny. Or nagging. Something that he would never have said to his dad, or Lily, but his mom always had a way of making him feel like a little boy.

"Need a ride?" A man in a white truck pulled up beside them. Ryan peered in and thought he recognized him from the boat. He might have even been on the bus from Terrace. Yes, he could see the man's bandaged hand on the steering wheel and remembered him in the seat in front of them. Cars were piling up behind them on the road. He looked at his mother, and she smirked, poked him with her elbow.

"See. You worry too much. Just like your sister and your father."

"I know, I know. The universe provides." Ryan looked at the man leaning across from the driver's seat and wondered what else there was about him. Something he couldn't quite put a finger on.

"We're looking for my sister. She works for Totem Timber," Ryan said.

"Well, that's where I'm going. Get in," the man said.

Ryan turned to his mother again, weirded out by the coincidence. But Arlene wasn't even looking at him. Her eyes were wandering around the place, taking in the blue water beyond the big white ferry. The lush green of the brush along the road. They had just gotten to the islands and she had already disappeared.

"Mom! Should we go with him?" Ryan asked.

"Why not?" she said.

Lily thought the universe was Arlene's biggest excuse for failing them. The times she forgot to pick them up from school, but someone else's parents had offered a ride, or when she wouldn't bother to buy groceries, but a friend would call to see if they wanted the extra trout that her husband had brought home from the river. Arlene had horseshoes up her ass. Why fight it?

Ryan looked at the guy with his bandaged hand. He seemed harmless. So he threw his pack into the back and squeezed onto the hump, then Arlene climbed in and pulled the truck door closed.

"Your hand looks pretty bad. You okay to drive?" Ryan immediately felt like a worrywart again.

"Yep. I still got one good one," Larry said.

"What did you do to it?" Ryan tried not to picture a zombie apocalypse as he watched the man's wrapped hand slip off the wheel. Too many video games. Too high a score on the driving exam.

"Long story. Might have been the worst mistake I've ever made. Or maybe the second, the first one could still turn out okay. So Lily's your sister?"

The truck rolled onto the road and Ryan figured he'd let his mother chime in. But her shoulders had stiffened and she seemed to be shrinking into the back of the seat. She pressed her sunglasses up against her face and Ryan watched her fingers crawl toward the door handle, as if she might be getting ready to fling it open and jump. He'd never seen her with so little to say.

"I never mentioned her name," Ryan said finally. How smart had it been to get into a stranger's car?

"Only one girl out there," said Larry, "unless you count the kitchen witch."

Arlene's head turned a bit at that comment and Ryan wanted to ask who the witch was, but Larry just kept nattering on about places they were passing, the weather. The rough ride on the ferry in the storm. He pointed at a totem pole, a village. Never stops talking, Ryan thought. He is nothing like Lily.

"Where you people from?" Larry finally paused long enough for someone else to get a word in, but Ryan kept it simple. "Frontier."

"That a town or the edge of the known universe?" Larry laughed at his own pathetic joke. Like they'd never heard that one before. That where John Wayne came from? Or Wyatt Earp? Arlene usually had some saucy retort. Ryan thought she might have fallen asleep, but then they rounded a corner and he saw a huge boulder floating above the the rocky beach.

"Balance Rock," she whispered.

"So you have been here before?" Larry said, as if confirming. Confirming what, Ryan did not know. Larry didn't wait for her to answer. "Quite the story about that rock. Miners tried to dynamite it. Some guy with his D6 Cat tried to knock it over, but it still stands. Some kind of equilibrium. Like two sides to a story, I guess."

The ravens rose from the ground at the back of the cookhouse as Larry rounded the corner into camp. Larry thought of the scraps Cookie would leave out for them and how that infuriated Rick. Rick would just as happily shoot the vermin as have them hanging around. He slowed the vehicle as they passed the stench of the garbage cans. The ravens had more than scraps. They'd pulled the meat-stained cardboard boxes out, but something had torn through the camp's detritus first. A bear maybe? Everything's gone to pot.

Larry stopped the truck and nodded to Lily's brother. "Breakfast time. She'll be in there." He didn't look at the mother. Didn't want to recognize her. Didn't want to hear her name. *Not unless they breed in Kleenex.* Isn't that what he always said?

The boy's mother opened the truck's door and they were getting their things out of the back when Larry saw Lily's car go by. That damn little Colt that he'd made her leave at the ferry terminal. Somehow she'd left it up in the woods by Yakoun Lake. He never did get that story straight. When the hell had they found time to go and get that? He would have to give Chaz a talking to. They had layout targets to reach.

Larry was about to point out the car to his passengers when it slid to a stop and the barefoot hippie got out. The one he'd seen at the dance back in Skidegate. What the hell was he doing in Lily's car? And before he could wrap his mind around that, Rick strode out of the mess hall and whacked the hood of the truck with his fist.

"Whoa, boss." Larry shut the engine off. "What the hell?"

"What are you doing back here?"

"I work here?" Rick looked like more of a prick than ever. What had Larry done to piss him off this time?

"Or do you work for them?"

"Who?"

"The blockaders!"

"Blockade?" said Larry.

"Don't try to pretend," said Rick. "You're the only one that could have given them all the details. Every freaking canoe tree. Every goshawk."

Larry stood by the stairwell that led to the shack where he'd eaten breakfast and dinner for more than twenty years. Rick yelling in front of him, the ravens tearing at the garbage behind. He did not like to be cornered.

"Maybe it was Chaz." Larry fought back. Tried to press the knife in, but he wished he could take the words back as soon as he'd said them, because somewhere in Rick's eyes he could see that Rick had now won.

"You are such a weasel. And to think I've trusted you for all of these years." Rick came at him like a raptor. "All this time, I've thought maybe you were Chaz's father. Maybe that was the secret in all of this. That the least I could do is give the kid a job and let you two work it out. But a real father wouldn't throw his own son under the bus."

Larry tripped over a discarded vodka bottle as he backed away. A raven dropped an eggshell and squawked, rising off the ground. Larry could feel the breeze from its feathers brushing his face. The hippie was coming up behind Rick. Larry was about to turn toward Lily's mom.

"Hey, dude. Remember me?" Blaize said to Larry.

Rick spun his head toward the voice. "Who the hell are you?"

"I'm looking for Lily."

"Don't get me started. She's gone. Long gone. Stole a truck and now it's behind enemy lines," said Rick.

Everyone's looking for Lily, Larry thought. He looked around for the brother, the mother, but they'd disappeared. This was all a little too much. He could feel the weight bearing down. The thud of wood hitting the ground. A secret. A demand. A woman backing away. Plates broken. Tables. Chairs. He had a sense of how it all fit together and it made him want to jump into the truck and race away. But when he scrolled back through the last few seconds, he realized what Rick had just said.

"Wait. What do you mean Lily's gone?"

41

Walker stood at the top of the cliff looking down at the greasy rocks and the dark green water. The wash from the swell splashed and tore at the yellow monkey flowers and the purple vetch. He'd brought a net bag of glass balls and started spilling the treasures onto the grass a few steps back from the edge. He'd found so many over the years, digging through graveyards of driftwood, past detergent bottles and old fishing nets. Searching for them had kept him busy, as did leaving them in unexpected places. As did this ritual return to the cliff.

He could hear the waves exhale through the crevices and liked to kneel with his face above the whispers. His one chance to feel another's breath on his skin. Sometimes he yelled her name into the breeze. Sometimes he saw lights from the fishing boats. Some days he did nothing more than sit and watch the light drop from the sky.

Today, the surge poured overtop of the rocky islet just offshore and the clouds tumbled toward him in a darkening line. He picked a ball from the top of the heap and threw it. The plop, as it hit the water, did not satisfy him, so he raised the next one above his head and smashed it onto the staircase of rocks jutting below. That was more like it. More like the breaking of his heart. He threw another and another and the glass shards skittered down the slope. He thought of his mother and her constant cigarettes, the smoke curling around her yellow fingers. Oh, she'd been surprised to see him when he'd returned home.

Another orb hit the rocks. His father had been jaundiced in the back bedroom—not dead, but close—and demanding another bottle of gin. That terrible man had been smaller than Walker had ever seen him. Not strong enough to grab and hit, but—once again, as always—able to punish his son. Walker tossed a few more balls and thought of the war he had refused to fight and the words that labelled his father's disdain. Draft dodger. Traitor. Coward. He was none of those things, and he'd never intended to see either of his parents again.

Walker set another glass ball on the grass and kicked it. This one went farther than expected and hit the rocks on the far side of the churn, but he still didn't smile.

That night at the bar with the raven-haired woman had made him smile. She'd taken him home and then he'd snuck out in the morning without saying goodbye. Maybe his father had been right.

The note he'd found tacked to his door was a deeper mystery. His mother calling him back. *I need you. Come home.* A phone message, supposedly, taken at the grocery store and delivered to his shack in the woods. But after he'd travelled across provinces and borders to see her, she'd looked as if he'd arrived from the moon. *I had no idea where you were, let alone how to call you*, she'd said. But she'd needed him—that much was true—so he'd stayed. Thinking of it made him dizzy. As if he was looking through the blurred glass of a fishing float.

When the old man finally relented and unclasped from life, his mother had begged Walker to stay longer. Walker kicked another ball off the grass into the sea. He'd hoped she might become someone else once the stranglehold of his father had disappeared. But in the end, she remained the same as when the asshole had been alive.

If you think that slut that you moan for is waiting for you, you should think again, his mother had said. At that, he'd finally had enough.

Walker watched the swell gather and felt the thump against the sea cave. The exhale came through the crevice and onto his cheek. Her lips on his face.

When he'd finally crossed the border again and returned to the islands, his mother had been right. He'd come all the way back to find out that she'd disappeared. He would never forget the look on June's mother's face, when he knocked at the door. *June's gone*, she hissed. As if he'd tossed her away himself.

But the child? He shouted the name and threw the last glass ball into the air, hoping to kick it as it dropped. When the ball slipped past him and bounced down the grassy side of the cliff, Walker watched it roll onto the beach. That meant something. Didn't it? He shouldn't get rid of them all. He needed one last gift. The least he could do was leave one last glass ball, before he threw himself into the sea.

He would follow the trail down and get it, then set it on a pedestal somewhere, just like he'd done in her mother's yard. All those surprises he'd left for the boy meant something, surely. But as he stepped on the grass, the cliff slipped out from under him. The ground rose up with a *whoosh*.

Just before he hit the sand, someone called his name. Must be the girl, he thought.

Who was she in all of this?

42

Ryan had been tiptoeing through the garbage trying to fathom everything he'd just seen on the drive to the camp. The giant trees, the massive clearcuts. A huge truck loaded with logs that almost ran them off the road. Larry had gripped the steering wheel with his good hand and swerved into a pullout just in time. Muttered something about the road being a place for suffering, before the real work begins. He said people should feel a bit sick after the ride, then whatever happens in the bush is a genuine effing relief.

Then some short tubby guy in coveralls whistled and yelled "You tell him, Rick" as he walked past Larry and the other guy shouting at each other. Blockade? Goshawk? Weasel? Had some dreadlock guy gotten out of Lily's car? It was just getting good when his mother disappeared through a door and he followed her into the darkness.

"Alberta girl?" said a lady with a French accent. "Holy sheet. I didn't tink I'd ever see you again."

Ryan's eyes adjusted to the dim light and he saw a woman with a glittery purple scarf tied over her hair.

"Same," said Arlene.

"You have a lot of nerve showing up after what you did," said Renée.

Arlene shook her head. "After what I did? You're the one who ditched me. Left me in that cabin all alone."

"Ya and dat place was destroyed when I got home. You were long gone."

"What?"

"Table turned over. Dishes broken. Firebox open and smouldering embers on de floor?"

"Okay. Stop." Arlene turned and saw Ryan shrunk up against the wall. "I don't want to talk about this right now. Especially not in front of my son."

"Dis your son? And Lily's your daughter? Seems like tings work out for you okay."

"Sure. Sure. Everything's been peachy. Anyway. You look good. Life seems to have been treating you well. How's June?"

"You don't know about June?"

Arlene shrugged. "Know what? It's not like we exchanged Christmas cards."

"Well. She's dead."

"What? That's terrible. What happened?"

"What happened? You stole her boyfriend and she went crazy. Den she got pregnant. Or maybe it was de other way around."

"I stole her boyfriend? What boyfriend?"

"Dat Walker guy. From Port."

"The guy we'd see carrying geese over his shoulder? Since when was he her guy? And why would anyone think I stole him?"

"June and him got together right around the time you left. You had the hots for him back den too. You told me yourself."

"We all did, remember? He was some kind of superhero. Mild-mannered by day, but once he was out in the bush? Look out," said Arlene.

"People say you left together. On de ferry. Dey saw you."

Ryan's head swivelled as if he were at a tennis match. He wished he had snacks.

"On the ferry?" Ryan could see Arlene thinking. But not in her I'll-find-a-way-out-of-this-no-matter-what-you-try-to-pin-on-me way, she really looked as if she was trying to conjure up a memory.

"He *was* on the ferry the night I left. I remember now. Pacing, circling on the outside deck. I tried to get him to sit. I tried to talk to him. I needed someone to talk to myself."

"I knew it!" said Renée.

"I remember wondering where he was going."

"Ya, well you and him both just disappeared."

"He never even stopped. You don't get it. I was lost. You and June always amped each other up. Always left me out or found something to blame me for. And now I'm responsible for some, some... loner ditching her? I just went inside and never saw him again."

"Merde, nobody did," Renée said. "Au moins, not in time to help."

43

Walker heard the woman shouting, but he couldn't care less. He had stopped moving and that was enough.

The pebbles on the beach scratched against his skin and he opened his eyes. Why could he see his foot? The angle didn't seem right. His left knee ached and he felt the heat at the back of his head. He could smell the pungent green of the ocean, the clinging air he'd inhaled for the last fifteen years—but something new too.

A blackness enveloped him again. On the ferry back to the islands, the two women had tried to make him come inside, but he wouldn't. The French one. What had she said? That June left the islands to go look for her son's father. She just dropped that detail like a knife. When the rain started ripping out of the clouds, they left him alone on the deck. Panic tore through him, but he kept moving, past the lifeboats, past the lines smacking in the wind. He stumbled around the prow and crossed back via the port side. Salt water hit his shoes. The rain lashed his face. Walker remembered leaning over the rail and the deck buckling as the ship twisted. When the huge wave walloped the side of the boat, he couldn't remember if it lifted him off his feet or if he'd jumped in.

Things had gone black. Waves. Cold. Then finally, dull light. He could see himself inching his way, on hands and knees, up the shore, sliding backwards with each surge. The green eelgrass that tangled around his eyes. He'd almost let go and slid back into the underwater world, but a blade of grass whipped through the corner of his mouth. The razor-sharpness had forced him to resurface again. He remembered collapsing onto the gravel beach.

He'd spotted an animal moving at the dune-edge of the forest. Had he followed it into the trees? Is that what started his life in the forest? Or had he turned toward the village to look for June instead?

44

Lily landed in the sand by the man's head and his eyes flung open.

"Oh my god. Are you okay?" Lily touched his shoulder lightly, afraid to bump him. His body was crumpled like something the ocean puked up.

"June?"

"No, I'm Lily. It's going to be okay. I think I spotted a boat offshore. I'll get them to call for help," she said. His skin was translucent. Just barely covering his bones. How had he survived all this time? Could it be true that he'd been wandering the woods for so many years?

"Let's get you warm first." Lily pulled a sweater out of her pack and put it over his chest. Did he need splints? A head board? She had wondered who this man was, but as she looked at him, the truth couldn't be denied.

When a raven squawked, she looked up and saw it flap its wings after landing in a nearby hemlock tree. The branch took a deep swing under the bird's weight. When it regained its balance, the raven called out again. Lily followed its gaze and saw a glowing blue moon on the beach. She leapt up and grabbed it, then held it up to the man.

"Is this yours?" she said.

Walker looked at the ball and winced.

Chaz saw someone on the beach, jumping in the air and waving their arms. It had to be Lily. He got out the binoculars and she came into focus at the base of the bluffs, right where Uncle had said she'd be. He tried to zoom in on the lump by her feet too. It wasn't a pile of seaweed, but what was it? Then the boat shifted and a head came into view. Lily lifted her hand. Chaz thought he could see blood.

He started moving quickly, unhooking the ropes that lashed the small aluminum skiff to the deck of Uncle's fishing boat. He called to Banger to help lower it down. Banger had the gas can out and made sure the motor was topped up. Chaz ran back into the cabin and grabbed some cheese and crackers. A tin of fish. A box of cookies. Uncle stood at the wheel, but reached over and handed him a bottle of water. He put it all in a garbage bag.

"You need me to come with you?" Banger said when Chaz came back out.

"I need you and Uncle ready out here in case anything goes wrong." Chaz slipped into the seat and pulled the cord on the outboard as Banger threw him the rope.

"Go safely, brother," Banger said.

The surge from the storm pushed the waves into piles and the tide was higher than Chaz liked—rocks could be covered by a pillow of water, or they might be just under the sheen. At least the beach looked as if it was mostly sand. He had a plan. He'd surf one of the rollers, and at the last possible moment, pull the motor up and ram onto the beach.

He bobbed in the water near the *Slayer* and looked for Lily again. She was dead straight ahead. Chaz jammed his wrist down on the throttle. He would not lose sight of her again.

f

Was it really Chaz? Lily recognized the way he tilted his head. Who else was on the fishing boat? Chaz's uncle and Banger?

"It's okay," she said to Walker. "He's coming."

"Who?"

"Your son."

"Is he?"

"Yes, I believe he is."

"Why?"

"Renée told me."

"The gypsy woman."

Lily laughed. So Renée had not been delirious when she'd come back to their room the other night. Everything she said must have been true.

"She loved you, you know," said Lily.

"Who?"

"June."

"June." He said her name with a smile and then started to cry.

Lily cried too. Renée had been drunk. Talking in circles. Almost asleep. Lily hadn't believed her at first. She'd wanted Walker for herself. The wild man of the woods. Besides, Chaz hated the woods. He belonged to the sea. Lily belonged nowhere. She had been looking for a sense of belonging through every room in the forest, and Chaz already had his uncle and gran. The Trina trio and Banger. It wasn't fair.

Still, Lily couldn't help smiling back at the man. Walker. Then she turned her head toward the water and saw that Chaz couldn't manage landing the boat on his own.

"I'll be right back. With your boy." She ran to Chaz, calling his name.

Chaz had to tug the skiff up out of the surf or it might be pulled away and they'd be stuck there. He held on by the bow rope, dug in his feet and called back.

"Lily! Help me."

"Okay. Quickly though. He might not have much time," she said.

"Who?"

"You'll see."

They pulled the boat as far onto the sand as they could.

"Come," she said.

"Just a sec." Always tie your boat, his uncle was probably saying this as he watched through binoculars from the deck of the *Slayer*. To a rock or a tree. Never leave things dangling or you could trip, get your foot caught. Chaz could hear his uncle's boat growling as it bobbed offshore in the surge. He breathed in and took the time to coil the rope.

"Chaz!" Lily called. "Hurry!"

"Coming!" He looked out at the water again and tried to judge the tide. It continued to push forward, inch by inch. He dropped to the sand and dug around a good-sized rock. When he'd loosened it, he tied the rope around the rock and buried it again.

When he finally moved toward the crumpled body Chaz watched as Lily pressed a compress bandage against the man's bleeding head.

"It's you." Chaz remembered the man at the door.

The man held a fishing float in his hands, the icy blue almost the same colour as his eyes. He offered it to Chaz.

"Did you bring me these before?" Chaz said.

"Yes."

"I don't understand."
"I know."
"You left..."
"I tried to come back. But it was too late. I'm sorry."
"Sorry doesn't cut it."
"I didn't know about you. I didn't know anything," Walker said.
"I didn't know about you either," Chaz said.
"Okay, you two. I think we've just found a way to get Walker out of here." Lily jumped to her feet and waved at the sky.

45

"There's a mayday out on the west coast." Larry heard Grayson spout this tidbit as he marched toward the crew of people amassed around Larry's white truck. Rick was still snorting like a raging bull at him, and Mac leaned against the truck box. That dirty hippie flopping around in his bare feet. Larry felt as if he was in a movie—either that or a bad dream. At least Rick shifted his attention to Grayson, giving Larry a chance to breathe.

"Details," Rick demanded.

"Chaz and his uncle think there's a body on the beach. They're up coast, just offshore."

"Up coast? I thought they went fishing?"

"Yeah, they did. I guess when they found out Lily was missing, they went looking for her," Grayson said.

"What is wrong with everyone? Why can't they just stay where they belong?" said Rick.

The screen door of the mess hall slammed and Arlene charged at them like a grizzly bear. "Went looking for Lily? What does that mean? Where is she? What the hell have you done with my daughter?" She jabbed her finger at Rick's chest.

"Look lady, she left on her own," Rick said. "Stole a vehicle, in fact. Now I can't even get it out from behind the protest lines."

"What protest?" said Arlene. "What have you got my daughter mixed up in now?"

"What have I got...?" Rick said. "Wait a second. Don't I know you?"

"Oh, I know you. That's for sure," Arlene spat back at him. "You always were a prick."

"And you... you were involved in that monkeywrenching, all those years ago. You destroyed that loader."

"How dare you try to blame me for something like that? I don't even know what a loader is," Arlene said. "And don't try to change the subject either. Where the hell is my daughter?"

The plot kept rolling and Larry just let the scenes ride out. He didn't know about the protest. Or the body on the beach, or what Chaz was doing on a boat, or how anyone knew where to look for Lily. He just wanted to get out of there. Time to skee-daddle. He shouldn't have come back to the islands. He should have disappeared. He should have done that a long time ago.

"Okay. Focus people," Grayson shouted.

The racket was too much. Larry looked at his hand and saw blood seeping through the bandage. He wondered if he might pass out.

"Helicopter coming in." Grayson again.

Larry just shook his head. How could it get here that quick? The kid had been trying to get heli-surveys going since the summer began. Larry had told Rick it wasn't worth the money, but as soon as Larry almost cuts his hand off, what does that kid do but call the choppers in? No. Larry reminded himself. He didn't care. He was out.

"Get the spine board and tell him not to shut down," yelled Rick over the whack of the heli blades.

"I'm coming with you," said Arlene, pushing her finger into his chest again.

"No, you aren't." Rick stepped forward and pushed her back.

Larry watched his boss put his hands on Arlene's shoulder and something snapped. "Don't touch her." Then he cracked Rick on the chin. Rick came back at him and was about to plow his fist into Larry's face, but Larry held up a bandaged hand in defence.

"You pussy," said Rick. "You won't even fight."

"This is bullshit," said Arlene, marching toward the helipad. "I didn't come here to deal with whatever you two are going on about. I'm going to find my kid."

Larry couldn't argue with that.

46

Chaz held his jacket around the man's head like a shield as the chopper buzzed above them. The blades whopped and whined and sand ripped at his cheeks, hot and sharp like a rash. When the racket finally quietened, Chaz expected Larry or Grayson to appear, but instead he heard Lily gasp as a woman got out.

"Mother?" she whispered, as if talking to a ghost.

Chaz reached up to touch her arm. "Go."

She took off running and Chaz saw a young man hop out too. Lily looked from one to the other, then her mother stopped and the boy kept coming and they hugged. They disengaged and Lily headed over to the chopper. She yelled at the pilot and then Chaz heard the boy yelling too. The boy was now crouched over the mother, who seemed to have collapsed to the ground. She rubbed at her ankle and Chaz could see a rock jutting up from the sand. He turned to look back at his skiff, which was still holding. The *Haida Slayer* still hovered on the edge of the waves. Jeezus, thought Chaz. What else?

And then, as if to answer all questions once and for all, a body emerged from the co-pilot seat. The movement, so familiar yet so estranged, caught Chaz off guard again.

"Rick?" he whispered.

Chaz turned from Rick to the man on the ground—a stranger, but as familiar as a photo of himself. Not the child on the wall of his Gran's house, but Chaz, the adult. His reflection in this bleeding man.

The man croaked something into the air and Chaz had to get closer to hear what he was trying to say.

"You look like her," Walker said.

Lily was commandeered by the pilot to help get the spine board out. She followed his instructions—pull, lift, shift—but twisted around to see where her mother went. Had she been a mirage? No. Arlene was truly on this remote beach on the west coast of Haida Gwaii, but what was she doing on the ground? Ryan tried to help her up but she swatted at him. Amid the wind and waves, Lily couldn't hear what they were saying. She wanted to rush over to them, but the pilot yelled at her again.

"Okay, I'm going to need your help with the patient. You ready?"

"Yes." But Lily did not believe her own voice.

"Looks like we have a major injury here," the pilot said as they approached.

"Head wound," said Chaz. "Could be a problem with his back and leg."

"What happened?" the pilot said.

"I made a mistake," Walker whispered.

"I've got the spine board. You just hold tight," said the pilot.

Lily held Walker's head and shoulders still as Chaz and the pilot got his leg straightened and splinted, then they lifted him enough to get the board underneath. Once his head and body were strapped and immobile, Lily, Rick, Ryan and Chaz carried him back to the chopper.

"Roll him right," the pilot said, as they slid the board diagonally into the six-seater.

"Somebody better come with him. I got room for one, maybe two. Does he have a next of kin?" said the pilot.

"I guess that's me," said Chaz.

"What's your relationship?"

"Um. I'm his son."

"You don't sound so sure."

"It's still sinking in."

Lily came forward again and hugged Chaz. His body felt stiff. "It's going to be okay," she said into his ear.

"Will it?"

"You found me. I'll find you again." She felt him loosen. Finally, he reached his arms around her back, rested his head against her cheek and sighed.

"Okay, we've got to get this man to the hospital," said the pilot. "Anyone else coming?"

"Wait," said Chaz. He ran to the skiff and got out the garbage bag of supplies and gave it to Lily. "Just in case."

f

Ryan stood back as the pilot closed the door.

"Are you going to be okay out here?" the pilot yelled out of the din. "I can still take one of you."

"Mom," Ryan yelled. Arlene still hadn't risen from the sand. "Get up."

His mother always said he was her one true love. She'd make him say it back to her, *You're my one twu wuv*, back when he was little, before he could speak clearly. Before he knew what it all meant. Then they'd rub noses. That was a long time ago. He knew better now.

He had never been as harsh on her as Lily had been. Ryan looked from one to the other—the two women in his life. The whipping blades. The ocean waves. The wild rock towers offshore. The dark green that edged along the white of the sand. Ryan could not believe where they had landed and even more so couldn't believe where they were about to be left alone.

"Mom, the helicopter's leaving. You should go."

"All of us?" she yelled.

"No. He only has room for one more." His mother struggled to get up.

"Is she okay?" yelled the pilot.

Arlene nodded her head.

Lily walked toward them. "Mom, stop being a baby."

"Rick? What about you? We've got to get going," said the pilot.

"Why don't you just go?" Lily yelled at her mother. Rick waved the pilot away and Arlene pulled herself to standing with Ryan's help.

"I'm not leaving without my kids," said Arlene, pressing her weight onto her foot. She grabbed Ryan's arm and then Lily's, even though Lily tried to back away.

The pilot rummaged around in the back of his chopper and pulled out a blanket, a first aid kit and a bottle of water. "Here's some supplies. If no one else is coming, we're lifting off."

Lily pulled her family closer to the water to get out of the way and then stared at the sky as the helicopter rose. Chaz was in there. He'd come looking for her, but he'd found someone more important, and now he was gone. And here she was on a beach in the middle of nowhere with barely enough to skills to survive on her own, let alone look after her mother and brother. She still had no father.

Static from a radio startled her and she turned to see Rick fiddling with the buttons and looking out at the fishing boat. "Look, I'm sorry about your sister. I should have said that a long time ago," Rick said into the hand set.

"I'm sorry too. Where are they taking Walker?"

"To the hospital in Charlotte for now. He might need a medevac. Chaz is with him."

"His son?"

"Yes. Chaz is his son," said Rick.

"I thought that might be the case," said Chuck.

An eagle circled the beach, rolling in the air currents, watching, waiting. Lily thought of the baby sandhill crane out on the flats. The limping father. The mother hidden in the grass and then coming out to join him.

"Who is he again?" Ryan asked, nodding toward Rick.

"The boss," Lily said. He wasn't Chaz's dad anymore. And Walker wasn't hers. That was clear.

"I thought I was doing the right thing. For me. Then for Chaz. But I messed up pretty bad with her," Rick continued.

"We all did," said Chuck.

Lily and Ryan moved farther away to give Rick some privacy. Chaz's uncle's boat bobbed on the swell and Rick was kicking at the skiff. A few minutes later, Lily heard Rick more loudly on the radio again. "I think I can get this boat off the beach."

Arlene had picked up the garbage bag Chaz had given to Lily and was rummaging through it, but stopped. "You're just going to leave on that little boat?" She looked terrified.

Lily tried to imagine herself in Arlene's situation, back then. Pregnant, but no family planning clinic to walk into. What if Lily had slapped Jeremy in the face and shoved the girl with the Coke t-shirt to the side? She might have had a baby with a father, and how would that have all turned out? But she had chosen her path and ended up on this beach on the west coast of Haida Gwaii. For better or worse, Lily had come to the forest and survived.

"It's going to be okay, Mom." Lily said the words, but she had no idea.

The radio squawked again and Chuck signed off. Lily bumped up against Ryan. He was her constant. The only one she could trust. The two of them went over to Rick to help him with the boat. She dug up the line that she'd watched Chaz bury.

"Are we going on the boat?" Ryan asked Lily, wiping his hands on his jeans. Rick was fiddling with the motor and Lily still held the rope.

Rick looked up. "I'd have to ferry you one by one," he said.

Lily imagined they could probably all get on it and Chaz's uncle would bring them back to civilization. But then she looked over at the cliff covered in yellow monkey flowers and knew she wasn't ready to leave. She threw the rope to Rick and waved.

"No," Lily said. "We're going to walk."

47

After Rick left, Lily's mother brushed the sand off her backside as if nothing mattered.

"How far did you say?" Arlene said.

"Three days, Mom." Lily tried to appear casual. A raven swooped down from a cedar branch and clucked at them. "Two along the beaches and one straight up through the trees to the nearest road. We better get going."

"You've got to be kidding."

"I wish I was," Lily said. "If we move fast, maybe we can make it in two."

"Okay, okay. We'll make it. We're survivors."

"You're unbelievable, Mom."

"What?"

"You left us to fend for ourselves all the time," Lily said. "Then you took off for Costa Rica or wherever you went. I thought it was for good. But now, all of a sudden you've swooped in as if this were some sort of fairy tale."

Lily shouldered her pack and grabbed the bag of food Chaz had left. She kicked at the emergency stuff the pilot had pulled out of the helicopter, but left it in the sand and started walking. Lily could hear her mother yelling above the waves. "You think you're better than me? It's not as if you've been hanging around. Not at home—not even at this job you left your father for. What the hell are you even doing out here?"

"Mom..." Ryan started to interject. Her little brother was always trying to save his mother from herself. Lily glanced back and saw him stumbling through the loose sand at the top of the beach. She wanted to tell him to get closer to the water. That the packed sand in the intertidal zone offered the surest footing. But she had her mother to deal with instead.

"I was looking for someone, okay?" Lily yelled back.

"Oh my god. Who?" Lily spun around and saw Arlene digging

through her purse. Why did she carry it? There was nothing of value in it. No money or food. Just mascara and shades of scarlet lipstick.

"Never mind."

"They said you were chasing some hermit through the trees. Oh my god. You didn't think he was your father, did you? Lily, listen. I've done a lot of messed up things in my life, but if there was one thing I did right, it was giving you a dad. Brian has loved you for your entire life. And what have you done to repay that?"

"Seriously? I'm the bad guy all of a sudden?" Lily had been walking backward but she stopped and let her mother approach.

"You and I are more similar than you'd like to admit, young lady."

"Why can't you two get along?" Ryan piped up.

"Don't worry, son. We get along fine."

"Bullshit, Mom. What are you even doing here?" Lily said.

"When I heard you were coming to these islands. I... I don't know. I guess I didn't want you to get lost."

"How was I going to get lost?"

"Look at you. Out here in the freaking wilderness. Chasing after some strange man that you don't even know. What were you going to do if he *was* your father?"

"I don't know. Who is my father?" Lily said.

But Arlene just shook her head.

A blast of wind hit Lily's face and reality came flooding back. Whatever she wanted to yell at her mother could wait. The clouds started draining and Lily looked down at her mother's shoes. They weren't sandals, that was something.

"There's an A-frame cabin at the far end of the beach," she yelled over the surf.

Arlene stomped forward, sand spraying. "Okay. Let's go."

Larry stood in the middle of the road by the cookhouse for a long time. The helicopter never came back. Rick never came back. Even Grayson had gone. He'd taken a work truck to go find the truck Lily had left at the end of the road.

Now what? Larry looked at Lily's Colt. He walked up to it and saw that the keys were still in it. Ready to race off down the road. He couldn't take it. Could he? He should leave it for her and her family. That would be the honourable thing to do.

"You're a twat."

Larry heard the voice. Knew who it was, but didn't want to look. Mac. He could always count on Mac to remind him of his failings.

"Why don't you just man up and apologize?"

"To who?" Larry could still pretend he didn't know what Mac was talking about and maybe it would all go away.

"To Arlene, you idiot. Or April, I think they called her back then."

"Oh."

"And to Lily," Mac said. "Jesus, Larry. I was there, remember?"

Larry remembered alright. That awful night at the cabin after the pub fight. The day before, Mac had been so hungover that he couldn't be roused to go into the field. So Larry had recruited Walker. Then at camp, June had dropped her apron to come too.

Larry remembered a high-line had been swinging logs down a big slope criss-crossed with fallen trees. Men were yelling and darting in and out. Giant trees being limbed and loaded onto those great square-front trucks. Larry had always marvelled at the order and chaos of logging. Men with specific jobs—felling, wrapping the choker, pressing the whistle. Wires taut, large objects moving. Stay out of the bite had been the first thing he'd learned on a logging show. Never put your body in a situation where stored energy could suddenly be released. Where two objects could change position without warning. You don't want to be caught between them.

The rest of that day had been spent in the old growth. He, June and Walker counting and measuring trees so that other men could puff up their chests and make a big clearcut out of it all.

It had been a beautiful day with June acting so natural and free around him again. Walker and her up ahead, getting along like a house on fire, and Larry keeping their bearings straight. June had said she didn't need a compass. That she knew the direction back to the truck, but he'd check her line and she kept veering the wrong way. Once they were back on the road, she said she had to pee, so they'd stopped by the clearcut. With the yard crew long gone, she'd snuck behind the loader, done her business and they'd continued on.

That was Friday. Then Saturday had been the night of the brawl and all of the events afterward. On Monday, when the landing crew came back, the machine was hooped. Kool-Aid in the tank or something. Everyone had been freaking out and he'd had to think quick because his had been the last truck out of the woods.

48

By the time Lily, Arlene and Ryan got to the cabin, the tide was rising, the day darkening and the rain getting worse. They'd made it across the creek but the headland would be challenging.

"Might as well wait for the tide to fall again," Lily said. Probably better to stay the night anyway. Ryan wanted the tent and Arlene wanted the cabin, but she didn't want to stay in it alone, so Lily got stuck with her mother.

The two women set themselves up in the scrunched little space and then Lily crawled outside to brush her teeth.

"You okay out here?" she called to Ryan.

"Snug as a bug in a rug," he said. "You?"

"Ya. Why?"

"Just checking. Night, Lily."

Why indeed. If Lily were to ask her mother why, it wouldn't be why did you leave. Or even why did you come back. Lily wanted to know why her mother kept a child she hadn't wanted.

When Lily tunnelled back inside, her mother had wrapped herself in the blanket and was already breathing with a familiar stutter. Talking to herself with little moans. Lily pulled a corner out from under her and curled up beside her mother's scent. Wind thumped against the little shack and Lily finally fell into fitful dreams. One where she walked through the forest and found a man with a moustache frozen into stone. She walked past him and he jingled the keys in his pocket. When she stepped on a stick, the snap released him and she saw herself frozen on a bed of moss. Then Brian was running around the house checking the fire alarms. The beeps transformed into shrieking as he moved back and forth between them. The house is on fire, the house is on fire. Wake up your mother.

Lily woke and felt gusts hit the cabin, then the quiet returned—back and forth as if the weather was some kind of morse code. She pulled at the covers, and the blanket slid toward her with no resistance. She slapped her hand at the space Arlene should be in, but she was gone.

Outside the wind tore at a royal blue tarp covering a pile of firewood. Pitch black and cold, the waves broke in a silvery gleam. Lily yelled, her voice carried away as a violent gust thudded in. She heard a crack in the forest behind her and a thud as a tree whacked the ground. She called again, quickly before the next shriek came from the sky. In the falling tones of her biggest question—*Mother?!*—Lily heard a response. *Here.* Something? Was it? Lily whistled, two fingers from each hand, tongue curled, blowing in desperation. Ryan in the tent answered back and Lily tried to shut that out. Then another call. From the sea? Lily couldn't see, but she ran toward the sound anyway, tripping through the top layer of wet sand with its squeaky dryness underneath.

She found her mother on the beach, near the creek's outflow, struggling in the sinking mud.

"Where were you trying to go?" Lily helped her mother up, her hair slashed against her face, one foot stuck in the sand.

"I don't know," she said. "I wanted to run."

"Stop running and tell me who my father is."

"Cripes, Lily, help me get her up." Ryan must have followed Lily down to the beach. "It's not always about you." Ryan pulled their storm-tumbled mother against him as they made their way back to the cabin and Lily hated him for the security he felt. His place in the world. A mother who loved him and a father he knew better than he knew his own dreams.

The next morning, Lily rationed out the granola bars. She looked out at the clearing sky. The tide was out and they rounded the headland easily. Marching like a little unit in the sand. Arlene spun with her arms out, as if she hadn't gone wild and almost disappeared into the night.

"Hey," said Ryan. "Somebody's coming."

Lily looked down the beach at the male figure walking toward them. She couldn't help it. She wanted it to be him. Whoever he was. Or Chaz. But as they got closer, Lily saw the straight-laced redneck. Grayson? She didn't understand.

"Nice string line," he said when they reached each other. "I followed it all the way from the truck to the beach."

"Wow. Why?" said Lily. "What are you doing here?"

"Scoping out cutblocks, obviously," said Grayson. Then he laughed. "No. That's not why. I wanted to make sure you were okay."

Renée always had an escape route. Asti, tabarnac. She knew how easy it was for things to go wrong. That fight in the bar all those years ago. Prochaine chose, she'd woken up on June's parents' couch and tout le monde avait disparu. She could vanish too. Renée wasn't one to stay stuck. June's car had been out front and Renée found the keys in a pair of jeans on June's bedroom floor. Below John Travolta in his *Saturday Night Fever* stance.

Thing was, she hadn't expected to arrive back at the cabin to find it about to burst into flames. She screamed for April, but as far as she could tell, no one was there. The wood stove door was wide open and a pile of wood stacked like a log cabin smouldered in the middle of the floor. Outside, Renée could see a delivery had come. She'd wondered who had brought the firewood and what they'd gotten in return.

Fucking for firewood had been kind of a joke, but she'd never been against the idea herself. June and April, they were both fussier about those things.

Renée had tossed a bucket of water at the pile. She remembered how April hadn't known how to get the woodstove going. Renée had taught her to cut the kindling and criss-cross the pieces into a square. Then fill the centre with paper. She also remembered the Alberta girl's frustration when the cabin wouldn't spark to life.

After April had disappeared, the shit had hit the fan. A fight in the pub and news of logging machines ruined with sugar or sand. Everyone had been looking for someone to pin it on and the next thing Renée knew April's name was being passed around.

Why would she disappear if she wasn't guilty? That's what everyone said.

Thing was that Walker had disappeared too, but no one had mentioned his name.

Except June.

Now Renée was stuck listening to Larry as he drove to the ferry terminal in Lily's car. She felt as if she was some kind of priest and the bucket seats had become some kind of confessional wall.

He needed to tell her the story, but she didn't need to hear it. She already knew. April, May, June. It was twenty years later—time to move on.

She would get on the ferry too, but she sure as hell wouldn't be hanging around with Larry. Renée planned to hide out in the bathroom stalls if she had to. She wasn't going to tell him or anyone her part in it all. The blue bins with the supplies. And those air photos. She was still trying to impress that Haida fisherman. But when Lily's mother arrived, Renée decided it was time to lay low.

Cookie said she could make real money in Fort McMurray—in kitchens and at whatever else she was willing to do. She would save her paycheques for once, so she could buy a little place of her own. A shack in Port where she could line the walls with preserves. Dried mushrooms. Deer stew. Hell, she'd learn to shoot her own geese if she had to. Learn to survive on her own.

49

Arlene couldn't believe she'd survived two nights in this godforsaken place. When they finally found the piece of flagging tape Lily had left and got off the beach, Arlene tumbled into the forest and curled up on the moss like a little bird. She lay there chirping while everyone else recalibrated their boots and packs and Grayson scouted around for the string line that Lily had left.

Arlene remembered picking herself up off the mouldy carpet in that cabin she'd shared with Renée and June, and she hadn't known what to do. She couldn't stay there any longer. A man had come to the door, dumped his load and moved on. She'd looked at the firewood and decided if he could, she would as well. Arlene remembered stealing one of Renée's scarves and wrapping it around her favourite shells. Then she pieced some small pieces of wood into a log cabin on the carpet and struck the match.

She'd started walking toward the highway and heard the same rattly, bugling sound that had haunted her each morning. This time she saw where the noise was coming from. Two giant birds dancing together. One bowed and dipped, then jumped in the air, flapping its wings, while the other pirouetted and rattled back. They hopped and skipped around each other. June had told her that sandhill cranes mate for life. They made their prehistoric noises again and veered across the clearing, as far away as they could get from Arlene.

Arlene found the grey feather with the orange tip on the path. She'd picked it up and thought of Brian. How he'd wanted to dance with her, but she didn't know the steps. Arlene had been so busy trying to run away, she hadn't had the patience to follow him around a dance floor. She'd gone as far as she could though—to the edge of the world—and that hadn't worked out. The least she could do was bring a feather back.

Arlene couldn't remember what ever happened to that feather. That had been so long ago. Arlene groaned. She didn't want to get up from her mossy bed. She looked up at her daughter and wished everything hadn't gone so wrong. She used to watch Lily, sitting on all those couches in the furniture store, playing games by herself. She always had a little smile on her face. As if she was satisfied to be right there. Humming while clicking the lever, level by level, on the reclining chair. Arlene could never find that peace. She patted the moss beside her and then lay back as if the forest was a big canopy bed. She felt Lily lower herself to the ground and Ryan did too. Arlene closed her eyes and started talking, hoping it would come out the right way. "I didn't tell you that Brian wasn't your father because that wasn't true. He is your father. He's loved you since the day you were born. The other man isn't important."

"He's important to me. Wouldn't you want to know where you came from?" said Lily.

"Sometimes things happen and there are no good reasons. Other times— maybe it's better for you not to know," Arlene finally said. She reached across the moss for her daughter's hand.

"It's my fault," said Ryan, bubbling up from the other side of Lily. Her little boy. Always trying to make things right.

"Shh," Arlene said. "It's not your fault. It's not even mine."

"I told her. I thought she'd want to know."

"I did want to know! Thank you Ryan."

"I wish I hadn't though. Mom's right. Knowing doesn't help."

Arlene started crying. "That man didn't have anything to do with what I wanted."

"Mom. He had to do with me."

"You don't understand."

"You're right, I don't," said Lily, but Arlene felt her daughter squeeze her hand anyway.

Lily couldn't believe Grayson was being so nice. He dropped them off near the ferry terminal after a stop to fuel up in Skidegate. They had all survived. Arlene had finally picked herself up and made it up the slope. They'd seen Banger at the gas station and he'd reported that Chuck and Rick had gotten back safely. The two men had reached a kind of truce: the blockade would continue and Totem Timber would be shut down for a while. Chaz had gone with Walker to Terrace, where the hospital had an intensive care unit, but Banger said Chaz would be back soon.

Of course, now that they were back in civilization, Arlene was no longer contrite. She grumbled around, desperate to leave, hopped up like an incoming storm. Why had she come, Lily wondered again. To find her daughter or to ensure she hadn't been blamed? She was the hippie chick who'd supposedly put sugar in the logging equipment's tank. Or she wasn't. Story of Arlene's life. Truth was, Ryan had some kind of soccer finals he had to get back to. And Brian? He'd be in the back room at the furniture store. As always.

Lily looked at the gaping maw of the ferry. A black bird cawed and then made one of those gurgling noises. Raven or crow? Lily watched it swoop out of the dark green forest, swaying, wings akimbo as it landed above her head on a telephone pole. Old One-Leg? Was it staring at her? What secrets did it know?

Lily thought of Walker and Chaz looking at each other as if seeing a silhouette finally coming into the light.

The big ferry steamed against the dock and Lily's Dodge Colt sat in the exact same spot she'd left it when she went up to the logging camp with Larry and Chaz. On the edge of the road hunched like a little lost dog that had waited for her in the rain.

Stupid thought. Things don't wait. People barely wait.

Lily pressed at her pockets for her car keys. Wait. No. She'd left her car back near Yakoun Lake, the first time she'd tried to go off on her own.

"Hey. This *is* your car. I saw some dreadlock guy driving it when we were back in the logging camp," said Ryan.

"Blaize? What? That's weird." She looked in the gas cap where she'd left her keys and, yep, there they were.

Arlene piped up. "This is your car? You think all of us will fit into this little tin can?"

"It'll be fine, Mom. It's quite comfy. Hey, you can drive."

"Me, drive across a whole province. That would be…" Arlene continued on, but Lily wasn't listening anymore. She'd opened the door and was looking around for a note. Had Blaize and Sissy brought it back? She thought she'd seen it in their camp. Maybe they'd be on the ferry. But Lily stopped short when she saw that someone had left a large grey feather beside the one she'd already stuck in the dashboard. She picked the feather up and brushed it across her face. The bird that painted its body a rusty red to attract a mate. Who pretended to have a broken wing to protect its child.

The one Larry knew so much about.

50

"Okay, boat's leaving. If we are going, we better go." Arlene sat in the driver's seat, tapping her fingernails on the car door. "Toot, toot, next stop Frontier."

Ryan looked over from the passenger side. He'd called shotgun, meaning Lily would have to sit in the back seat with her giant pack.

Arlene turned the key in the ignition and gunned the engine. Lily teetered on the side of the road and watched the current of Haida Gwaii flow by. Cars. Bikes. Was that Dually-guy in his big black truck? She still had no history, but she knew a carved pole stood by the beach before the curve. Beyond that, a huge rock balanced on a fulcrum and farther on, because of Haida gods fucking, the earth had cracked near a spring. She hadn't drunk the water there yet. She'd been in the depths of the forest, and on the edge of the west coast, but it wasn't enough. She wanted to taste whatever else she could.

She walked around to check the tires and noticed a white truck coming along, just like the Totem Timber ones she'd been driving into the field. Lily didn't even know what she was doing, until she stuck out her thumb.

The truck stopped and the passenger window rolled down. She wasn't sure which face she hoped would appear.

"Stypes," she said.

"Brown noser. Heard you found the Gogeet."

"What? How did you know?"

"Small town. Never mind. Where you headed?"

"North Beach?"

"Excellent idea," he said. "Work's shut down, might as well go dig some razor clams. Hop in. I can drop you at the campground."

Lily turned to look at her mother and Ryan. They sat perched in her little red car and would return to Frontier, where it all began. She didn't have to go with them. That was a different story. This one was hers.

Lily tossed her pack in the back of the truck and patted the Colt's hood. "Change of plans," she said to Arlene and Ryan. "I'm staying on the islands for a while. Say hi to Dad and tell him I'll give him a call when I get to a phone."

Acknowledgements

The Haida have long asserted title and sovereignty over their entire territory, and after many years of nation building, taking stands, negotiations and governance the Gaayhllxid • Gíihlagalgang "Rising Tide" Haida Title Lands Agreement was signed in April 2024. This wasn't an ending, but a movement away from the colonial era. Haida laws protecting cedar, goshawks, culturally modified trees and more will continue to gain ground as Haida jurisdiction over their territory expands.

This work of fiction is set in 1999, before the name Queen Charlotte Islands was put in a bentwood box and respectfully given back to the province. Before the west coast of Graham Island, also known as Duu Guusd, was recognized as a protected area by the province (the Haida protected it in 1982). Before the Village of Queen Charlotte (once known as Queen Charlotte City) reverted to its ancestral village name, Daajing Giids. This book is set in a time before cell service reached the islands. Before the internet took hold.

I lived on Haida Gwaii for ten years (2004–2014) and mostly worked as a reporter for the local newspaper. Many important shifts happened in that time: the Islands' Spirit Rising movement, Protocol Agreement signings with all the non-Haida communities and the opening of the Haida Heritage Centre at K̲ay 'llnagaay, to name a few. As a participant in and observer of island life, I wrote or worked for various magazines, the Haida Gwaii Museum and Gwaii Haanas National Park Reserve and Haida Heritage Site. In all roles, I learned valuable stories and perspectives and witnessed the great diversity of individuals who call the place home. Thanks to my partner, I was also part of the forestry family—said to me as if they were some kind of mafia!

Although I have been inspired by many people on Haida Gwaii, all characters appearing in this work are fictitious (okay, there are a couple of cameos). I've kept the general geography true to what I remember, but in the more remote parts of the islands, I've taken a few liberties.

I am also aware of concerns around a person of settler descent writing from a Haida perspective. But I couldn't conceive of writing a book set on Haida Gwaii without Haida characters. I sincerely hope my portrayal of Chaz, his gran, his uncle and others will be received with the generosity and love that I respectfully tried to imbue into them.

I've tried to be accurate in what I've written about forestry work, fishing, plants, birds, seasons, etc., but any mistakes are my own. For a more fulsome discussion of an important stand the Haida took in the years before this book is set, please read *Athlii Gwaii: Upholding Haida Law at Lyell Island*, published by Locarno Press in 2018.

To those who have read early versions of this manuscript, thank you for helping me keep going, especially Jacqueline Baker, Maureen Bayless, Percy Crosby, Barry Windecker and Alex Rinfret. Pam Robertson ended up as my editor after reading an earlier version, so thank you twice to her.

So many friends have provided support and words of encouragement about my writing over the years: Wendy, Jim, Carrie, Laurie, Ruth, Hilary, Tyler, Laurel, Ricardo, Natalie, Nathalie, Lynn, Leandre, Sandra, Margret, Deb, Maggie, Dinah, Marilyn, Donna, George, Dean, Emily and many, many more.

Thank you to all those who saw early versions in classes and workshops at UBC and the Banff Centre for the Arts. This novel was my thesis, so special thanks to supervisor Susan Musgrave and to my thesis committee members, Kevin Chong and Maureen Medved.

I want to say haawa to Jaalen, Kwiaahwah, Nika, Jags, Captain Gold, Guujaaw, Diane, Judson, Linda, Barb, Christian, Robert, Gitkinjuuwaas, Stephen, Aay Aay, Herb and Terry as just a few of those who shared knowledge with me while I lived on Haida Gwaii, especially while I worked on two books for the Haida Gwaii Museum.

A Room in the Forest is a love song to a place that I once called home. Thank you to everyone at Caitlin Press who helped bring this novel into its physical form.

Finally, thank you to Tom for being my muse and partner for all of these years. And to my parents—especially my father, who saves everything I've ever written in a binder.

About the Author

Photo Zoe Mix

Heather Ramsay lives and writes in unceded Ts'elxwéyeqw territory (Chilliwack, BC) and is heavily influenced by place: the ten years she lived on Haida Gwaii; the seven years she lived in Wet'suwet'en territory (Smithers, BC); her childhood in Tsuut'ina and Blackfoot territory (Calgary, Alberta)—it's all in there somewhere. She has an MFA in creative writing from UBC and has been published in *The Fiddlehead*, *The Antigonish Review*, *Numero Cinq*, *Canadian Geographic* and more. She has also co-written two books for the Haida Gwaii Museum: *Gina 'Waadlux̱an Tluu: The Everything Canoe* and *gyaag̱ang.ngaay: The Monumental Poles of Skidegate*.

About the Cover Artist

Maryanne Wettlaufer grew up on a farm in Southwest Ontario where the seeds of her connection to the land began and her formal art training at the Ontario College of Art (OCAD) took place. She is an explorer and passionate about the Canadian wilderness, her work has been influenced by the adventures of the Group of Seven and after moving to British Columbia in 1996 by Emily Carr as well.

In 2006 after a year of exploring Western Canada and living in Inuvik she moved to Haida Gwaii. It is here that Wettlaufer began her journey to develop a creative language that helps her to express with oil paint and watercolours the vast emotion embodied in the Canadian landscape. "I feel on a map Haida Gwaii may be tiny in size but in all its mystery, harshness and beauty it is the epitome of the whole of vast Canadian Landscape."

Artist Statement

The tree in Maryanne Wettlaufer's oil painting, Nadu Cedar, stands where patches of colourful bog give way to forest giants shaped by relentless bouts of prevailing southwest winds. Wettlaufer has lived on Haida Gwaii since 2006, but grew up on a farm in southwestern Ontario. She went to the Ontario College of Art and her work has been influenced by her adventures into nature, the Group of Seven and Emily Carr.